"I do not fear you."

Magnus's hand grabbed hold of Reena's finger and he brought it near his mouth. His warm breath whispered across the sensitive flesh. "Are you sure of that?" He kissed her finger, and then gently suckled the tip.

Her eyes turned wide, her mouth dropped open, and though she searched for a response, all she could do was moan—in pleasure, not in pain.

"Let me taste that moan," he whispered, and captured her lips with his.

She thought to move away, her body already in motion, but his arms were quick and strong, wrapping around her and pulling her toward him. Her hands pushed against him, and the feel of the soft leather over his hard, muscled chest tingled her fingers.

In an instant she was lost in the taste of him. There was no thought, no choice—just response—and she responded without reason.

There was only a need, and she surrendered to it more completely than she had ever thought possible . . .

"*Legendary Warrior* is a terrific tale. A great hero, an appealing heroine, and an intriguing story. This is what romance is all about. They don't get better than this."
Patricia Potter, bestselling author of *The Diamond King*

W9-CBY-422

Other **AVON ROMANCES**

AN AFFAIR MOST WICKED *by Julianne MacLean*
ALMOST PERFECT *by Denise Hampton*
THE DUCHESS DIARIES *by Mia Ryan*
KISS ME AGAIN *by Margaret Moore*
NO ORDINARY GROOM *by Gayle Callen*
SEEN BY MOONLIGHT *by Kathleen Eschenburg*
THREE NIGHTS . . . *by Debra Mullins*

Coming Soon

IN MY HEART *by Melody Thomas*
THE PRINCESS MASQUERADE *by Lois Greiman*

And Don't Miss These
ROMANTIC TREASURES
from Avon Books

ENGLAND'S PERFECT HERO *by Suzanne Enoch*
GUILTY PLEASURES *by Laura Lee Guhrke*
MARRIED TO THE VISCOUNT *by Sabrina Jeffries*

DONNA FLETCHER

LEGENDARY WARRIOR

AVON BOOKS
An Imprint of HarperCollinsPublishers

AVON BOOKS
An Imprint of HarperCollins*Publishers*
10 East 53rd Street
New York, New York 10022-5299

First Avon Books paperback printing: March 2004

To my agent, Grace Morgan,
for performing miracles.

Prologue

Ireland, 1500s

"He stands three heads above other men. His strength is that of a dozen warriors. With his claymore in hand he enters every battle without fear, devastating his enemies with a single blow and leaving in his wake death and destruction."

The wind whistled around the stone and thatched-roof cottage, sounding as if someone cried out in fright, and interrupting the telling of the tale. The children who sat gathered at the storyteller's feet shivered, and their eyes grew wide. The young girl nestled on the big, burly man's lap snuggled closer to his warmth and the protection of his thick arms.

When the wind ceased its anguished cries, Patrick Cullen continued, raising a beefy hand. "His hands possess the might of one hundred men and his weapon of choice—fear." He stopped and looked

1

cautiously around the single-room cottage, causing the children to follow his glance, their small bodies tense, wondering, Was he near? Then he once again settled into telling the tale. "It is told that to face him in battle means certain death. No one has seen his face, for he wears a black helmet designed and crafted especially for him. It conceals all but his eyes, mouth and jaw. Men shiver and women weep in his presence, for he shows mercy to none."

The big man held firm to the young girl in his arm and leaned forward, his deep voice a husky whisper. "Kings fear him, the Lord rejects him and the devil wants nothing to do with him."

He leaned back in his wooden chair and continued to captivate his young audience. "It is told that he lives far north, where the winters turn bitter cold and no one dares trespass on his land. Those brave enough to seek his help pay a dear price, for he does nothing out of the kindness of his heart—but he is always victorious. He has a legion of men that follow him, follow him because they owe him their souls."

Several mouths dropped open, and the children huddled closer to those beside them.

The man pounded the arm of his chair with a beefy fist. "Some insist he is a myth, others think he is a ghost, but he has forever been called—" He paused for a moment, and the children waited anxiously and fearfully, their breaths caught in their throats. The big man glanced at each child, then announced in a deep booming voice, "The Legend!"

Silence struck the room, and even the crackle of the fire in the hearth quieted in reverence.

John, a brave lad, spoke up though his voice trembled. "We live north and our winters are cold. Does that mean"—he stopped and swallowed hard, afraid to speak the name, so he whispered—"the Legend lives nearby?"

The man rubbed his chin slowly, and the children waited in anxious anticipation. "Could be the Legend lives not far from us."

Reena snuggled closer in her father's huge, warm arms. Her deep blue eyes rounded in fright as he continued to speak of the Legend. His booming voice filled the small cottage along with the warmth of the stone hearth, though shivers were common among the children when Patrick was in the thick of his storytelling.

Patrick rubbed at the stubble of gray whiskers on his thick chin. "Could be," he nodded slowly, "that the Legend hears all and knows that we speak of him."

Another young lad leaned forward and tapped Patrick's leg.

"Whisper," the tiny lad said with a finger to his lips.

Patrick nodded again, keeping his smile concealed. "A good point, but I fear he would hear us anyway. He hears and sees much." He looked out at the anticipating sea of young faces. "I know, for I have seen the Legend with my own eyes."

A round of gasps rushed around the room then settled, all the children eager to hear more.

"On one of my journeys I came upon a group of warriors sitting around a campfire. They looked battle worn and seemed frightened of their own shadows, jumping at the barest sound and casting anxious glances at the surrounding darkness.

"They bid me to join them as though my presence would make a difference to their safety. I did so though with a bit of reluctance, their fears contagious. I sat with them, shared their meal and waited, for what I did not know."

"The Legend," said Reena's best friend, Brigid.

"Shh," admonished John. "You speak his name too loud."

In a solemn tone Patrick agreed with the young lass. "Ah, it was the Legend they feared, for they had recently battled with him and his warriors, and it was said that no enemy was left untouched when faced by the Legend and his legion of warriors. They told me of the battle and how in the end the Legend was left standing alone on the battlefield, dozens of dead and dying men at his feet. And while victory was his, he did not stop until every last enemy was captured, which meant the Legend was coming for them."

Reena sat spellbound on her father's lap and listened to him weave his magic. No story fascinated her as much as the one about the Legend. She had heard it many times, and it never failed to send the shivers through her small body or cause her blue eyes to round in fright. She held her breath, as did the other children, waiting for the moment when the Legend entered the story.

Patrick continued. "The dark woods grew silent, the chilled wind ceased blowing and not an animal could be heard." He lowered his voice. "Then out of the darkness stepped four big men; they surrounded the camp not in haste but in confidence. They drew not a single weapon; they simply stood and waited."

The children huddled closer together.

"Then as though the black night gave birth to him and spit him forth from its belly, the Legend appeared." Patrick closed his eyes for a moment, shook his head and shivered. He opened his eyes and looked at each child. "He was a giant of a man and looked to have the strength of twenty. His metal helmet gave no hint to his features, and every man there shivered in fright, for no one knew what the helmet concealed. Was he man or beast?"

More gasps circled the room.

"With fearless strides he advanced on the battle-worn warriors, and they instantly fell to their knees begging for mercy. The Legend raised his hand and pointed to the darkened woods. The blackness swallowed the men whole as they marched one by one into the woods, not a protest made. The Legend followed last, but not before he glanced at me; his look warned me that I should not follow. I bowed my head, rubbed my chilled hands together near the fire, and when I raised my head, all were gone. I knew then why the Legend was feared; he feared none, not man, not beast, not God."

"I never want to meet the Legend," Brigid said and moved closer to huddle against Patrick's leg.

"Nor do I," echoed another child until there was a resounding chorus of agreement from all the children.

Reena joined in, echoing the same sentiments. "Never, never do I want to meet the Legend."

Chapter 1

"You cannot do this, Reena," Brigid begged her best friend. "It is not a wise choice."

"It is the *only* choice I have." Reena stopped packing the cloth sack with the few food items she had managed to scrounge together. With a heavy sigh, she lowered herself to the wooden chair at the table in front of the hearth—an empty hearth—leaving the small cottage cold, though it was but early autumn. What would happen when winter set in with all its force and fury?

"The villagers are starving and there is not enough firewood for the winter—" Reena suddenly grew silent.

"It is not your fault," Brigid insisted. "The new earl has caused our hardships."

"True, but who in the village is strong enough to stop him from causing more harm? And who is left to protect you?"

Brigid sat and fought the torrent of threatening

tears that ached to spill. "I cannot believe my John is gone."

Reena said nothing, the memory of Brigid's tragedy fresh in both their minds.

The tragic day had brought a horrible change to their prosperous village. All had been well in the small earldom of Philip Kilkern, earl of Culberry. He had been generous to the tenants who farmed his land, and the land had prospered along with the villagers. But two summers ago, the day after Reena had celebrated her twenty-year, the earl had taken ill and died within the week. With no immediate heirs of his own, his land passed to his nephew.

Peter Kilkern arrived in the village that fateful day in early afternoon. The sun was bright, the sky a brilliant blue and the crops grew fat in the fields, which meant there would be a bountiful harvest and more than sufficient food for the winter.

The villagers had gathered to share the midday meal, talk, laugh and hear Patrick Cullen tell a tale or two. They watched as Peter Kilkern rode in on a fine steed, looking as if he was prepared for battle, wearing fine body armament of leather and metal. He had dismounted his horse with ease and stood tall and straight, his six feet or more height impressive as well as the strength of him, his bulk being more muscle than fat. He had sharp features, his nose narrow and ending in a defined point, his lips thin and his dark eyes intent, as though with one swift glance he could take in all and know all.

Reena remained by her father's side, though he blocked much of her slim body with his bulk. She appreciated her father's protective stance, for she shivered at the sight of the new earl.

Peter Kilkern introduced himself and announced in a clear crisp tone what he expected from his tenants. "I care not how hard you work or what revelry you make, but my fee for farming *my land* will be seventy-five percent of all harvested crops."

The crowd had gasped, and he in turn had silenced them with a raised hand. "I am not finished."

The crowd's mumbles faded, and it was with heavy hearts they continued to listen.

"Tenants will not be allowed to hunt on my land—"

That was when Brigid's husband John spoke up.

"How are we to live?"

Peter Kilkern turned glaring eyes on him. "Who asks this?"

John stepped forward without fear. He was a large man in height and width, and handsome. All the women in the village had vied for his attention, but he had lost his heart to Brigid, for how could he not? Brigid was beautiful, tall, slim, long reddish-blond hair and the face of an angel.

"I am John, and we have lived well under Philip Kilkern's fair rule, and his lands thrive because of our care."

Peter Kilkern's voice turned harsh. "*My lands* best continue to thrive because of your care. And you will not hunt off Kilkern land; the animals are for my hunting and feeding pleasure, not yours."

John tried to reason. "Your land stretches far and wide; it will take days for us to reach land where it is permissible to hunt for food."

"That matters not to me."

"How can it not?" John asked. "Do you not care if your tenants starve?"

Peter Kilkern's dark eyes glared like an animal ready to attack. "You dare question me?"

Brigid stepped forward, her instincts to protect her husband, but Reena's father stilled her steps with his large hand and whispered, "Do not be foolish."

John kept his tone calm and reasonable. "Hungry tenants cannot work hard."

Peter Kilkern advanced on John. "Tenants work hungry or not." And to everyone's horror, and before anyone could react, Kilkern pulled his knife from its sheath and struck at John, slicing his arm open from shoulder to wrist.

"No one is to challenge my edicts," the man raged, his face red with anger.

Brigid screamed and ran to her husband as several men nearby reached out for John as he dropped to the ground in agonizing pain.

Brigid had worked frantically to stem the bleeding and to piece his savaged arm together. Fever soon set in, and within a week John died, after having suffered greatly. Everyone in the village had offered Brigid their help, but that winter proved difficult for all. There was barely enough food to feed everyone, and without game from the surrounding woods, many went hungry. Reena's father had gone hunting in an attempt to find food; he suffered a broken leg, and by the time he managed to return to the village, his leg had begun to heal, though not properly. Her father lost much weight, and now he walked with a severe limp that limited his ability to farm the land.

Reena had taken over her father's farming chores, but they proved more demanding than she had expected. Average in height and slim, she had never lacked strength or fortitude in completing any task, but the constant struggle with the land overwhelmed her, and she began to lose weight until she barely resembled herself. Her once full breasts shrunk to a mere handful, her curving waist, which had flowed to curving hips, were no more, and her face had lost its fullness. If it were not for her long, shiny black hair, many would think her a young lad; it fell to the middle of her back and was straight, not a curl or wave to it. She wore it tied back, rarely pinning it up, preferring it loose and free.

When possible, she had helped Brigid attempt to keep up the parcel of land that John had so successfully cultivated. There were many nights when she had been too exhausted to eat and fell into bed only to begin her arduous chores again at sunrise. The second winter proved more disastrous—several older villagers died, along with two babies, barely two years.

Reena could not, *would* not allow another horrendous winter to pass. All the villagers had worked together to help one another, giving food to those who had none, helping to farm another's plot along with their own, but it had taken its toll, and they were beginning to hoard their food for themselves for fear of starving.

It could not go on, especially with what had recently happened to Brigid. Peter Kilkern had mostly kept to himself, his men keeping count of the tenant fees paid with the harvest. One day Kilkern rode up on his steed as the villagers arrived at the keep to pay their fees. Brigid had been among them, and her beauty had caught his eye. He had approached her and made it known that she would do well to please him, for then she and her friends would not go hungry.

Reena knew that her friend considered the option. So many people were suffering, especially the children. What did Brigid have to lose now when a part of her had died with her husband? And she did not wish to see Reena's family suffer any more than they already had. Her father was crippled and her mother rarely left her bed. Reena was the only one capable of taking care of her family, and she planned to do just that.

"I cannot let you do this," Brigid said with a determined swipe at one last stubborn tear on her damp cheek.

Reena stood and continued packing the cloth sack. "And I do not want you selling yourself to the man who killed your husband to keep me and my family fed or any of the villagers from starving."

Brigid reached out and grasped her wrist. "Think about what you do."

"I have thought. I have thought long and hard, and it is the only chance for us all to survive."

"You do not even know where to go."

"But I do," Reena said as she reached in the sack and pulled out a rolled piece of parchment. She spread it out on the table, moving the sack to the side and placing the candlestick with the half-burned wick closer so that Brigid could see clearly.

"A map," Brigid said, surprised, and looked more closely at it. "A good one too, so it must be one of yours." Her fingers traced the intricate lines and drawings.

Reena smiled, something she had not done in many months. But then drawing maps brought her much pleasure—at least it had before Peter Kilkern had arrived. When she had grown old enough to travel, she had accompanied her father on his map-making expeditions, and he had taught her well the ways of recording the land. Reena possessed a natural ability to draw and had an acute eye for detail and memory. She'd remembered much of what she had seen on her travels and had recorded all she could.

Her father and her travels had come to an abrupt halt when Peter Kilkern had arrived. There had been no time for anything but work, and when her father had suffered his broken leg, they'd both known that he would never again map any lands, far or near.

Patrick attempted to encourage his daughter to continue her mapmaking skills. He would whisper at night when her mother was asleep that she should go and travel and not return home.

She understood that he wanted her safe and happy, but she could be neither if she left her family and friends behind to suffer, especially when she had it in her power to help them.

"How do you know this map is accurate?" Brigid asked. "You have never been there."

"But I have," she said with a sad smile. "My father's tales have taken me there so often that I know the way without even glancing at the map."

"Then you also recall that anyone that trespasses on his land suffers a terrible fate."

Reena rolled up the map. "I will not be trespassing." She shoved the valuable parchment in the sack.

"What will you be doing if not trespassing?"

"I will be offering my skills as a mapmaker in exchange for protection of our village."

Brigid shook her head. "What would he want with a mapmaker?"

"I have charted many areas with my father. When he sees my work, I am sure he will see how it could benefit him."

"In exchange for protection? He will lead his army here in exchange for your mapmaking skills?" Brigid disagreed most vehemently. "I do not think so. He will want more than that."

"I will negotiate with him."

Brigid attempted to make her friend see reason. "Do you not remember your father's tale? There is no negotiating with him. The man demands and no one dares defy him."

"I do not intend to defy him. I will provide a good exchange for his services."

"Mapmaking."

Reena stuck her chin out. "Whatever it takes."

Brigid's mouth dropped open. "You cannot mean to offer yourself to him?"

Reena laughed softly. "Do you really think he would want the likes of me?" She held her arms out from her sides and turned slowly. "My body is so thin that I fear a gust of wind will pick me up and carry me away."

"You are a stubborn one, you would demand the wind release you," Brigid said on a gentle laugh. "And you underestimate your beauty."

"I do not think so and I do not care about beauty. I care that the villagers starve and that you are in danger. Something must be done."

"Your strength and courage always amazed me. If it had not been for your strong support, I would never have survived John's death. And even now it takes strength to go do what you plan. If your father or mother knew of your intentions, they would never allow you to go."

Reena reached out and grabbed her friend's arm. "You will not tell them. My father believes that I go off to map, and he hopes—" She could not continue.

"He hopes you find a new home," Brigid said. "Your father and I talk, and you would be wise to listen to him—there is nothing here."

"There is everything here; there is family and friends, and I cannot turn my back on them. We need help, all of us, and we need it before winter sets in. You know as well as I do that there is not a sufficient food supply for everyone. Many will starve, many innocent children. I cannot have that."

Reena slipped on a wool jacket and tucked her hair beneath a cap. "You must promise me that you will tell no one of this."

"And if you do not return with help?"

"I will," Reena said adamantly.

"How long should I wait before I begin to worry over your safe return? Though you have not yet left I worry already, dressed like a young lad." Brigid shook her head.

"A young lad traveling on his own is less likely to be bothered than a young lass on her own. These garments afford me protection; they are my armor. Now as to your waiting, from my father's descriptions and my own calculations I do not think I have to travel far. I would estimate that if I do not return in two weeks' time that I am in trouble, in which case there is nothing you could do."

"I will come search for you," Brigid insisted. "You are my friend; I would not leave you to another's mercy."

"You will, for I will not have you hurt. I do this of my own free choice, and whatever befalls me is the consequence of my own decision. You must promise me that you will not come after me. You are needed here. Who will look after my parents? Who will help the other women with their sick and hungry babies? Promise me, Brigid, please. I need this promise from you."

She hesitated. "I give you my promise reluctantly and because I know that your stubbornness will help you to succeed in an impossible task."

Reena smiled and hugged her friend tightly, the thought of possibly never seeing her again a distant worry in her mind. She would do as she must and she would succeed. She had to, or many would perish.

She grabbed her sack, slipping her arm through the opening beneath the knot that held all the necessary items for her trip. "Fret not. I go off to continue my father's most famous tale—I go to meet the *Legend*."

Chapter 2

R eena stared at the line of trees in front of her. They looked like a row of soldiers guarding the woods behind them; one after the other they stood, their heavy branches resembling arms stretched out, ready to prevent intruders from passing. It was odd that they should grow in a perfect line, for in their oddity they intimidated. They actually looked ready to attack anyone who dared attempt to pass them.

Reena gave a little shiver. The weather had chilled in the last two days, and she was glad for the wool leggings, tunic, jacket and leather boots. That she resembled a young lad mattered not to her; that she remained warm mattered greatly. The change in weather reminded her how very important her journey was. She simply could not fail.

She studied the line of trees; if her father's mappings were accurate, she was standing at the border of the Legend's lands.

A sudden wind rushed around her, swirling up leaves on the ground and sending a stronger shiver through her. The sky was heavy with clouds, making the woods darker than usual for early afternoon and making her wonder at the wisdom of her decision. But there was no going back—she had to find help for her village, or many would die this coming winter.

That thought reinforced her courage. With her sack firmly in her grasp, she breathed a hefty sigh as she approached the line of soldier trees.

She almost expected the trees to march forward and forbid her entrance, but they remained stoic sentinels and allowed her to pass. She proceeded several feet, thinking the woods too dense to harbor any keep or cottage. How, then, did the Legend live? Her father had never spoken of seeing the Legend's home, only his land.

Not allowing herself to grow discouraged, she moved on, climbing over large stones, fallen trees and bending down to pass through an arch of thorns. One thorn caught at her shoulder as if warning her not to go on, to turn back now, while she had the chance.

She did not heed the warning; she simply dislodged the thorn from her jacket and proceeded past bushes and saplings. Stepping out into a large meadow, she could see, with a squint of her eyes, a high stone wall in the distance.

"What do you want here?"

The deep voice so startled her that she jumped in fright, stumbled and fell, her backside hitting the ground hard.

With her elbows braced on the ground and her bottom throbbing, she stared up at a tall man who was so thick with muscles she wondered how he could move. And his face? She had to blink and look again. His face would win no heart, his nose appearing to have been broken more than once. Scars mapped his face and bald head in a mismatched fashion, and the corner of his lip looked to be missing, though Reena had to admit he had compelling eyes, soft blue like the sky on a perfect spring day. His clothes were clean and finely stitched, their colors dark. His boots were fine leather, and the only weapon he carried was a knife tucked in the scabbard attached to his belt.

"Are you deaf?" he asked loudly and pointed to his ear.

She shook her head and hurried to her feet, feeling much more confidence on them than on her bottom. At least she thought she would, but when she reached her full height of barely two inches past five feet she realized she did not even reach the man's chest.

"What do you want?" he demanded.

If he could demand, then so could she. She was on a mission, and her fears would just have to be ignored. She spoke up. "I have come to speak with the Legend."

The large man snickered, grinned and then broke into a fit of laughter.

"When you finish finding my request humorous I suggest you pay it heed, for I am not leaving here until I speak with him."

The man stopped laughing and stared at her. "That sounds like a demand, and he does not take well to demands."

"I am here to barter for his services."

The large man looked her over quickly and shook his head. "What could a young lad like you offer the Legend?"

He thought her a young lad, but that had been her intention when she'd donned the garments. It had worked. Her weight loss and her meager height served her disguise well, but she did not wish to deceive this man, only those who would mean her harm.

"Do you have a hearing problem, lad?" the large man nearly shouted.

"Nay," she said quickly and removed her cap, letting her long black hair spill past her shoulders.

The man's face turned bright red, and he sputtered in an attempt to talk.

Reena felt guilty for causing him unease. "I meant no deception; it was for my own protection I dressed as a lad, my intentions being to travel here and offer my mapmaking skills to the Legend."

With his face glowing red, the man asked, "Mapmaking?"

"Aye," she said quickly and set her bundle on the ground to pull out one of the maps she carried with her. She handed it to him. "See for yourself."

The man took it from her and looked it over. "You mapped this area?"

"My father mapped the area on a visit here. I copied his details and added the ones he spoke about when telling of his journey, but I have personally mapped places myself."

"It is done well."

"Thank you." Reena smiled, proud of her skill.

"But how do I know that is why you are truly here? Many seek to meet with the Legend and not all with good intentions in mind."

Reena took the map from him and stuffed it in her bundle. "Do I look like someone who could cause the Legend harm?"

He looked her over while rubbing his chin. "You are a scrawny lass, but appearance can deceive."

"I can assure you my only motive is to secure his services to help my village in exchange for my mapping skills. I mean him no harm; I give you my word of honor on that."

He nodded. "I will accept your word, but I warn you, a high price will be paid for any deception."

"I wish to deceive no one."

He introduced himself. "I am Thomas."

"Reena," she said and shared a quick handshake with him.

"I know not if he needs a mapmaker, but that is for him to decide. I will take you to him"—he paused, and his smile challenged—"that is, if you have the courage to face the Legend."

Reena shoved her black hair beneath her cap. "Lead the way."

They reached the keep as dusk appeared on the horizon. Her legs were tired, having to take several strides to match Thomas's one large stride, but she complained not. She kept pace no matter how tired she felt, though at the moment she wished for a pallet of any kind to lay her tired body on.

The stone wall that surrounded the castle grounds stood a good eight feet or more. Reena and Thomas crossed a thick wooden plank with heavy chains attached to each side; once raised, it would make the castle impregnable. Reena tilted her head back as she passed under the portcullis and admired the skilled craftsmanship.

The interior of the walled fortress amazed her. It contained a village larger than her own. The many cottages were well kept, the thatching on the roofs fresh and thick. The individual gardens had been harvested along with the large fields that occupied most of the land opposite the cottages. She caught sight of the fully stocked storehouses and envied their harvest.

She passed metalworkers, weavers, and masons who were busy constructing a tower, and it was just past the tower that Reena saw the keep. It was impressive in size and solid in structure.

Villagers called out and waved to Thomas. The people appeared a cheerful lot, but then they had plenty of food and the protection of the Legend. What did they have to fear?

A small chapel sat to the right of the keep, and a short, stout man dressed in brown clerical robes was busy stocking chopped wood beside it.

Thomas waved to him.

The man waved back and smiled. "The chapel will be nice and warm Sunday, Thomas. See you at Mass."

Reena could not help but comment. "There is a fireplace in the chapel?"

Thomas answered without breaking his stride. "Cleric David believes the chapel should be a place of comfort for his flock, so when it was built he insisted on a fireplace."

Her own village had never had a chapel and had limited access to a cleric; the new earl insisted that religion was wasted on heathens.

It was then she felt the rumble beneath her feet; it was as if the ground trembled. She looked to Thomas to see if he had felt it, but he continued walking undisturbed. She rushed to catch up with him, but the steady rumble beneath her had her casting an anxious glance over her shoulder.

She noticed the villagers hurry off the pathway to hover near their cottages and fences as they looked anxiously toward the portcullis.

Was someone approaching the castle?

A fine mist suddenly appeared and crept slowly along the ground as if in answer, but it was not the mist that concerned her.

The rumble turned into a distinct thunder and Reena realized that it actually heralded approaching men on horseback. She heard the unmistakable sound of horses' hooves pounding the planks of the drawbridge before she caught her first glimpse of the warriors.

They entered with a flourish and villagers ran to get out of their way, the massive steeds and powerful mares demanding that no one cross their path— the path where Reena stood.

She froze watching the mighty beasts and their ominous dark riders approach. She wanted to move; she had to move, but the sight of the warrior who led them rendered her powerless.

He was like nothing she had ever seen before.

There was not a speck of light to him. His garments were black, blacker than the darkest night, and his black metal helmet concealed all but his eyes, mouth and chin. He resembled a demon spawned from the depths of hell ready to devour anyone in his path.

"Move away," Thomas shouted at her.

Her fear of the descending demon kept her legs

frozen. Her mind screamed for her to do as Thomas warned, but she could not move as her legs refused to obey her.

The mist swirled around her feet, night devoured the dusky sky, the ground shook and the devil descended upon her.

Again she silently screamed, to run and hide, escape, but she cringed and braced to face death.

She was suddenly swept up by a strong arm and landed with a thud on the horse. With a quick yank her back slammed against his solid, leather-clad chest and his arm remained firm around her waist.

She thought she heard him angrily grumble, "Fool." But she could not be certain.

It was not long before he brought his beast of a steed to a halt at the foot of the steps to the keep. After the horse settled under his skillful hand, he grabbed her arm and swung her off the animal, depositing her on the ground just as Thomas caught up with them.

The dark warrior dismounted his horse, handing the reins to a young lad who waited nearby. He walked up to Thomas. "I will see you and the lad inside."

Thomas watched as the warrior walked up the steps and disappeared behind the massive wooden door. He then turned to Reena and with a grin said, "You have just met the Legend."

Chapter 3

Reena's legs trembled so badly that she thought she would not be able to take another step, but she did. The Legend already thought her a fool; she could not allow herself to appear even more foolish. He would never wish to retain her as his mapmaker.

She entered the great hall behind Thomas, giving a peek past his massive shoulders. The Legend motioned with his hand, and the few people in the hall emptied without protest. He pulled his helmet off his head and laid it on the table beside him before turning to face her and Thomas.

Her breath caught in anticipation, and she clung tightly to her meager sack. She almost gasped at the sight of him. She had expected a beast and instead saw beauty. She had not thought a man's face could be beautiful, but his was a work of art—every bone, each muscle, the texture blended perfectly together.

She could imagine drawing his face, the ease with

which the charcoal would flow, and all because he was crafted so magnificently. And coloring, his eyes were the deepest of browns, like the rich soil just before planting, and his long hair was a lighter shade of brown with streaks the color of golden wheat raging through it. And tall, he was so very tall, at least a head past most men. And his expression?

Thomas quietly voiced her thoughts. "He is angry."

The Legend removed his black leather gloves and tossed them on top of the helmet before walking over to Thomas.

"The reason for this lad's foolishness."

It was not a question; it was a demand, and Reena suddenly wondered if she truly was *foolish* for thinking she could convince such a powerful man to help her. But then, she was here; she had made it this far into the Legend's home, she could not retreat now.

She stepped from behind Thomas before the large man could answer, and she removed her cap, a gesture of respect and to clarify her gender. She did not wish the Legend thinking that she deliberately deceived him.

Her long hair spilled down around her shoulders, and she pushed the silky dark strands behind her ears, away from her face.

His response was to cross his arms over his broad chest and stare at her.

No simple stare, but one that intimidated her to the depths of her soul. Without speaking a word, he demanded an explanation.

She gathered every ounce of courage she had. "A lad fairs better on the road than a lass with no companion. A lad's garb was as necessary as my journey here. I have come to ask for your help."

The Legend looked her over. "What man in your village would allow a bit of a lass like you to journey on her own?"

"It was my choice," she said, a defensive edge to her tone.

"Do you always make unwise decisions?"

She clung tightly to her cap to keep her hands from trembling and her anger from flaring. "I make necessary decisions. My village is starving. We have lost two people already; I will see no more die."

He remained silent for a moment as though in contemplation. "Come join me in food and drink while we discuss this matter?"

The scent of the roasting lamb that cooked on the spit in the hearth had her mouth watering, as did the full platter of breads and cheeses, and she was hungry, having taken only a meager portion of food from her deprived village.

She could not deny her hunger, but the guilt of filling her belly while those she cared about starved caused her pain. "I would be grateful for your hospitality."

The Legend walked to the table nearest the hearth, but before he sat, a plump little puppy came running into the great hall and jumped up and down in front of the dark lord, happy to see him. The Legend ordered him to sit, but the puppy ignored his edict and continued jumping.

The Legend attempted again to make the puppy obey, but it was futile; the plump animal intended to have his way. The Legend shook his head and sat with the puppy cuddling at his feet.

Thomas took a seat beside the Legend, and Reena

sat across from the two men. Ale was poured, bread broken and sliced lamb was served before any words were exchanged.

"Your name?" Once again the Legend ordered.

"Reena," she answered after hastily swallowing a bite of delicious black bread.

"I am Magnus." He offered her his hand, a show of respect she appreciated.

She took his hand, her small one insignificant compared to the size of his, and she realized he softened his handshake to accommodate her meager strength.

"Now what is it you want from me?"

This was why she had come here, and she had to make certain she succeeded. Otherwise, her village would be doomed.

"My village is starving, though our harvest is bountiful. Philip Kilkern, earl of Culberry, was a fair and decent landlord, but he passed unexpectedly, and his property went to his nephew Peter Kilkern, who is not at all fair and definitely not decent. He demands the impossible from his tenants and forbids us to hunt on his land—and he strikes out without provocation. We are at his mercy, for many fear his heavy retributions."

"Why come to me?"

Reena felt his question fair, and he asked it without malice or disregard to her plight—he simply wanted a reasonable explanation. She gave it.

"I have grown up hearing stories about your bravery and how you help others—for a price, of course. I knew of no other who is capable of helping my village."

"What do you offer in exchange for my help?"

Thomas smiled and popped a piece of cheese into his mouth.

She raised her chin and spoke with pride. "I am a skilled mapmaker, and I offer you my services in exchange for your help."

"She is a good mapmaker," Thomas said, his words garbled, since he had not finished all of the cheese.

Magnus turned to him. "You saw her maps?"

Thomas nodded as he swallowed, then pointed to Reena. "Show him."

Reena quickly dug several maps out of her sack, moved the food out of the way and spread out one map after another. "This one is of the village and the earl's land, including his keep."

Magnus looked it over carefully. "You drew this?"

"I have a fine and steady hand with a quill—good eyes and a mind that remembers what I see."

He studied the map for several minutes, then rolled it up to glance over the second map.

Reena was fast to explain. "This is of the land that sits adjacent to Culbery land. It is Dunhurnal land; I have mapped some but not all. It is beautiful, though the keep is in sad neglect. Some believe that Peter Kilkern is attempting to gain the land to advance his holdings and wealth. If that is so, my village will surely starve, for our men travel there now to hunt."

Magnus rubbed his chin while he studied the map with intent interest.

Reena felt a sense of hope. The Legend—she silently corrected herself; Magnus, his name was

Magnus, and she must remember to refer to him by his given name—looked truly intrigued with her maps.

He rolled the map up and looked at the next one. "This is my land."

"Aye," she said with pride.

He looked at her. "You have been here before this visit?"

"Nay, I learned my mapmaking skills from my father. He was in this area and recorded the landmarks. I simply copied his, though now I could do a more detailed map of your property and your keep."

"And the price for a map of my land and home would be my helping your village?"

"Nay," she was quick to say. "I offer my mapmaking skills to you whenever you would need them."

"You would then be my official mapmaker."

"If that is what you wish in payment for your help, then so be it."

He considered her offer and she prayed hard—very hard that he would agree.

"Why did the village send *you* and not a man?"

She took no offense at his question. It was odd that she, a woman, and a small one at that, should journey on her own to request help from the infamous Legend. "The village does not know I have come here seeking your help, and if my father had known what I was about he would have forbidden me to come. He would be more upset with himself that he could not journey here himself."

"He is ill?"

"He suffered a broken leg while hunting for food for the village. He now suffers a severe limp and is limited in his activities."

He leaned forward, bracing his elbows on the table. "You are a wee bit of a lass to be traveling these parts on your own."

"I can see to myself."

Thomas disagreed. "A good gust of wind would pick you up and carry you away."

"I would like to see it try," Reena said defiantly.

"She has courage," Thomas said, looking to Magnus. "She did not fear me and spoke right up about wanting to see the Legend. Most quake in their boots before they meet you."

"I heard the Legend was feared but that he was also a fair man." And seeing him now, the puppy asleep at his feet, offering her food and listening to her plight, Reena knew this to be true. But she also understood why he was feared. It was simple; he feared nothing. "Your skill is fighting, my skill is mapmaking. Think how much easier it would be for you if you knew the lay of the land before you proceeded into battle."

"I have men who supply me with that information."

"But you will have the information there in front of you for you to study again and again. You will know where paths and streams connect, where rivers flow and merge, and the boundaries of lands. It will all be at your fingertips whenever you wish to see it for yourself."

Magnus remained silent, though he kept an eye on her. He looked to be considering her offer, and again she prayed for a favorable decision.

"How do I know this is your work?" Magnus asked.

"A fair question," Thomas said with a nod and broke off a chunk of bread.

Reena agreed. "Aye, it is, and I will be glad to demonstrate my skills for you."

Magnus's silence once again filled the hall, and Reena realized he grew quiet when in thought. She waited.

"You could map the keep and the village. If I find it adequate, I will then consider your offer," Magnus said, as if declaring it done.

His response was not good enough for Reena. "Time is of the essence for my village. I cannot waste time mapping for you if in the end you will only consider my request. I ask that if my skills prove adequate, my offer be accepted—not merely considered."

Again he grew silent, but this time Reena did not wait.

"Time is a factor that can win or lose a battle. I will map your keep and the village in a day's time, and you will then see how my skills can be used when time is of the essence for you."

"You are sure of your skills."

"I am."

"One day's time," Magnus said.

"Tomorrow at this time I will present you with a map of your keep and the village, and you will let me know if my skills are adequate enough for me to be of service to you."

She offered him her hand, binding their agreement.

He took it and held it for a moment. "Tell me if there is anything you need."

Need.

There was so much that she needed, food for her village, protection for the villagers and hope—hope that once again life would be good for them all—and this man could provide it all.

"I have everything I need right now, thank you."

She intended to get right to work, but Thomas stopped her with his question.

"What made you think the Legend was real? Some think Magnus a myth."

"Nay," Reena said with a soft smile that had both men staring at her oddly. "I never thought the Legend a myth. The tales spoke of his strength and courage, and while it was said he was feared by many, they never spoke of brutality. To me the Legend fought with honor and dignity—a difficult task in this brutal world."

"And what do you think of him now that you have met him?" Thomas asked, looking from her to Magnus.

"You are not bound to answer that," Magnus said. "It matters not what others think of me, and Thomas well knows this."

"I do not mind answering," she said. "I think you are a man of many mysteries."

"What mysteries?"

Reena placed her elbows on the table and rested her face in her hands. "You are considerate and accommodating, yet demanding and commanding, and I find it easy to speak with you."

Thomas's whole body shook with a laughter he attempted to contain.

Magnus ignored his friend after giving him a

rough shot to the side with his elbow. "There are not many who would agree with you on that."

Reena yawned; with a full stomach and the warmth of the hall relaxing her, she was about ready to fall asleep. "They do not see you as I do."

"You have only met me. What makes you think you see me more clearly than others?"

"I have a good eye, which is the reason why I am a skilled mapmaker. I see much and remember even more. Your face tells me much."

Thomas wanted to hear more. "What does his face tell you?"

Another yawned attacked, and she moved her arms off the table to sit straight, as if the new position would keep her more alert. "Besides the obvious?"

"You mean that he is so handsome that women fall at his feet?" Thomas asked with a grin.

Both Thomas and Reena ignored Magnus's scowl.

"Aye," she said with a nod, then shook her head. Sleep was nipping at her heels fast and furious, and she had no time for it. She had to start mapping the keep now if she was to finish in a day's time.

"Tell us," Thomas urged.

"He is a man who respects honor and strength, and a man who commands with a demanding hand, and I sense compassion in his heart."

Both men sat speechless, staring at her.

Thomas leaned forward. "You know him well."

Reena smiled at the large man, and then at Magnus. "I see how you truly are a legend, and I hope you will help me in my time of need." She stood, yawning. "Now, I must begin my mapmaking."

"You are tired," Magnus said with concern.

"It will pass." Reena reached for her sack.

"Take time to rest." There was that demand again.

She ignored him. "Nay, there is no time."

"I say there is," he challenged.

"I know otherwise." She held firm to her annoyance and worry. "And I beg for you to understand my plight."

He remained silent for a moment, and Reena held her breath.

"Go do as you will and know that when you grow weary there will be a sleeping pallet ready for you in front of the hearth."

Reena could not contain the sigh of relief that rushed from her lips. "Thank you. I am free to look throughout your keep?"

"Aye," Magnus said. "You are free to go where you wish."

"Again thank you," she said and went through the arch that led to the cooking area.

"She is different than most women," Thomas said, staring after her.

"She is too skinny."

Thomas nodded. "Lack of food will do that."

"She does have courage."

"And she is honest."

"Aye, that she is."

Thomas waited a moment, then continued. "The question is, will you be honest with her?"

"In time."

"You will not tell her then?"

"There is no need," Magnus said.

The puppy woke, yawned, stretched and attempted to climb in Magnus's lap. He picked him up and held him close, the little pup licking at his chin.

Thomas shook his head. "No need to tell the small wisp of a lass that you already had every intention of paying Peter Kilkern, earl of Culberry, a visit?"

Chapter 4

Reena stretched her arms up as if reaching for the sky. She rolled her neck from side to side, lowered her arms, and gave a huge yawn. It had been a long night, with barely two hours of sleep, and the pallet before the hearth in the great hall had been most welcoming. Now that dawn had graced the land with light she needed to get busy.

She had mapped most of the keep, having started at the top and worked her way down. The tower room had fascinated her. She had recorded the area quickly, but she could not help but linger and look over the many interesting objects. Many were from distant lands, but many were foreign to her, their purpose unknown to her. She realized the room was Magnus's solar, his retreat that held his prized possessions, and it gave her a more personal glimpse of the Legend.

He had traveled extensively, and she envied him the sights he had seen and the memories he had gathered, though she realized not all were favorable memories. Weapons of all shapes and sizes hung on the walls, along with beautifully crafted tapestries. Wooden chests carved with the most interesting designs mingled with chairs carved in the same fashion. Goblets of silver and gold sat along flasks of the same metals, and bright-colored silks lay draped over chairs and chests. Then there were the skulls of animals and pelts of the softest fur and a silver metal shield imprinted with strange symbols and several large dents, making her cringe at the thought of the severe blows it had suffered.

She had lingered too long in that particular room, but then there had been so much of interest to look at. She had hurried on after that, recording with her charcoal and storing objects in her mind so that she could add pertinent details later.

Now that the sun had risen she wanted to take advantage of the light and the fine weather.

The keep was just coming to life, the smell of fresh-cooked food wafting in the hall from the kitchen. The delicious aroma made her lick her lips. But there was no time to eat if she was to finish mapping the castle grounds. Besides, there were many in her village that would not have food this day. And that reminded her of the consequences of her task at hand. She could not fail her people. They needed a champion, someone to defend them and to see that they had decent lodgings and adequate food—they needed the Legend.

And she intended to make certain they got the Legend.

She would map his keep and castle grounds so well that he would realize that he could not do without her skills, and though her agreement would bind her to him, she did not mind—the thought actually excited her. Being his mapmaker, she would travel with him and get to see and to record far distant lands, and she would learn and strive to improve her skills.

Reena felt confident, while her stomach quietly protested its hunger. With a hand to her stomach she said, "There will be time for food later."

"I think not."

The strong objection had her spinning on her heels to face the Legend. His good looks caused her stomach to flutter. She had never known or seen such a handsome man.

Today he wore all black, the leather on his tunic trimmed with silver metalwork over his shoulder and across his chest in a well-crafted, circular design. His brown hair was tied back with a few strands of golden blond falling free. But it was the sight of the plump black puppy he held in his arms that made him appear less intimidating.

"You will fill your protesting stomach before you set to work." He summoned a servant who lingered nearby.

The young woman's face lit with a wide smile as she hurried over to him.

"Fill this table close to the hearth with a hearty fare."

The lass nodded, her smile remaining as she hurried off.

Magnus directed Reena to the table flanked by two benches.

Reena felt it impolite to refuse his offer, and by the strong tone of his voice, he told her he would have it no other way. With little choice and not wanting to waste precious time in arguing, she joined him for the morning meal.

He placed the puppy on the ground, and the little animal wandered over to her. She picked him up before she sat down and cuddled him to her. He in turn licked her face, then his attention was caught by something on the ground. He squirmed out of her arms and went off to play with his discovery.

"What do you call him?"

Magnus sat opposite her, his arms braced on the table. "I had thought to give him a warrior's name, but he possesses more friendly traits than warring instincts. So I named him after a friend with a similar nature—Horace."

Reena smiled and looked at the plump puppy that frolicked in delight after whatever caught his eye. "I think Horace suits him."

"Perhaps, but I chose him from the litter, thinking him to be of a warrior's mind."

"Looks can deceive. He is plump and looks as though he will grow large and be strong."

"My exact thought when I first saw him."

Reena spoke in defense of the pup. "He is young and you can guide and train him."

"He runs behind me any time a voice is raised or someone unfamiliar approaches, and he pays no attention to my commands."

Reena could not help but laugh and watched as the plump pup scurried under the table when two servants entered the hall with trays of food. "He knows neither of them?"

"Sadly, he knows them both, so I should amend my words and say he runs and hides by me any time *anyone* approaches."

Reena continued to laugh softly while the young servant girls stacked the table with meats, eggs, cheeses, breads and hot cider. She could not help but think how this abundance of food would be appreciated in her village, and she felt a twinge of guilt for being able to eat so well this day.

"Your smile fades quickly," Magnus said and began to pile her plate with an assortment of food.

"I think of my village." Sadness filled her words and sorrow filled her blue eyes.

He piled his own plate high after filling their tankards with mulled cider. "The only thing you can do for them now is eat and stay strong."

Guilt swept over her. She thought of her mother and father and how Brigid was looking after them. She was probably finding it difficult to pretend that Reena was away on a mapping quest. Brigid would be able to hold out only so long before confessing the truth for her absence, and by then she hoped to be home—the Legend along with her.

"Eat," he urged.

She bristled at his order. She had a good appetite and ate heartily when food was plentiful, but food had been far from plentiful and she had relinquished most of her share to the children. She knew she had lost much weight, and it was obvious he thought the same.

He grew quiet, and she knew he gave thought before he spoke. "You do not need to rush with the mapping, you may—"

She interrupted him quickly. "We made an agreement and I will keep my end. I expect the same of you." With that she placed a piece of meat and cheese on a piece of the dark bread, topped it with another piece of bread, took a generous swallow of cider and stood. "I waste precious time."

She snatched her sack from the bench and slipped on her wool jacket. "When night falls, my mapping will be complete. I will see you then, and our agreement will be settled." She walked to the great hall doors, stopped and turned to him. "Thank you for your generous hospitality."

She opened the door and Horace raced out from under the table, chasing after her, squeezing out the door just before it closed behind her.

Magnus sat there grinning. She was a bundle of strength and determination for a skinny lass. She was right—looks do deceive. No one would credit her with strength, yet she possessed a remarkable amount. And while her skinny features did not attract, there was something intriguing about her. She did have beautiful hair, shiny black and long to the middle of her back and straight—not a wave or curl to any silky strand. Then there were her eyes—blue, the bright blue of a summer's day. And there was the fact that she did not seem at all interested in him. The women he met either sought to catch his eye or cowered at the sight of him, yet Reena did neither. She spoke her mind with courage and conducted herself with respect.

He had never encountered a woman like her and that itself presented a challenge to him.

He would enjoy getting to know her better.

Thomas entered the great hall shaking his head and laughing. He joined Magnus at the table, helping himself to Reena's plate of food. "Horace is sticking close to Reena, especially since she is sharing her food with him."

Magnus cringed. "Now he will not only be a coward, he will be a spoiled coward."

"She is fast and accurate in her mapping skills. I watched her and was surprised by the details she included. I never noticed that cleric David stacks his wood in a particular order, but Reena did and drew it exactly how he stacked it. She also made certain to include where all weapons and tools were located."

"What you are saying is that her skills could prove useful to us?"

Thomas refilled his plate. "Aye, very useful, since most maps are crudely drawn and lack detail, but Reena includes things one would not expect on a map. It is as though her eye must record whatever she sees. And your plans were to go to Culberry regardless of the plight of Reena's village."

"It would not be wise for her to be aware of my plans."

"Or the truth behind them?"

"That is for me alone."

Thomas shrugged and reached for a thick slice of bread. "Stubborn as usual."

His remark did not bother Magnus. "My stubbornness is my shield."

"Your stubbornness is your prison. Reena seems a good lass and her talents could prove useful. Why not just tell her you go her way, offer the assistance you know you will not deny her and give her a position as your official mapmaker—that would settle everything."

"I could do that, but I think what brought Reena to me was more than just help for her village."

"What else does she seek?"

"Life."

"Then your plans do include her? For you can teach her much of life."

Magnus smiled. "Aye, my plans include her."

"I like her."

"Do you, now?" Magnus said.

Thomas blushed a bright red. "Not that way. She is a nice woman and has courage."

Magnus leaned his arms on the edge of the table. "What you mean is that she was not intimidated by the sight of you."

Thomas shrugged, as if a woman's reaction to him mattered not. "She faced me with courage and spoke her mind—and shortly after, she talked with me as though we were friends."

Magnus felt for his friend. While Thomas had known women, he had never known love. Deserted at the young age of five, he had been raised by the brutal innkeeper at the inn where he had been abandoned. The man had physically abused Thomas, breaking his nose several times. It was by chance—though Magnus often thought it was fate that he had stopped at the dismal inn—that Thomas had come to a much welcome rescue when a band of thieves had attempted to rob Magnus. Afterward they had shared several ales and talked well into the night; by morning Thomas had left with Magnus. That had been eight years ago, when Thomas had barely been twenty and Magnus twenty and three. They had been together ever since, their friendship growing stronger with the passing years.

While Magnus never lacked for female companionship, coins were the only way Thomas could find a companion. Magnus hoped that one day his friend would find a woman who would accept him for who he was.

"Reena is much like me," Thomas said.

Magnus found his remark curious. "How so?"

"Many misjudge her. They think her weak because she is small and thin, like many think me stupid because I am large and ugly."

"Looks deceive," Magnus said. He had been surprised to learn that Thomas was more intelligent than anyone could imagine and could even read and write. A man who had traveled extensively with a troupe of performers had stopped at the inn and taken a room. He had been penniless, and with no coin to pay the innkeeper, he had been put to work at the inn, and he and Thomas had formed a friendship. The man had taught him to read and write before sneaking off one night with a troupe of performers passing by.

"Your looks deceive also."

"Aye, they do," Magnus admitted. "My fine features make many think me a fine man."

"Until they see you dressed for battle," Thomas said and shivered. "You put the fear of the devil in the devil himself. Your eyes turn cold and empty, your features grow taut and the air around you grows heavy with fear."

"It is who I am—the Legend."

"It is not who you are." Thomas said no more. There was no need; both men knew and understood each other well. Their bond of friendship was strong, their insight into each other that of loving brothers.

"It is who I am out of necessity."

"Aye, life does that to us all—teaches us to deal out of necessity."

Magnus turned silent and looked deep in thought.

Thomas remained quiet for a few moments, giving him time, then he spoke. "You knew it would come to this, it was but a matter of time."

"Aye, but I did not expect interference from a skinny young woman who prides herself on her mapmaking skills, and now—"

Thomas laughed. "And now, for her own protection, she must become your official mapmaker."

Chapter 5

Magnus studied the maps with surprise and admiration. The young woman was skilled and possessed an eye for detail. He knew well his lands and had them guarded wisely, which Reena had seen and recorded accurately, even to the guard tower in a large tree west of the portcullis. Few realized it existed or knew that a guard was ever present, but Reena had seen and she had recorded the man—sleeping. He would see to that matter later, but for now, her skills could prove advantageous to him.

Reena stood silently in front of the table on the dais, nervously waiting for the verdict.

Thomas sat beside Magnus, his head bent over the maps as Magnus examined each paper. She was simply remarkable—even with poor-quality paper she produced an excellent and accurate map. He had not thought anyone capable of such talented mapping skills; most maps he possessed were crude and often inaccurate.

"You have done a fine job," Magnus said, his interest still held by the maps in front of him.

"Fine job, you say?" Thomas tapped the one map with his finger. "That is more than a *fine* job, that is"—he tapped the map again—"that is—is—"

Magnus waited, amused. Thomas rarely had difficulty articulating his opinion—except around women. He would grasp for words that simply deserted him and be left floundering like a fish abandoned of water.

"The best map I have ever seen," Thomas blurted.

Magnus slapped his friend on the back. "Then that settles it, Reena is my official mapmaker."

Reena thought her trembling legs would fail her at that moment, but her courage kept her standing. She had done it; the Legend was returning with her and all would be well in the village. Tears of relief almost filled her eyes but she fought them back; she would show no weakness, only strength, in front of this man.

Magnus stood. "We leave tomorrow at dawn."

Relief flooded her like a rushing wave and she braced her hand on the edge of the table.

"You need food and rest," Magnus commanded. "Your day has been long and you have not eaten since the morning meal."

"There was too much to be done—"

"And now that it is done, you will rest."

It was a stern command and it took Reena a moment to realize that he had the right to command her, for she was now under his charge and direction. "As you say."

"Come join us," Magnus offered and pulled out the chair beside him.

Reena looked along the dais, which was empty

but for Magnus and Thomas. The evening meal had long been finished, and now few men sat conversing near the hearth while several servant girls chatted at another table. She hesitated before joining the two men. The dais was for more important members of the lord and lady's keep, not a mapmaker such as herself.

But Magnus had invited her, and besides, she was terribly hungry.

Reena helped herself to the fruit and cheese piled high on a silver platter in front of where Magnus sat. He moved the platter closer to her.

"What else would you like?"

"Cider, please."

"No more food?"

She shook her head, her mouth full with a bite from a juicy apple.

"Tell me more of this village of yours." Magnus poured her the cider.

She quickly finished the apple and downed a mouthful of cider, anxious to tell him all she could about her village. "The villagers have made Culberry a prosperous land. We have worked hard to produce hardy and abundant crops, and our animals are healthy. The cows provide us with tasty milk, and the sheep, fine wool for spinning."

She paused a moment to nibble on a piece of cheese and then resumed talking with a bright smile. "My father is the village storyteller. He entertains everyone with exciting and marvelous tales. Midday you will find many gathered in the village to hear a story. Brigid and I would rush from wherever we were to listen, even if we had heard the tale again and again. My father finds a way of making a redundant tale new and exciting so no one tale ever sounds the same."

"Brigid is a friend of yours?" Magnus asked.

Reena laughed softly and Magnus was caught by the beauty of the delicate sound, like soft chimes ringing in a warm breeze. And the pleasantness of her smile amazed him; it radiated over her entire face.

"We are best friends. Growing up together we would get into mischief, fight mythical dragons in the nearby woods and of course search for those ever elusive wood fairies that all children attempt to find."

Her smile faded. "Brigid was married to a wonderful man, but Peter Kilkern caused his death, and now she mourns a husband and a life that is no more."

"Magnus will see to Peter Kilkern," Thomas said with certainty.

Reena felt assured by Thomas's declaration, and the long day fast caught up with her. If she rested her head back she was sure to fall asleep, and a yawn surfaced to prove it.

"You need a full night of sleep," Magnus said.

"Aye, that I do, especially since we leave early tomorrow."

"I had a room prepared for you."

"The sleeping pallet I used by the hearth last night will suffice."

"You are in my employment now and as such will do as directed."

He spoke with authority, and Reena, now being in his service, had to accept that. But he also had to accept that she would speak her peace, in a respectful manner, of course. "I am grateful for the opportunity to map for you in return for protecting my village, but I must ask how long this will indebt me to you."

"A fair enough question. I will expect six months' time from you in return for my services, and then you may decide if you would like to remain in my service for a fair coin."

Reena thought that was more than fair; he actually was being generous with her. And she would accept his generosity with a simple, "Thank you."

"You are most welcome, though know that I will expect much from you and you will have little time for much else but mapping for me." Her skills would serve him well for what he had planned.

"I understand and I will serve you well; you will not be disappointed."

Magnus summoned a servant with a wave. "Show Reena to her room."

She bid the two men goodnight and followed the servant from the hall.

"She is a good and brave lass and deserves a good man," Thomas said. He stared at Magnus for several moments.

"What is it?"

Thomas nodded as if agreeing with himself. "Reena would be good for you and you for her."

"And why is that?"

"You do not like women who have a need for attention. They annoy you."

"You know this, do you?"

Thomas nodded again, though agreeing with Magnus this time. "I have watched you with women, hoping to learn your skills with the fairer sex so that if I am lucky enough to attract one I will know well what to do. And I have learned that women who demand attention and praise irritate you."

"You are right," Magnus admitted freely. "I cannot abide a demanding woman or a weak-willed woman, for that matter."

"Reena is strong and not at all demanding."

Magnus gave a quick laugh. "I think Reena can demand when she wants to."

"She defends, not demands."

Magnus grinned. "You have a way with words— you make them go your way."

Thomas ignored his remark. "You have been alone too long."

"So have you, so when you find a woman, then so will I," Magnus challenged. His tone turned serious. "Besides, Reena has much to learn about me yet, and when she learns, she may fear me as most do."

"I think Reena is wiser than most."

"We will find out soon enough."

Reena climbed beneath the clean bedding and snuggled comfortably under the wool blanket, a roaring fire in the fireplace adding to her warmth. And though she yawned with fatigue she found her active thoughts keeping her awake.

The Legend confused her. She could see how many believed him a fearsome man who frightened and intimidated people, for she had thought the same of him at first. But there was more to Magnus the man. It was as if he were two men in one.

He seemed a true friend to Thomas and was generous with her. He made her feel welcome in his home, and she had not expected that from the Legend, especially after their first encounter. She had trembled and shaken with fear and had been worried about asking for his help. And while he continued to intimidate her at times, she also felt a sense of ease with him. How? Why? She simply did not understand.

She quickly raised her head, listening to a noise that caught her attention, a scratching sound, a faint whine and then more scratching. She reluctantly got out of bed and went to the door. No sooner did she ease the door open to peek out than a round ball of black fur came rushing into her room and hurried to the bed.

Horace stood next to the bed, wagging his tail even faster as Reena approached. He pounced at her legs, jumping up and down.

She scooped him up and put him on the bed, returning to the warmth of the wool blanket. The pup waited until she was comfortable and then snuggled next to her chest; after a quick lick to her nose he went to sleep.

"The Legend's own pup is docile and pays no heed to his commands."

The little animal was one of few who did not fear the Legend. But was that fear not why she was here, to hire the infamous Legend to do what he did best—make men fear him. She wanted Peter Kilkern to fear him and leave her village in peace.

She no longer needed to worry about that, for Magnus would see to it. They had struck a bargain, her mapping skills in return for his protecting her village. He had given his word, and that was all she needed, for in all her father's stories the Legend was a man of his word, and meeting him she could see the truth of it.

Her body relaxed, and she knew sleep would soon claim her. That was fine. She was anxious for the morning to come and eager to return home. She hoped all was well in the village and that Brigid did not overly worry about her.

She missed her friend and her family, and she would probably miss them even more when the time came to leave with the Legend. She had not given the idea much thought; if she had, she would have hesitated in her decision. Her whole life had been her village. Now she was the official map-maker to the Legend. She would live at his keep, travel with him and obey his commands.

Life was certainly going to be different.

Chapter 6

Reena stood on the keep's steps, clutching her makeshift satchel in her arms and watching with excitement as the Legend's men prepared to embark on their journey. It was an orchestrated effort, everyone working together in unison. They were an organized and practiced troop, impressive in size, mostly large men, bulky with muscles and superior strength. They were clad in dark brown shirts covered with black leather tunics and black leggings. Swords, bows and arrows, and battle-axes were being strapped to horse and man alike.

She could see how the sight of them could intimidate, though she felt not the least frightened by them. They were pleasant and well mannered toward her. One man had even handed her a brown wool cloak, explaining that the Legend's troop all wore the same distinguishing colors—brown and black.

She had wrapped it around her immediately,

pleased that she was so easily accepted by them. And pleased that soon she would be on her way home.

Wagons were packed, their drivers ready, reins in hands, and several women, in brown cloaks, stood alongside prepared to walk. How this large troop had managed to prepare for a journey in one day's time certainly spoke highly of their skills and dedication to their leader. They seemed prepared to follow him anywhere.

She wondered why women were joining the troop, since it seemed like the men were preparing to go off to battle. But then, the Legend had his way of doing things, and she was not one to judge them.

Thomas suddenly walked out of the keep, and all the men quickly mounted their horses. He was dressed as the others, though his bulk and bald head made him appear much more intimidating. He went to his horse and mounted, then all eyes turned to the keep's open door.

Reena smiled knowing they all waited for the Legend.

Her smile vanished in a flash as she took several hasty steps back from the dark figure that emerged from the keep.

Complete silence filled the cool autumn air, not a voice was heard, not a bird sang, and the bright sun hurried behind a dark cloud.

Reena remained frozen where she stood, her mouth agape and her body trembling as she watched the Legend walk forward.

He wore complete black except for the silver studs that accented his leather tunic in a random design. But it was not his dress that left her speechless, it was his metal helmet, black as night covering nearly all of his face except for his eyes, mouth and jaw. It looked as though it had been made for him, rounding over his head and fitting snug to his face.

She shivered, for his appearance certainly helped make him a legend.

His eyes slowly canvassed the area, searching the sea of faces until his intent gaze settled on her.

He walked down the steps and toward her, and if she were not still frightened from the sight of him she would have run. Instead she clutched her sack to her chest like a shield, fought to keep her trembling legs from collapsing, and waited.

He stopped mere inches away from her, and while she was familiar with his height, he seemed taller, broader and more like a stranger. "Do you ride?"

She nodded, finding that her voice had deserted her.

He signaled, and two men on horse rode up to them. One man held the reins to a beautiful dark gray mare with a black mane. The other rider held the reins of a magnificent beast of a black horse that pranced and snorted and appeared agitated until he caught sight of the Legend. Then he calmed instantly.

The Legend took the reins of the gray mare and handed them to Reena. "She is yours, treat her well and she will serve you well."

Before she could thank him he reached out, grabbed her by the waist, and hoisted her up on the horse. Her breath caught with the ease and swiftness of his actions. It was as if she weighed nothing to him. He could move her about like a simple reed in the wind with no effort at all. His strength suddenly intimidated, and she reminded herself to pay heed to it.

He mounted his own horse, the stallion's demeanor obedient in the presence of the Legend.

"You will ride behind me and Thomas unless I order otherwise."

She nodded again, her voice, she feared, lost forever somewhere in the depths of her trembling stomach. She followed behind him after Thomas rode forward and easily directed the horse behind the two men. She was a compliant mare, though not docile. Reena could feel the strength of her body beneath and against her legs, and she knew without a doubt that the mare possessed power.

Reena kept a steady eye on the Legend's back, and it was not until at least an hour later that her body finally relaxed and her voice returned, though she remained silent. Her mind had a difficult time releasing the image of the Legend emerging from the keep.

He was as her father had so often described him—fearful to look at. A tactic that she was certain served him well in battle, but he was not presently in battle and still he was dressed as he was. No wonder he was so feared; he looked forever ready to battle. Who would dare oppose a man who was always prepared to fight?

She forced herself to remember Magnus and his fine qualities, but her urgings did little to comfort her. The dark-clad man in front of her was too imposing to even think that Magnus resided within him.

And she was indebted to this dark lord for six months. She sighed. Had she been too hasty? She shook her head, her answer obvious. Her village needed help and she needed to remain brave no matter how much she trembled.

Clouds continued to drift past the sun intermittently throughout the day. A chill autumn wind swept around the band of travelers, reminding them that winter was not far off and now was a good time for a journey.

If the weather held, they would have no trouble reaching her village in two days' time. She was glad to be returning home. She had worried about family and friends even though she had been gone for a mere six days. It took only one day's time for an incident to change lives completely.

Reena kept a steady eye on the Legend's back. His dark side was necessary to her village. She wanted Peter Kilkern to pay for Brigid's husband's death, and she wanted him gone and the Legend to be the lord of their land. She hoped then that joy would return to Brigid, laughter to her village and the abundance of food they once shared to be theirs once again.

This was her hope, her dream, for then her village would never need to worry about survival—the Legend would forever protect them. If she had spoken of this to anyone they would have thought her foolish, for they would have insisted there was no way Kilkern land could belong to the Legend.

But then no one in the village would have believed that the Legend would have agreed to help her. Yet here she was returning to the village on a mare he had given her, a part of his legion.

Her being in service to him partly united him with her village. Marriage, however, was the only way to permanently keep her village under his protection, and who better to marry him than Brigid? She was beautiful, and he, handsome. They would have fine children and Brigid would be happy, having a home and a husband once again.

The thought had been a seed, restless in her mind, that had suddenly sprouted and flourished. With the two wed it would mean that she would not be alone in her service to the Legend. Her friend would always be near and then she could remain in his legion when her debt to him was fulfilled. And she would always have her best friend close by and well protected.

They stopped for a brief repose, though many of the men remained on guard around the group. Thirst and hunger were quenched, conversation punctuated with laughter—a common sound.

Reena sat alone, braced against a decaying stump, munching on an apple. She enjoyed the sights and sounds in front of her, for they reminded her of how her village had once been and how it would soon be again. In time she would get to know these people and make friends, but for now she preferred to watch and learn and, of course, sketch the sights in her mind.

She picked up a slim branch nearby and snapped it in two, choosing the pointed end that best fit her needs. She then began to draw the man and woman talking a few feet away.

Their interest in each other was obvious, and she smiled as she reproduced their faces in the dark soil in front of her.

"So your talent extends to drawing people."

The familiar voice did not startle her, since the

heavy crunch of fallen leaves warned her of someone's approach. She was, however, relieved to see that Magnus joined her, the helmet removed and with it, the Legend.

He sat alongside her, giving her enough room to complete her drawing. "I think they favor each other."

"Aye," she agreed. "You can see it in their faces."

"It is an excellent drawing. Why not commit it to paper?"

"My paper supply is limited and I must conserve it for mapping."

"You map for me now. I will supply you with paper, quills, ink and paper enough to draw, besides map."

She stopped, her eyes wide and her smile bright. She reminded him of a young girl who had just been surprised with the most wonderful gift yet doubted what she had heard.

"Truly, I will have paper to draw besides map?"

"Aye, you have my word."

He was shocked by her actions that followed. She dropped the stick, turned, and flung her arms around him and hugged him tightly, her face pressed to his.

"You are wonderful and I am forever grateful." She released him and gleefully scooped the stick up to return to her drawing. "I will draw anything you wish, a place, an object, a person." She turned her eyes to him, the drawing stick idle in her hand. "Is there someone you favor who you wish me to draw?"

He thought she had startled him with her actions, but now her words gave him a start. To his own surprise, he answered her. "There is no one I presently favor."

She looked delighted by his response and he assumed she was attracted to him, hence her probing question. Oddly, he found her appealing, though why he couldn't say. She was too thin, with barely a shape to her, yet her creamy skin was flawless and looked soft to the touch. Her long silky black hair was forever escaping the combs that fought to contain it. She did not pretend or falter falsely; she was honest in word and action. She was a talented artist, and he had enjoyed the few conversations they had shared, finding her more knowledgeable than most women he had known.

And though he attempted to ignore it, he found himself easily aroused around her. He had tried to determine the reason, since usually he did not find plain features and a thin body attractive. But damned if he did not grow hard when near her.

He did not notice that while he was deep in thought she replaced the couple she had been drawing with the face of a startlingly beautiful woman.

When he did, he could not help but remark, "She is stunning."

"Brigid, my best friend." She smiled. "She is a loving and caring person and would make someone a loving wife. Children and a home are important to her, unlike me, who prefers to explore and map my explorations or draw the many wonders I see."

Was she attempting to find her friend a mate? And was she considering him a good prospect? The thought annoyed him. Did she not find him attractive or interesting enough to pursue for herself?

Thomas approached and prevented further discussion.

The large man craned his neck to view the drawing. His breath caught and he stepped slowly around to view the face more clearly. "She is the most beautiful woman I have ever seen."

"Her friend Brigid, who is a loving and caring woman." Magnus noticed his response pleased her. Did she think him interested?

Thomas continued to stare. "It shows in her lovely features."

"She would make a good wife," Reena said and looked to Magnus.

Thomas grinned, his eyes following Reena to Magnus. "A good wife, do you hear that?"

"I hear it well enough. Do you wish me to meet this friend of yours?" Magnus asked with a curtness that caused Thomas to raise his brow.

Reena paid no heed to his sharp tone. "If it would please you."

He stood abruptly. "I am always pleased to meet a beautiful woman."

Reena was overjoyed. "I will introduce you as soon as we reach the village."

"You will ride beside me," Magnus ordered her. "There are matters I wish to discuss with you."

Reena nodded and reached out with the stick to erase her friend's face.

"Nay," Thomas said, his beefy hand grabbing the stick. "Leave her beauty for the trees and birds to admire."

"Aye, she would like that, since she admires the trees and birds and considers them her friends."

"Then she toils in the soil with enjoyment?" Thomas asked as they walked toward their horses.

"She loves digging, planting and growing, and

she is an excellent cook." Reena spoke loud enough for Magnus to hear, since he walked a few feet in front of them.

"I already have an excellent cook," Magnus called back to her.

"Then that gives her time to stitch, since she is an artist with needle and thread."

"Is there anything she cannot do?" Magnus nearly shouted.

Reena was quick. "Defend herself."

Magnus shot back just as quickly, "A weakness in all women."

Reena bristled at his remark. "I can defend myself well enough."

"Can you now?"

Before Reena could blink, Magnus had turned and was upon her in an instant. He grabbed her by the shoulders and just as quickly took her to the ground, his legs straddling her while his hands had her shoulders pinned against the hard earth.

"Now can you defend yourself?"

"Aye, I can," she said with a calmness that belied her quivering stomach.

He laughed.

"I only need to ask you to remove yourself from me."

She forever startled him, whether in action or words. "And you think a foe would honor your request?"

"You are not a foe. I would not be so foolish as to ask a foe, but then I would not be so foolish as to place myself in a position of defending myself against someone more capable than me."

"She defends herself well," Thomas said with a laugh.

Begrudgingly Magnus agreed. "Aye, she does; she uses her intelligence and does not waste her strength in battling someone she cannot defend against." He stood and offered his hand to her.

She took it and got to her feet, brushing off her cloak. "If I had no choice I would give a foe a worthy battle, though knowing full well victory would not be mine. I would not meet my demise without a fight."

The thought that Reena would be in such a helpless situation and in need of defending herself infuriated Magnus. "You are under my protection now."

The three continued toward the horses.

"I am grateful to know that, but I also know that each day can bring the unexpected and I must remain aware and keep my eyes wide and my ears alert."

Magnus reached out suddenly, grabbing her around the waist and hoisting her up onto her mare. "You do that, but know that anyone who dares to harm one of mine will suffer my wrath."

He walked over to his horse, mounted, and reached out to take his helmet from one of his men, who held it up to him.

Reena watched as the thoughtful and gentle Magnus disappeared and the fearsome Legend returned, and she shivered from the darkness that appeared to consume him.

A sharp yapping sound broke through her musing, and she looked to see plump little Horace running toward them. He stopped near her, plopped down on the ground for a second, then jumped up and down barking.

Magnus rode over. "Sit, Horace."

The puppy jumped up and down several more times before he sat, his plump body leaning to the side and his tongue lolling out of the side of his mouth.

"I did not know you brought him along," Reena said, delighted. She favored the pup, for he had followed her around yesterday like a dutiful guardian.

Magnus's deep brown eyes peered at her through the slits of his helmet. "He has been riding in the wagon since our departure, too lazy to walk, and now he wants to join you on your horse."

Horace seemed to understand and jumped up near Reena as if insisting she reach down and lift him up.

"He is welcome to ride along with me."

Horace barked and continued looking to Reena, completely ignoring Magnus.

Magnus dismounted and leaned down to scoop the pup up, but Horace, upon seeing the large dark figure approach him, scurried like a frightened rabbit beneath Reena's horse and whimpered.

"He is threatened by you," Reena said sympathetically, understanding the small pup's reaction.

Magnus grumbled for a moment, then ordered the pup out from under the horse. Horace whimpered louder.

"I will get him," Reena offered.

"You will not." Magnus was curt. "He will obey me."

Reena defended the pup. "But he is terrified of you."

"He must learn." Once again he ordered the pup from beneath the horse.

Horace started to shiver.

Reena did not hesitate as she slipped off the horse, scooped up the petrified Horace, and looked to Magnus. "Fear teaches fear. Strength teaches strength."

Magnus felt as if he had just been reprimanded and taught a lesson. He reached out to hoist Reena back onto her horse, and Horace hurried to bury his face in the crook of Reena's arm. He shook his head and placed a heavy hand on her leg. "I need no reminding of how to handle my dog."

She would have argued otherwise but thought better of disagreeing. She was in his service now, and that required obedience. Besides, the pup was safe and comfortable in her arms.

"I am sorry if I offended."

Her apology seemed to irritate him even more, and he marched off without a word, leaving a decisive chill in his wake.

Reena hugged the pup to her. "Do not worry, Horace. Brigid will calm the Legend."

Horace whimpered and snuggled closer to Reena, tucking himself soundly in her arms.

"Brigid will be good for him," she whispered so only she could hear.

Why, then, did the thought upset her?

Chapter 7

Reena sat by the campfire, perplexed. They were not that far from their destination, yet Magnus had ordered them to camp for the night. She had hoped they would continue and arrive near nightfall, but not so.

She huddled in the comfort of the brown wool cloak, grateful for its warmth, for the night had chilled considerably. Frost would soon be thick and heavy on the branches, and winter was not far behind. And a sorrowful winter it would have been if she had not enlisted the Legend's help.

She knew even at this moment that while she sat warm, her stomach full, many in her village huddled before a dying hearth, their stomachs aching for a scrap of food.

A good reason why they should have continued on and not camped for the night when they were so close. Her village could have had food tonight and eased the torment they had suffered.

Thomas joined her, draping a wool blanket around her, adding more warmth and much more guilt. It hung heavy on her shoulders.

"Why do we stop? Why not go on? The village is so close." She heard her own annoyance.

Thomas simply shrugged as he stretched out on the opposite side of the fire from her. "I do not question his decisions. They have always proven to be wise."

"My people are hungry." Her annoyance was replaced by a sense of defeat. What if she failed one person by being so close and not arriving on time? Losing one was as bad as losing ten, for they were all connected—they all cared for each other, thus one survival meant everyone's survival.

"Do not worry yourself," Thomas urged. "This night will make no difference to anyone in your village. If one should die of hunger, our arrival would not have saved him for he was too close to death to save. What matters is that tomorrow your village will have an abundance of food once more and the winter will see no one go hungry. Magnus will make certain of it."

Reena stretched out on her pallet. "Thank you, Thomas, your words help."

"Good, now sleep, for tomorrow we rise early and there will be much work to do when we arrive at your village."

"Aye, much," she agreed and smiled to herself. She would help distribute the food and assist the healers with the ill, but first she would hug her parents to her—and Brigid as well. Tears threatened her eyes, but she fought them with a deep strength, as she had so many times in the last few months. It would do her no good to show weakness. After all was settled and everyone taken care of, she would go to a place of solitude and release the abundance of tears that needed shedding—alone, where no one could see or hear her. Only then would she allow herself to cry.

Reena rose with the sun, happy that it was a beautiful day for her homecoming. The camp rose as well and packed in mere minutes, no food being cooked or distributed. Magnus had given orders that they would share the morning fare with the village.

He approached her with strong and hasty strides where she stood beside her horse, and she fought the urge to retreat. He intimidated when dressed for battle, especially when he wore his helmet. He resembled the dark lord of the underworld who rose from the earth to instill fear.

He stopped beside her, so close that his arm brushed hers. His slight touch sent a shiver through her, the likes of which she had never felt before. And it perplexed her, for she had tasted fear on more than one occasion and his touch felt nothing like fear.

"You are chilled?"

She focused on his eyes, for in them, beyond the helmet, was Magnus. "Nay, I am fine and eager to return home and see my family and friends."

"I need not remind you that your loyalty is now with me?"

She nodded. "I understand."

"Then no matter my edict you will follow?"

She hesitated a moment. What was he asking of her? She gave his words thought and then spoke up. "As long as it brings no harm to my village."

He smiled and she had to fight down the shiver that raced over her, for his expression looked ominous framed by the dark helmet.

"You have courage and you are honest with your word—I would ask nothing of you that would bring you dishonor."

"Then I will follow your command without hesitation."

His hands went to her waist, but before he hoisted her up on her horse he bent his head and whispered, "Trust me."

She had no choice but to trust him. Her fate and the fate of the village were in his hands.

He swung her up onto her horse and walked off to mount his own horse and lead his troop. All followed him without hesitation, as did she.

Reena rode beside the Legend, and she grew anxious on their approach to the village. Everyone knew of her absence, Brigid having told them she was on a mapping expedition that could possibly provide the village with another source of food. They would be relieved to see her, but cautious of the troop she rode with.

From what she could see at first glance nothing much had changed. The village looked as she had left it—defeated and on the verge of utter starvation.

The villagers eyed the entering troop with suspicion and caution, whispering among themselves. A few hurriedly crossed themselves in protection, uncertain of their fate and fearful of the iron masked man who led them.

She called out to a few and waved to others, alerting them to her presence. While they responded in kind, they continued to keep a suspicious glance on the man in the iron helmet.

"Reena," Magnus said, catching her attention. "A place where I can address your people."

She nodded and called out to the people to meet them in the center of the village, for she had important news to share with them. All followed, eager to hear from Reena and whoever it was she had brought to them, though they kept a safe distance from the stranger on the large black stallion.

"Introduce me, Reena, so that the villagers' needs can be seen to."

Reena nodded, proud that concern glared in his dark eyes, Magnus's eyes, but it was the Legend she introduced.

"I left here but five days ago to seek help for our village. I have returned with that help. I bid you all welcome to our home . . . the Legend."

Gasps and cries rang loudly in the air, and the children, having heard tales of the infamous warrior, scurried behind their parents in fright. Reena caught sight of Brigid. Her friend was helping her father, who leaned heavily on a crutch, and her mother, who looked more pale and thin than when she had left. Her father's eyes widened in shock, though they softened quickly enough, and tears followed a smile as he looked on his daughter with pride.

Magnus made no move to dismount; he sat in complete silence, waiting as the crowd quieted to a hush and silence once again reigned.

"Your village is truly blessed to have one so brave among it. Reena came to me and offered her mapping skills in exchange for protection of her village."

He did not wait for the rushed murmurs to settle before he continued, "I accepted her offer, her mapping skills having been proved worthy of such an exchange.

"My people have food for you and healers to help the ill. After you have feasted I shall speak with you all again." He turned to his troop. "See to all their needs." He then looked down at Thomas, who stood beside his horse. "Place guards with extras in the tall trees to the north."

"It will take Kilkern time to learn of our arrival, since he appears a poor leader with no extended sentinels in watch of his lands."

Magnus lowered his voice. "By then we will be gone."

Thomas nodded and walked off to see to his orders.

Reena walked up to his horse. "I would like you to meet my parents and my friend."

Magnus dismounted, slipped his helmet off, and handed it and the reins to one of his men, who stepped forward without a word having been spoken to him. Curious and cautious eyes followed him and Reena as they approached her parents. A few brave souls nodded and whispered their thanks, though none looked directly at him.

"Magnus, may I present my mother, Anona, and my father, Patrick."

Magnus gave a curt bow to her mother. "Your daughter is an exceptional woman, and I am pleased to have her in my service."

"Thank you, sir, for such kind words."

Magnus turned to her father and extended his hand. "Your daughter speaks highly of you and your talent."

Patrick accepted his offer of friendship, giving his hand a firm shake. "She far surpasses my meager skills and does me and mine proud."

Reena was quick to introduce her friend. "This is Brigid, my friend since forever."

Reena had not wasted a moment in introducing her friend to him. Brigid was as beautiful as her drawing. She had hair the color of freshly sown wheat, eyes that mirrored the blue skies, and a faint blushed skin that looked petal soft, with a body that captured a man's breath.

But it was her all too skinny friend who stood beside her that caught his attention, especially since he caught her shiver and thought for sure he heard her stomach grumble. She required food and rest, but he had learned fast that Reena put others before herself. He would soon change that.

"I am pleased to meet you and I look forward to becoming better acquainted, but right now I am sure you all must be looking forward to the morning fare." He turned to Reena. "Take your family and friend and feast. We will talk when you are finished."

"I am grateful for your generosity," she said before walking with her parents and friends toward the wagons, where the women were busy arranging blankets on the ground and handing boards filled with breads, cheeses, meats and more to the crowd to take and eat in the bright sunshine.

"Reena."

She turned and hurried over to him.

He placed a finger under her chin and gave it a slight lift. "You make certain you eat well."

She smiled. "I will try, but I am so happy to be home, I do not know if I could eat a morsel right now."

"I expect you to eat more than a morsel."

"Is that an order?" she asked on a laugh.

"You are too skinny, and I require strength in those who serve me."

She bristled. She knew her unintended weight loss made her appear frail, but her determination kept her strong.

"Do not underestimate my strength. I will serve you well." She turned and walked away without waiting for him to dismiss her.

"Damn," he murmured. His concern was for her, and yet he'd made himself appear selfish. It disturbed him to know that she had gone without food and shed weight, which had left her looking thin and frail. And it disturbed him even more to think that she thought him a better match for her friend Brigid, never thinking that he would find her attractive.

"Damn," he said beneath his breath once more. What was it about her that he found attractive? The thought plagued him, and he would not rest easy until he discovered it for himself.

He walked off to find Thomas and set his plans in motion.

Merriment returned, if only briefly, as bellies were filled, tales were told, and hope filled hearts once again. Reena was thanked over and over again as she joined her village in a feast the likes of which they had not shared in far too long.

But merriment turned to serious discussion when many spoke of the repercussions Peter Kilkern would inflict on them when he learned of the Legend's interference. After all, this was Kilkern land, and the Legend had no right here. What then?

Reena wondered herself, and her concerns grew when she realized that food was not being distributed to cottages but kept in the wagons. What were the Legend's intentions?

It was not long before she had her answer.

Thomas informed her to gather the villagers once again, for the Legend wished to address them.

Children were still stuffing their mouths with honey cakes as they leaned against their parents and stared in awe at the Legend. Women openly admired him, though they kept their eyes from his. The men waited with caution, though less caution than before, since their stomachs were full.

Reena remained by her parents' side. As she glanced around the crowd, she could see that many villagers had food in their hands, fearing that if they did not hold on to every morsel they could once again be close to starvation.

Magnus raised his voice for all to hear. "I will make this brief and easy for you all to understand. I have no right to this land and I cannot force the earl of Culberry to treat you fairly."

Sighs were heard and tears soon fell.

"He rules this land as he sees fit, fair or unfairly. But you have a choice." A sudden silence descended over the crowd. "You can stay and tenant his land for unreasonable fees, or you can tenant my land for reasonable fees."

Grumbles and whispers rushed like a gust of wind through the gathered crowd.

"We have paid our tenant fee for the year," one man called out.

"And you have nothing left for yourself. How will you feed your family?" Magnus asked.

"How do we pay you when we have nothing left?" asked another man.

"I will take no fee from you for one year's time. You will have time to till the land, and I will provide food and shelter for you while you work the soil."

"And in return?" asked a man suspiciously.

"You pledge your loyalty to me and tend my land with the care and love that you once did this land."

Two men, their wives and children in tow, stepped forward. One followed the other, though their words rang the same.

"I pledge my loyalty to you."

Reena was not surprised by William and Paul's hasty decision. Both had six children between them, and William's wife was heavy with another child. Both men felt their duty was to provide for their family and keep them safe.

Old Margaret, the healer, stepped forward. She was seventy and five years, but no hunch marred her back. Her face was aged, though ageless, and all in the village loved her and sought her talent and wisdom for healing.

"My loyalty I pledge to you." She paused a moment. "As long as I have enough time to dig up my herbs and ready them for a new patch of soil."

"My people will help you with whatever assistance you require."

Margaret nodded. "Then you have my loyalty and I will serve you and your land."

"I thank you—" Magnus waited.

"Margaret, I am Margaret, the healer."

"I welcome you to my family, Margaret, and pledge my protection to you."

The word *protection* caused an outburst of villagers

to step forward, and in the end all in the village had decided to pledge their loyalty to the Legend.

It was little Daniel, the bowman's son, who stepped forward with courage and asked, "Where is our new home, sir?"

Magnus patted the young lad's head and looked out over the sea of anxious faces. "My land is not far, for you have just pledged your loyalty to the new earl of Dunhurnal."

Chapter 8

~~~~~⌒◯◯⌒~~~~~

Reena was stunned by the announcement, but when she reexamined the last few days, she realized that everyone at his keep had been busy preparing for a planned departure. Magnus had had all intentions of traveling to Dunhurnal, and he would have passed through Kilkern property.

She recalled his interest in the Dunhurnal map and now she understood why, and she wondered if it had any relevance to his decision to trade his protection for her mapmaking skills.

He was not obligated to tell her of his plans, so why did she feel a sense of betrayal? The Legend owed her no explanation, and yet she felt he should have told her of his intentions. She attempted to settle the nagging accusation with the thought that the villagers had a new lord and would be safe. But that knowledge did little to ease her unrest and concern regarding the fact that he had not informed her of his being the new lord of Dunhurnal. Why had he felt it necessary to keep the information from her? And was there more he refused to share?

The villagers set to work gathering their personal belongings and items of importance they wished to take with them. Several women helped old Margaret dig up many of her herb plants and bundle them adequately for travel. They bundled her dried herbs as well, for the plants were an essential part of her healing skills.

The few animals that remained were not in the best of health, Peter Kilkern having taken most of their prime stock, but they were not to be left behind and were tethered to the wagon.

Reena worked hard helping as many as she could, and it was only after her mother and father were comfortably settled in a wagon, along with the few villagers too ill to walk, that she saw to her own meager belongings.

There was not much to take. The important items—her quills, inkbottles and papers—were already packed in her satchel. Her garments consisted of one linen shift, two tunics, and an old bone comb for her hair. The most difficult part of gathering her things were her memories of the only home she had ever known.

It was here in this small cottage that she'd been raised. She remembered much laughter, good food and her daily studies, her mother having taught her to speak fluent French and Latin, she in turn having learned from her uncle, a cleric who felt knowledge was important. And then there had been her father's patience in teaching her to draw. He would smile at her efforts and encourage her. Her mother would attempt to teach her to cook, the lesson often ending in laughter, since no food Reena prepared ever proved eatable. And then there had been those moments of silence when she'd sat snuggled in a blanket before the hearth, her father busy at the table with his maps and her mother sitting in the rocking chair, stitching.

She had good memories here, but it was time to take them with her to her new life.

Reena's mother held out her hand to take her daughter's small satchel as she approached the wagon.

Reena smiled, seeing the plump little pup curled in her mother's lap, fast asleep. He had exhausted himself making new friends and begging for food, which all willingly shared with him.

"You will ride with us? You look fatigued," her mother said, taking the bundle from her. "It will be good to talk with you at length."

"That is up to Lord Dunhurnal," her father said.

The title gave her a start. He was a lord and she could no longer call him Magnus. The thought upset her, for she had fast considered him a friend, enjoying his company and his smile.

Smile?

Feeling flustered and considering her father's words, she excused herself so that she could locate her new lord and seek his permission to walk alongside her parents' wagon. She would not ride in the wagon when there were many who needed it more.

All was in readiness, and excitement was high in the air. Laughter, smiles and children's giggles were heard, and Reena's heart swelled with joy, for merriment had returned to her people.

She found Magnus in the lead, his warriors dispersed throughout the line of villagers. Her horse waited next to his, and she realized he expected her to ride beside him.

What surprised her was that Brigid stood speaking with Magnus, and while she was pleased that her plan to put them together had taken little effort on her part, she felt a strange ache in her stomach. She ignored it and thought on how well they looked together, Brigid beautiful, and he handsome—a perfect pair.

"You are very kind, my lord," Reena heard Brigid say as she approached. Both of their smiles widened when they caught sight of each other. It was so good to be back with family and friends, and she could not wait to be alone with Brigid and ask her what she thought of their new lord.

Magnus summoned Thomas with a wave, and it was brief and hasty orders he issued. "Thomas, assist Brigid with her needs."

The big warrior hesitated a moment, as if debating Magnus's instructions, then he lowered his head, stepped aside, and waited for Brigid to lead.

"Your name is Thomas?" Brigid asked, stepping closer to him.

"Aye, Thomas," he repeated.

Reena watched them together. Thomas was obviously uncomfortable in front of Brigid, but her friend would see to his unease, and she was sure they would be friends in no time.

"I am pleased to meet you and grateful that you will help me," Brigid said and walked slowly so that he would walk along with her.

Reena looked to Magnus. "All is ready for departure, my lord?"

He studied her for a moment. "You will call me Magnus."

"As you wish." She was relieved that he did not insist she use his title. She felt more at ease, more of a friend, referring to him by name.

He raised his hand slowly, all the while keeping his eyes on hers as he tucked a stray lock of hair behind her ear. "You have gone without sufficient sleep these last few days and require rest."

His touch was cool and feather light so that she barely felt it, yet it affected her like no other touch. "We all require rest; we have all worked hard."

Had he taken a step closer to her? He felt nearer to her somehow, and yet she did not recall him moving.

"My concern is for you."

"No need," was her hasty response.

His hands went to her waist and rested there, pausing over hers and squeezing gently, as if it were a common touch they often exchanged. Their eyes remained on each other, and for a brief moment in time the world seemed suspended around them. Then the spell was broken and he lifted her and placed her on her horse. "You will ride beside me."

He mounted his horse, put his helmet on, and directed his stallion beside her. "You will tell me all you know of Dunhurnal land."

She wondered if she would ever grow at ease with the change the helmet brought. Magnus was easy and enjoyable to converse with, but the helmet hid this side of him away from her; his dark eyes were more ominous behind the metal holes, his look more fearful, and he, more unapproachable.

"Something troubles you?"

She focused on his dark brown eyes, hoping she

could see Magnus in them and thus put herself at ease. "My thoughts but wander." She immediately turned her attention to his command. "Dunhurnal land is rich in soil and the woods wealthy with game. The keep is in disrepair, though a fine size. It was built on a small rise and situated so that from the battlements all approaching directions held clear views, thus no enemy could approach without Lord Dunhurnal's knowledge. The tenant cottages surround the keep and are in need of repair, and the land itself is thick with useless vegetation. The previous lord passed, and no heirs stepped forth to claim the property."

A thought struck her silent. Lands passed to heirs; how, then, had the Legend become the new lord of Dunhurnal?

"Did you travel to Dunhurnal land alone when you mapped the area?"

"Aye, I did. It takes time to map the land and the buildings, and none in the village could spare the time to accompany me, but it was necessary for the village to know the land. We needed a place to hunt for food once Lord Kilkern forbade us to hunt on his property." She paused, a frown on her face. "If the land had been mapped, my father might not have broken his leg."

"You blame yourself for your father's injury?" he asked.

"I know it may seem foolish, but I feel my skills in mapmaking can help in many ways, thus preventing unfortunate and sometimes dangerous results. That is why I detail my maps so precisely; you never know what might be helpful." A yawn rushed up and out before Reena could stop it, and her

shoulders slumped slightly, fatigue fast catching up
with her.

"You have done far too much, on far too little
sleep."

He sounded annoyed, which frustrated her, since
she was well aware that he thought her too skinny
and weak and she did not wish him to think so. "I
am strong and can do what is necessary."

"I did not question your strength." His tone softened.

Another yawn attacked her, and she realized that
she would not be able to continue the journey without some sleep. It would be nightfall before they
reached Dunhurnal land.

Reena was about to admit her fatigue and seek the
comfort of her parents' wagon when she was suddenly plucked off her horse and deposited in front
of the Legend.

One of his men took charge of her mare, directing
the animal away from them.

"Lean back and rest," he said with a sense of command, his face near to hers and his breath a warm,
faint breeze on her cool cheek.

She was startled by his unexpected action. What
would everyone think? But then he had told her
once that he did not care what others thought of
him. He had just proved it. She was so tired that she
succumbed to his order, and she realized as she
rested back against him that her hand remained firm
on his arm, which was wrapped around her waist.

She thought to say something but could think of
no words, especially since she felt comforted by the
strength of him. Her eyes drifted closed, though she

fought to keep them open; why, she did not know. He had ordered her to rest, but sleep? She needed to remain alert, needed to finish the conversation with him about Dunhurnal land, needed to discuss Brigid with him.

The last thought startled her, but sleep was close to claiming her, and she could do nothing more but think of how she must look, wrapped in the Legend's arms, to those around them.

Brigid woke Reena the next morning, and she sat up with a start.

She looked around, sniffed the scent of fresh roasted meat, and saw that everyone was enjoying a substantial morning meal.

"I thought you would be hungry being you slept through supper," Brigid said and handed her a slice of black bread with cheese and meat piled on it.

Reena took it, her stomach eager for sustenance.

Brigid nibbled on a piece of cheese.

After a bite or two Reena had to ask the obvious. "The last I remember was riding with Magnus on his horse. How did I get here?" *Here* was a soft bed of blankets beside a comforting fire that kept the chilled air at bay.

"It was a sight for sure," Brigid said excitedly. "First the Legend ordered that a fire be built and bedding spread for you, then he handed you to Thomas—a dear man with a huge heart—to hold while he dismounted. He then took you from Thomas, carried you to this bedding, which I prepared with haste, and lowered you ever so slowly and carefully, as though he thought you would break or perhaps he did not want to let you go. Then he covered you with a blanket and commanded that no one disturb you."

Speechless, Reena stared at Brigid.

"There are whispers—"

Reena would not allow her friend to finish. "Nonsense. The Legend but looks after his people, and besides, he has expressed interest in you."

"Me?" Brigid placed a hand to her chest. "Why ever would he be interested in me?"

"You are beautiful, for one thing. And he is handsome beyond belief. You two would make a splendid couple, and I let him know this."

Brigid nodded, understanding her friend. "We shall see who interests him."

"I have no interest in him and he has none in me," Reena said with a defensive edge.

"We shall see." Brigid smiled, though it faded slowly. "I am glad the Legend moves us to his land. I left much behind in the village, including painful memories."

Horace ran up to Reena and sat beside her, waiting for any morsel of food. She couldn't resist him, and besides, she wasn't as hungry as she had thought. Reena brushed the crumbs from her hands after feeding the remainder of her meal to Horace.

"Kilkern did not bother you while I was gone?" Reena asked, concerned for her friend.

"Nay, there was gossip that he had traveled to see the king in regards to his property, but we could not be certain, and no one wished to approach his keep to see if there was truth to the gossip."

"You need not worry any longer, you are now under the Legend's protection."

"So Thomas informed me." Her smile returned. "He is such a tender man, I enjoy talking with him." She laughed softly. "Though I do most of the talking and he listens; he is a good listener, and since John died I have not known a man who would listen so patiently to my endless chatter. He even listened to me tell him about the garden I wish to plant in the spring, and he promises he will till the soil well for me."

"Aye, Thomas is a good man and I am glad you befriended him, since many fear his size and looks or they ignore him completely."

"The villagers will accept him once they get to know him. Old Margaret claims he is a special man. She insists that any man as large as he who can cradle a tender seedling and do it no damage has a loving touch."

Reena looked past the flames at her friend. "I am so glad to be talking with you again."

Brigid hurried over beside Reena and hugged her. "I worried so about you." She squeezed her friend's hand. "But I tell you true, Reena, a part of me prayed you would succeed, for I feared my fate with Kilkern if you did not."

"I did not intend to fail."

"And you did not—you returned a heroine to our village, and everyone is grateful to you, though many remain fearful of Kilkern, for they know he will seek retribution."

Shouts to break up camp and make ready for departure interrupted their conversation. The two women quickly saw to their area and assisted those who needed help.

Reena spoke with her parents briefly. Both understood that she now had duties that must be attended to, and they assured her there would be time to talk when they settled in their new cottage.

She received instructions that Magnus wished to see her. When she approached him where he sat on his horse, and she saw hers next to his, she knew she would ride beside him again, and she was pleased. She enjoyed his company and their conversations, and oddly enough she had felt content and safe falling asleep in his arms.

After a quick good morning from Thomas, the large man hoisted her onto her horse and mounted his own. The three led the procession of villagers and warriors as the journey began, though short it would be since they were already on Dunhurnal land and the keep was but a couple of hours' ride away.

Magnus turned to her and said, "Tell me all you know about the surrounding land." He paused his horse, cast an intense look around him, then turned to her once again. "Peter Kilkern approaches Dunhurnal land."

Chapter 9

$\sim\!\!\mathcal{OQ}\!\!\sim$

They arrived at the castle, and the villagers cheerfully sought out cottages for themselves. Even though most of the cottages were in need of repairs, it mattered not. They would have food, shelter and protection from the Legend.

The warriors and Reena were the only ones aware of Kilkern's impending arrival, and Magnus intended to keep it that way. He wanted no fear to mar the joy of the villagers' new home.

Upon their arrival, his men were positioned strategically. Many lined the battlements of the keep, while others covered the land. As soon as possible they would set to work mapping the area and making the village impregnable. It would take time and hard work, but Magnus had waited and planned for this, and he would not see it fail.

Reena's skills were an added benefit, and he intended to take full advantage of her talent. She had already proved useful detailing Dunhurnal land.

The specifics she had outlined in the maps helped him to position his men more favorably, and he would know when Kilkern was near.

He had removed his helmet and stood on the steps of the keep, looking out over his newly acquired land. Much was in sad neglect, but the fact that he was here filled him with a sense of accomplishment. He had achieved part of his desired goal; the rest would follow.

Thomas approached, shaking his head. "She helps everyone with the selection of their cottage and ignores her own need."

"Reena requires no cottage, she will reside in the keep."

"It is Brigid I speak of. She let Old Margaret have the cottage she herself first admired and then walked away from another, thinking it better left for a larger family even though she favored it."

Magnus pointed to a cottage close to the keep. "How about that one?"

It looked as though it was tucked partially in the woods. The thatching on the roof needed repair and it was overgrown with weeds and brush, but it was a good size, and Magnus knew Reena would be pleased to have her friend close by.

Thomas gave it a quick glance, then glanced from the keep to the cottage and back again several times. "Close," he mumbled and hurried off.

He returned in haste with Brigid in tow.

"It is a good cottage for you, and close to the keep, where Reena will reside. Now have a look and claim it so that it will be done." Thomas seemed adamant, so Brigid obliged him and looked over the cottage.

A chill wind had arrived with the pending storm

clouds. Brigid wrapped her dark green wool shawl more tightly around her and hurried into the cottage, Thomas waiting at the end of the path that led to the door.

His thoughts centered on the work that was needed, and it was not long before the shutter to one of the two windows was thrown open, only to fall off the cottage wall and crash to the ground.

Brigid laughed, looking out the window. "Thomas, this is perfect."

"Good, then it is yours. We will gather your belongings and move you in, and I will repair the roof—"

"Tomorrow," Magnus finished. "Brigid can stay in the keep until the cottage is ready; there are more important things that must be done this day."

Thomas nodded, understanding that protection of the village and keep was of the utmost importance; the rest would be seen to in time.

"Find Reena, Brigid, and both of you move your belongings into the keep for now," Magnus said.

Brigid bit at her bottom lip, cast a glance to the ground, then turned around from the window. A brief second later she walked out of the cottage toward Thomas. She stood half behind him, as if seeking his protection.

Magnus realized her reluctance to answer and instantly understood. "Where is Reena?"

Brigid hesitated once again.

"Answer me now," Magnus snapped.

Thomas looked to Brigid. "He protects what is his."

Brigid's worry eased a little, and she answered. "A portion of Dunhurnal land was mapped by her father, and she wanted to make certain no changes had occurred since it had been mapped."

Magnus swore beneath his breath. "Do you know where exactly she went?"

"Nay, but she seemed to feel it was imperative that she see to this area immediately."

Magnus wished he had Reena in front of him, for he would shake some sense into her. She must have thought it important to go off on her own when she knew Kilkern was not far off. Was she attempting to prove herself useful? "Has she been gone long?"

"Aye," Brigid answered with a nod.

"Did she tell anyone else of her intentions?"

Brigid shook her head. "But she is not alone. Horace went with her."

"That certainly relieves my concern," Magnus said. "A pint-sized woman followed by a cowardly pup."

He was about to direct Thomas to send a group of warriors out to search for her when one of his men approached them on a run.

Out of breath, he fast delivered the news. "Kilkern is in sight, and he has Reena with him."

Magnus issued orders to Thomas to ready the men. He instructed Brigid to alert the villagers to the situation, especially Reena's parents, and have them all gather in front of the keep.

Tension and worry soon filled the chilled air as the villagers hurried to obey their new lord, and the sky overhead darkened, causing many to whisper of ominous possibilities. They huddled together as thunder rolled in the distance, and Brigid, along with Reena's parents, stood in front of the crowd, anxious to see that Reena was unharmed.

Warriors lined the battlements, their bows and arrows in hand and ready for battle. A circle of warriors protected the villagers and the keep, and more were dispersed in the woods, where they could not be seen but their arrows would soon be felt.

Magnus stood in front of the villagers. His garments were all black, except for the silver metal studs that crisscrossed over his leather tunic, and his long hair framed a face that, while handsome, looked devoid of emotion. He appeared ready to destroy anything that stood in his path—even the devil himself.

Peter Kilkern approached at a slow gait with several of his men following behind. Reena walked beside his horse with a trembling Horace in her arms. It was not until they were close enough that Magnus saw the bruise on the side of Reena's mouth.

His hand curled into a fist at his side.

Kilkern stopped a short distance from Magnus, and when he did, Reena kept walking forward.

"I gave you no order to leave my side," Kilkern shouted at her.

She ignored him and kept walking with her head held high, straight to Magnus.

He wanted to grab her and hug her close to him, so relieved was he that she had returned safely, proud that she was confident in his ability to protect her.

"My lord," she said with a bow of her head, purposely honoring him in front of Kilkern. She then walked past him and joined Brigid and her parents, giving them a glance that warned they were not to fuss over her but to remain as they were, a show of true strength to their new lord.

Peter Kilkern dismounted, along with a few of his men. Dressed in his usual rich finery, his dark eyes alert to all around him, he approached Magnus with arrogant confidence, laughing as he removed his brown leather gloves, three of his men following close behind him.

Magnus remained as he was, forcing Kilkern to come to him, refusing to step forward and display any sign of welcome.

Kilkern felt the insult and lashed out. "I have come for my tenants, you have no right—"

"*You* have no right to starve them."

"Let them grow more food."

"So you can raise the tenant fees and take more from them?" Magnus's expression remained cold. "Their yearly fees are paid to you, and they owe you no more. They are free to go where they choose."

Kilkern appeared angry—very angry. He stepped forward again. "They have no rights. They belong to me and you will return them."

Magnus's words were for Kilkern's ears alone. "Make me."

Kilkern grew even more agitated. "One tenant fee has not been paid in full to me. That tenant will return and fulfill her obligation."

"Who is this you speak of?"

"Brigid."

Gasps rumbled throughout the villagers, and Reena quickly squeezed her friend's hand in reassurance.

"I will pay what she owes you," Magnus said and motioned to one of his men.

Kilkern was adamant. "Nay, she will serve out her obligation to me; I will have it no other way."

"Brigid remains here. You can leave with her fee paid or without it, but that does not change the fact that Brigid will not leave with you."

Kilkern spit out his words like venom. "Want her for yourself?"

Magnus's slow smile was like a warning. "What I want, I always get. Remember that."

Kilkern seemed at a loss, though he recovered his composure quickly. "Pay me her fee, but you will be sorry for taking this lazy lot; they are worthless."

Magnus tossed the coins at him and had Kilkern sign a paper stating his tenants were free of all debt to him.

"Kilkern," Magnus said as he turned to walk away.

"Earl of Culberry," Kilkern corrected.

Magnus ignored his title. "Who struck the woman?"

"She was being insolent."

"I did not ask why she was struck; I asked *who* struck her."

"It matters not."

"It does to me."

Kilkern ignored him and walked away, his men waiting as their lord walked to his horse and mounted safely.

"She is a worthless woman, too frail to work the fields and too skinny to be appealing to a man."

Magnus's fists were fast and furious, and before anyone realized what had happened, three of Kilkern's men lay sprawled out on the ground.

Magnus stepped over the fallen men and walked up to Kilkern. "Never touch what is mine." He turned his back on Kilkern and walked up to Thomas. "Make certain they are escorted off Dunhurnal land."

Thomas grinned. "With pleasure."

Magnus watched with his arms crossed over his chest as Kilkern's men gathered their wits, mounted their horses, and were led from Dunhurnal land by a large escort of the Legend's warriors.

When they were no longer in sight, Magnus addressed his new tenants as a fine mist of rain began to fall. "You are free of Kilkern. I will be fair in my dealings and I expect the same from you. There is much work to be done here, and I expect all of you to do your share. Now go and enjoy your new homes, and join me and mine this evening in the great hall as we celebrate our good fortune."

Cheers rang out, laughter was plentiful, tears of joy were shed, and everyone hurried out of the rain after paying thanks with bowed heads and smiles to their new lord. They were no longer fearful, for they had seen for themselves his strength and courage and how he protected one of his.

"Reena."

The summons was distinct, and Reena was not certain who she preferred not to face—her parents, who were ready to fuss over her, Brigid, who looked concerned, or Magnus, whose anger was obvious in his glistening dark eyes.

Horace seemed as undecided as she, though when Reena approached Magnus, the little pup hastily jumped out of her arms and made his way to Brigid to huddle at her feet.

Magnus turned and walked up the steps to the keep, a sign that Reena was to follow. She did, though with reluctance.

The great hall was busy with activity as women and warriors alike worked together to make it presentable for the evening meal. Years of neglect meant much hard work to restore the keep to its original condition. The land as well, for it had fallen in great disrepair, and much toil would be needed for a good harvest to be met. The soil was rich, though, and that alone would almost guarantee good crops.

Those thoughts brought a smile to Reena, a brief one, since her mouth hurt from the blow she had sustained, and which was the very reason Magnus summoned her. Was she in trouble? After she had departed on her brief quest to survey the piece of land she'd feared had been mapped incorrectly, she'd realized that she should have requested permission from Magnus. She'd been accustomed to doing as she'd pleased when it had come to her maps, but that was no more; she now answered to a new lord. She had hoped she would return to the keep before he knew of her absence. Then she'd met with Kilkern and his men, and she'd known she was in trouble.

Magnus continued through the great hall, down and around a narrow passageway and up spiral stone steps to come out into a large room. Debris and cobwebs occupied the place, and a tattered tapestry hung on a wall. A large fireplace occupied a whole wall and was made of thick round stones, the mantel being one solid beam of wood.

With his arms crossed over his chest, Magnus took a stance in front of the cold hearth.

Reena decided to offer an apology, hoping to avoid a confrontation. "I am sorry for not seeking your permission to leave the village. My only excuse, and a poor one at that, is that I have yet to grow accustomed to answering to anyone for my actions."

She shivered, not certain whether she was chilled by the cold room or by his chilled expression.

He remained silent, an indication that he gave her words thought. She waited.

He closed the distance between them to stand directly in front of her, so close that she could feel the warmth of his body. It eased her chill and brought her comfort.

An odd thought, and one she pushed from her mind.

"Tell me what happened."

"Kilkern's men appeared out of nowhere, though I had been too busy taking note of the land—"

"—to pay attention to your safety."

"Foolish, I know," she admitted with a brief shake of her head.

"Then you spoke up without thinking."

Her eyes went wide.

"I have learned you are not one to hold your tongue."

"I can when necessary," she defended. "But my confidence was strong, having the distinction of being the Legend's mapmaker."

"And this you told him."

"Aye," she said with her head high. "Straight and forward I was, letting him know that I was now under your protection."

Magnus held firm to his anger; that Kilkern would strike Reena knowing she was under his protection infuriated him.

"Your name seemed to anger him as much as his presence angers you." She hoped for an explanation, though she doubted he was ready to offer it.

"He lashed out at you." Magnus reached up and

gently touched the swollen corner of her mouth. "Perhaps Old Margaret can help alleviate your discomfort."

His voice softened, his eyes showed concern, and his touch was light, like butterfly wings whispering across her cheek. Her legs trembled, her knees grew weak, and she fought the urge to rest her head on his chest.

Instead she stepped away from him. "I will see what Margaret can do, and I thank you for what you did for Brigid. I know you will find her to your liking, for she is a good and kind woman."

"So are you."

She laughed, though it sounded sad to his ears. "Did you not hear Kilkern? I am useless and not attractive to a man."

"He is ignorant and blind."

"I have grown thin, and my features are plain and will set no man's heart to beating wildly."

Magnus closed the distance between them once more. "You possess the skill, the strength and the courage to travel the land and map it. How many among us can do as you do? And as for your features?"

He paused and stared at her in silence.

Did words fail him? Were her features so difficult to describe that he could find no words? And why did the thought hurt her so? She had never allowed such silly nonsense to disturb her before.

He spoke then in a whisper, as if his words were meant for her alone. "The only beauty that counts is the true beauty that is seen by a true heart."

Her laughter was soft, like a gentle breeze. "Then beauty escapes me, for a true heart will never find me. No man will love a woman such as I, and it is good that I know this, for I will not waste my time on useless dreams."

She turned and hurried from the room, rushing down the steps and out of the keep.

Chapter 10

Winter nipped at the last few days of autumn, and preparation was well underway to make certain all in the village and keep were ready. In the two weeks since their arrival at Dunhurnal, the villagers and the Legend's warriors had been busy repairing and preparing the cottages, the keep and the land. Much had been accomplished. Though more work was necessary, at least everyone would have a warm, comfortable cottage for the winter.

Warriors busily hunted game, while the women saw to smoking and salting the meat for storage. Wool cloth was distributed to the women, who immediately set to work sewing new garments. Wood was chopped and stored, and peat collected for a sufficient supply of fuel for the hearths.

Through all the activity Reena saw to it that Brigid was often thrown in Magnus's path. And she made certain that he was aware of how talented Brigid was with a needle and thread and cooking.

Brigid had helped in the cleaning of the keep's kitchen, a large room separated from the castle though connected by a covered passageway, which Magnus had ordered enclosed. He insisted that his servants would remain warm along with the food as they carried it from the kitchen to the keep during the cold winter months.

Reena divided her time between helping her parents settle into their cottage and Brigid in hers.

It surprised Reena that her own quarters were located in the keep. They were larger than she had expected, and the room was furnished with not only a good-size bed but also a large table more than sufficient for mapping. She would have enough room to place her inkwells, quills, maps and several candles.

Presently, she was on her way to the woods behind Brigid's cottage to look for bird feathers that would make good quills. She wanted to make certain that she had a good supply before winter set in. Magnus had promised she would have sufficient mapping material, including quills, ink and paper, but she favored making her own quills.

Thomas was outside Brigid's cottage, clearing the front of overgrown weeds and brush. He and Brigid had become good friends, and it was he who had seen to the repair of her cottage. Her roof thatching had been repaired, the window shutters were secure, and the hearth was in good working condition, Thomas having insisted she would be safe and warm when winter's chill set in. And he had promised her a fine garden in the spring, which was why he had set to work now clearing the land.

Thomas greeted her with a wave. "Good timing. Brigid just made fresh mulled cider."

Reena licked her lips. "She makes the best mulled cider."

Thomas brushed his hands off. "Magnus thinks the same, he is enjoying some now."

Reena felt the familiar tug to her tummy, but she ignored it. She'd realized over the last week or so that she found Magnus to her liking. He was handsome enough, but that was not what attracted her to him. She enjoyed talking with him on a variety of subjects, sharing opinions and being treated with equal intelligence. He expected no womanly chores from her and encouraged her to pursue her drawing skills and, of course, work on her maps. He often shared his experiences of other lands, detailing how difficult it had been at times to traverse unknown terrain.

And she knew in her heart that Magnus could be no more than a friend. She was not the type of woman he could care for; being small in size and having lost weight, she resembled a young lad. Even with weight she did not possess the appealing body that Brigid had, and she doubted she would ever have such an alluring shape. Then there were her simple features, nothing that would make a man take notice.

She was definitely not the type of woman Magnus could love, and she did not want to foolishly lose her heart to someone who could never love her. Magnus and Brigid suited each other well, and she would do well to remember that.

Therefore it was not surprising that she envied

her friend Brigid, though it was a friendly envy, since she wanted very much for Brigid to be happy again, and she would have Magnus as a good friend as well. Besides, she doubted she would find love, and she did not wish to waste time pursuing a dream that would never come true.

And she always had Horace. The little pup had grown a little bigger and followed her wherever she went, though the woods frightened him, and he would often wait for her at Brigid's cottage, where she would return to find him curled sound asleep in front of the warm hearth or waiting impatiently at the front door.

She followed Thomas into the cottage, Horace leading the way.

Magnus was laughing and Brigid was smiling when they joined them, and Reena smiled along with them, happy to see her friend enjoying life once again. Magnus was good for her, and she was glad she had seen to it that the two were often placed in each other's paths, though today their company was not of her doing.

"Reena," Brigid said, reaching to fill a tankard. "Just in time for cinnamon cakes and cider."

Thomas sat opposite Magnus at the table, and she sat at the opposite end from Brigid. Horace plopped down beside Brigid, knowing she would give him food in good time.

Reena had barely taken a bite of her cake when a knock sounded at the door.

Brigid bid her visitor welcome.

Justin, the tanner, entered. "I am truly sorry to interrupt."

"Is there a problem?" Magnus asked, knowing the

young man, since he found his talents useful in producing the leather tunics he favored. He was a personable young man, average in height and quiet in nature.

"Nay, my lord, I was hoping to have a word with Reena."

Reena grabbed her cinnamon cake and one for Justin, and she stood before she realized that Brigid was looking at her strangely and Thomas was holding a beefy hand to his mouth to hide his smile.

Reena mentally shook her head, not wanting to openly admit she'd once again given no thought to seeking Magnus's permission to leave when in his presence. Not that he strictly demanded such obedience, especially when he and she shared time together, but when in the company of others, it was proper and courteous for her to do so.

Justin quickly sought to correct her mistake. "My lord, I will only take a moment of Reena's time."

"That is good, since her cider will chill if she is gone too long."

Reena was surprised at his response; he seemed annoyed at her brief absence.

She hurried out the door with Justin, handing him a cake as they walked a short distance away from the cottage.

Justin was apologetic. "I am sorry to bother you, but I needed to talk with someone, and you have often lent a gracious and understanding ear to me."

She placed her hand on his arm. "I do not mind listening. What troubles you?"

"How do you know I feel troubled?"

"You have not touched Brigid's cinnamon cake, and no one can resist Brigid's cinnamon cakes."

Justin stared at the cake in his hand. "I have lost my appetite." He sighed again and shook his head.

"Only love can cause loss of appetite."

Justin shook his head and admitted with frustration, "She does not know I exist."

"Who is it you favor?"

"Maura, the young lass who helps Kate, the cook, in the kitchen."

Reena knew immediately of whom he spoke. "She is a pretty one, with that long red hair of hers."

"Aye, she is," Justin said with a heartfelt sigh. "And there are many men who agree with you, which is my problem. Do you think I have a chance with her?"

"Why would you not?"

"Look at me, Reena, I am not much to look at, a tanner by trade, not good with a sword—"

"But excellent with a bow and arrow, a skillful tanner who could provide beautiful leather workings for her, and a man who would love her deeply from his heart. How could she resist you?"

"Your confidence is appreciated, but how do I make myself known to her? My tongue deserts me when I attempt to speak with her. That is why I thought of you." He grew excited. "You have become acquainted with the women in the kitchen."

"A wise choice for one who cannot cook."

He smiled, hesitated, then asked, "I thought maybe you would introduce her to me and then—" He shrugged. "Well, then I am on my own."

"I go to gather feathers for quills now, but when I return we will go to the kitchen and I will introduce you to her."

"You will?" Justin could not keep the excitement

from his voice, though doubt soon followed. "What if words fail me and I make a fool of myself?"

"Words will not fail you, and I will be there to help with the conversation. Then I will make myself scarce, and you will be on your own and do well."

Justin threw his arms around her and hugged her tightly. "Thank you, and please tell no one of this. I do not want to look the fool."

Reena laughed and returned the hug. "Love often makes fools of us."

"Reena!"

The booming voice snapped the two apart, and they turned to stare at Magnus, who stood outside the front door, his arms crossed over his chest.

"I have kept you too long," Justin whispered. "Go, and I will see you when you return, and thank you again."

Reena nodded and squeezed his hand. "Until later." She hurried to Magnus.

"Is there a problem with Justin?"

"Nay."

"What did he want?"

"A small favor, nothing of importance," she said, wondering why he sounded irritated and thinking it wise to change the subject. After all, she had promised not to betray Justin's trust. "It is time for me to go in search of feathers for new quills."

For a moment she thought he intended to pursue his concern with Justin, then he asked, "Where will you hunt for feathers?"

She pointed past him. "Beyond Brigid's cottage in the woods."

"Your cider grows cold," Brigid called out from the cottage.

"Warm yourself with hot cider and enjoy more of Brigid's cinnamon cakes before you go to the woods," Magnus said and stepped aside for her to enter.

"Nay, I think it is wiser for me to go now when the sun is strong."

Magnus reached out to take her arm, but she hurried past him into the cottage, grabbed her cloak, gave Horace a pat on the head where he lay curled contentedly before the hearth, and was out the door.

"Wait," Brigid said, rushing after her friend, basket in hand. "You forgot this."

"I will not be long." Reena took the basket, smiled at Magnus as she rushed past him, and waved to Thomas, who was repairing the front gate. She brushed her long dark hair away from her face and hurried around the side of the cottage, only to have a gust of wind slip beneath her cloak and send it billowing out behind her. She laughed like a child at play, spread her arms as if she intended to fly, and hurried off, disappearing into the woods.

Magnus watched her as he walked over to Thomas, who kept his laughter low.

"You find this amusing?"

"Aye," Thomas said with a good nod of his head. "I have never known a woman who did not find you appealing and make her feelings known. Now I know not only one." He held up two fingers. "But two."

"I admire Brigid, for she loved her husband, but I do not interest her, nor does she interest me. While she is a good woman—"

"A very good woman," Thomas said firmly.

"Aye, a very good woman," Magnus agreed with a nod. "She is not what I look for, though"—with a purposeful pause he stared at his friend—"she would be good for you."

Thomas grew flustered, shook his head, and dismissed Magnus's words with a curt wave. "Nay, I am but a friend to her; she has no other interest in me."

Magnus placed a hand on Thomas's large shoulder. "You say yourself she is a very good woman."

"And what of you and Reena?" Thomas asked. "I see how you look at her and want to know her whereabouts, and how you provided her with large quarters in the keep. I know that you have sent for special drawing and writing materials for her, and that you have ordered Mary the spinner to spin a fine cloth for garments specially to be made for Reena."

"She is my mapmaker and therefore I provide for her."

"Really? Then why do I find you so often in her company and in conversation with her? And why did you grow so annoyed when she went off to speak with Justin?"

Magnus bristled. "I do not need to explain myself to you."

Thomas laughed and placed a hand on Magnus's shoulder. "Nay, my friend, you do not, but some advice. I would suggest you not harm that young lad Justin, who you obviously feel is interested in Reena."

"They hugged," Magnus said, his own irritation surprising him.

Thomas kept a restraint on his chuckle.

"You find this humorous?" Magnus asked, not at all amused.

"I find it humorous that you have denied your attraction to Reena."

Magnus shook his head. "I have been trying to understand why I found her interesting ever since I first saw her. She is too thin—"

"She has gained some weight," Thomas said in her defense.

"Not much, and her features are plain, though her smile is pleasant and she has no interest in womanly matters. She maps, draws and helps many in the village, and she does what she pleases without thought of seeking my permission."

"And still you find her attractive."

"Why?" Magnus threw his hands to the heavens.

"Why not find out why?" Thomas asked.

"A simple solution, you would think," Magnus said with a shake of his head. "I need to clear my thoughts."

"A walk in the woods," Thomas suggested with a smile.

Magnus ignored him, since a walk in the woods had been his intentions, and he entered the woods deep in thought.

He had much on his mind of late, securing land being the most important. Then he had to find a good woman to make his wife and see to a debt owed to him.

He had been granted lands for his allegiance and service to the king. He had learned early on that a king's wealth was more in land than in coin, so he'd made certain to gain his own wealth in more than just land. He'd made his wealth on foreign soil, and it far exceeded those in power, though he'd let no one know, for it would make him vulnerable for attack from the monarchy.

The monarch wanted his hired warriors loyal to him alone, and granting them land and securing marriages for them was one way of making certain they remained loyal. Magnus had accepted the land granted him, but a marriage contract he would not accept.

The choice of the woman he married would be entirely left to his discretion. He would not be locked into a loveless marriage as his mother had been, and he would not wed a woman who cared nothing for him but served him only out of duty.

Even with his thoughts heavily occupied he remained alert to his surroundings, and he caught sight of Reena climbing over a fallen tree and bending down, a wide smile filling her face.

He froze and stared at her, for her smile reflected her innocence. She shoved her long black hair away from her face, tucking it behind her ears, and her bright blue eyes shined with the eagerness of a child who had just discovered a treasure. She stared in awe at the ground where she bent down, and he knew she had found a feather that excited her, a feather that would make a good quill.

She was an unusual woman in her pursuits and that, in part, was what interested him. She was a woman of many talents. When he had conversed in French with Thomas at supper one night she'd joined in the conversation, her tongue fluid in the foreign language. She had shocked him even more when he'd discovered that she could speak Latin, a language he had never learned. It seemed as though she forever surprised him with her skills and knowledge.

He did not wish to startle her, but she was obviously more alert to her surroundings than he thought, for she realized he was near.

"Magnus, look what I have found." Excitement filled her every word.

He joined her, bending down beside her.

She looked up at him. Then, without thought to her actions, she gently brushed behind his ear a long wisp of hair that had fallen across his cheek, and she continued on as if she had done nothing out of the ordinary. "Look, Magnus, it is perfect, simply a perfect feather."

He glanced down as her hand tenderly brushed away the few leaves that covered the red-tipped brown feather.

"Turkey," Magnus said.

"Aye, turkey." She handled the feather with extreme care. "The tip needs further drying; the sun will do. It must dry slowly or the tip will turn brittle and not make a good quill."

She placed the feather in a narrow basket on the ground.

"What other feathers make good quills?" Magnus asked, standing and holding his hand out to her.

She took it and noticed how warm and strong his touch was and she reluctantly released it once she stood. "Goose feathers make sturdy quills, swan feathers, though I have never personally owned one, and black crow feathers. I hope to find a few today, since not all will dry well."

"I will help you," he offered.

She seemed surprised. "It is not necessary, you are busy with the keep, and I am accustomed to foraging for feathers on my own."

For a brief moment he grew annoyed that she did not want his help, for he felt it meant she also did not wish his company, and he grew more annoyed at himself for letting her rejection disturb him. Then he calmed, reminded himself of Reena's independent nature, and was more direct.

"I would like to help you."

"If you wish," she said, delighted to have his company. Recently she had been finding his company more than merely pleasant: she had found herself looking forward to spending time with him, enjoying the time she spent with him and even finding excuses to be in his company.

"Why do you not just collect feathers from the birds used for our meals?"

"I do sometimes, but many are damaged and I find I enjoy searching the woods, for I feel the birds leave their feathers behind specially for me."

She smiled, and for a moment it looked as though the bruise had returned to the side of her mouth. Then he realized it was the shadows of the tree branches playing tricks against her face.

The reminder of the blow stirred his anger, along with his fierce need to protect her.

He walked toward her, not realizing he looked more like a bird of prey in his dark garments and scowling expression.

Reena took a few hasty steps back, but not fast enough, for he reached out and grabbed her by the arms, pulling her up against him.

"You will not go into the woods alone ever again."

Anyone mindful enough to know her place and wise enough to fear someone larger and more powerful would respond sensibly. Reena, however, had been feeling the loss of her freedom to the Legend, and for him to rob her of the joy of gathering feathers for quills annoyed her. How was she ever to map terrain if she was forbidden to enter the woods alone?

"That is not possible."

His eyes widened, startled by her sharp tongue.

"It is necessary for me to traverse the woods, forests, hills, streams and more if I am your mapmaker, and it will not always be feasible for someone to accompany me. I am small and fast on my feet and I can cover much land in a short time, and I do not fear being alone."

"I fear you being alone, and *you* obey *me*."

"*You* are being stubborn, *I* am being sensible."

He lowered his face close to hers. "You think so."

"Nay, I know so."

"I will not tolerate disobedience."

"I will not be prevented from fulfilling my obligation to you, by you."

"You are stubborn," he said sharply.

"As are you." She was grateful it was her legs that trembled and not her speech, and grateful that he held her firm, for if he released her, she doubted her legs would support her.

"What do I do with you, Reena?"

She was surprised that his voice softened, though his gentle response tempered her own. "Let me map as I know how, and"—she smiled slowly—"help me forage for feathers?"

Her need to pursue her mapping skills, her soft smile and her gentle request melted his heart and tormented his senses, and damned if he possessed a shield strong enough to defend himself.

He moved his mouth close to hers and she tensed: for a brief moment she thought he meant to kiss her. Instead he whispered, "I, and I alone, will help you forage for feathers."

Chapter 11

⌒◯◯⌒

Reena hurried to gather Horace, and with a few quick words to Brigid and Thomas, she went on her way. Magnus had gone on ahead of her and disappeared inside the keep. The moment between them when his lips had been so close to hers affected her much more than she wished to admit. She was actually disappointed that he had not kissed her, and the emptiness of that missed kiss startled and upset her.

"I am a fool," she said quietly to the small puppy that bounced along beside her. "He has no interest in me; I am his mapmaker, and therefore he is concerned for my safety."

Horace barked as if in response, though whether in agreement or not it was hard to say.

She approached Justin's cottage, her mind active with the incident in the woods. It unsettled her and in so doing it refused to leave her thoughts. The idea that she thought he would kiss her haunted her, and that he had not kissed her troubled her more so. Had she not been the one to consider the Legend a perfect match for her friend Brigid? Her thoughts were near to traitorous, and she would not have it so. She would not allow herself to think of Magnus in any intimate way; it was unfair to her friend and also unfair to her. She knew that many women would favor a tryst with the lord they were in service to, but not her. Intimacy was something she did not take lightly. She intended a loving marriage to a trusting man before she allowed someone in her bed. The Legend and Brigid made a good match, and she would keep that well in her mind and chase all other foolish thoughts away.

Justin hurried over to her, filled with anticipation.

"Ready to meet Maura?" she asked.

"I . . . I . . . I" Justin stumbled to speak.

She hooked her arm in his and attempted to calm him. "I think Maura and you would work well together."

"Truly?"

They walked toward the kitchen, Reena filling him with courage, Horace yapping loudly once he realized their direction.

Magnus stood on the steps of the keep watching them, Thomas coming up behind him.

"A storm brews." Thomas studied the cloud-ridden sky. "Snow may fly before this night ends."

Magnus turned to his friend.

Thomas raised a brow. "A storm brews elsewhere. You look ready to battle."

"I grow annoyed that she speaks with a mere lad and looks happy in doing so." He sounded as agitated as he felt, and that annoyed him all the more. "Listen to me, I sound like a jealous lover, and over what? A woman I have only just met, and who thinks of me as her lord and nothing more."

Thomas laughed, though it barely could be heard, a mere chuckle of sorts beneath his breath.

"I heard that," Magnus accused with frustration.

"Reena has her own way about her, and she is determined to see you and Brigid together."

"That is not going to happen, and Reena is too stubborn to understand that."

Thomas did not hide the next chuckle. "Is Reena too much of a challenge?"

Magnus scowled, his eyes on the kitchen area where a young lass had joined Reena and Justin. The three stood talking in what appeared to be an enjoyable conversation.

"Justin is but a friend to Reena."

"He is a man," Magnus said as if the few words explained it all.

Another chuckle from Thomas received another scowl from Magnus. "I am glad you find this situation so humorous."

"I have never known you to be at a loss when faced with a challenge."

"I am not at a loss," Magnus said adamantly. "You know well enough that when I want something I go after it."

"Do you want Reena?"

Magnus nodded, then shook his head. "I want to know what it is that attracts me to the skinny lass, for I find myself drawn to her like no other woman I have ever known."

Laughter rang out from the trio several feet away from them.

Magnus grew more annoyed. "Reena ignores her work."

"What work?"

"She should be tending to her feathers she collected for quill making, and I have mapping I wish from her before the first snow falls."

"Then you best hurry her along, for I think this eve we will see a snowflake or two. What is it you wish her to map?"

It was Magnus's turn to chuckle. "Me."

Reena watched Maura and Justin as they all talked. At first Maura appeared shy, her gentle green eyes avoiding direct contact with Justin's dark ones. After a hesitant start Justin grew more confident, and the conversation began to flow smoothly. Soon Maura was smiling and laughing. Justin even caused her to blush when he mentioned what a wonderful cook she was.

"Would you like to sample the apple tarts I made? There are more than enough," Maura said, drawing her blue wool shawl more closely around her.

Justin was quick to answer. "I would love to, apple tarts are my favorite."

Maura's green eyes brightened. "Apple tarts are my favorite too."

Reena rolled her eyes to the heaven. The two were getting along well, and her presence was no longer necessary. "The two of you go and enjoy. I have work I must—"

"Reena!"

The three jumped, startled by the raw power in the voice that called out her name.

"I need you to map," Magnus said as he approached her.

Reena was elated. He had not requested her mapping services since their arrival at Dunhurnal.

She glanced at him with a smile that played havoc with his heart, not to mention his senses—but then he wondered if he had any senses left at all since meeting her.

"We can discuss what it is you wished mapped over apple tarts."

Reena failed to notice the smiles on Maura's and Justin's faces, but Magnus did not. The two saw how easily she spoke with him and how he did not deny her her request but acquiesced in silence. Gossip would soon spread throughout the keep about him and the mapmaker, and the thought did not at all disturb him.

"I will bring tarts to the great hall," Maura said.

"I will join you in the kitchen," Justin said enthusiastically.

She smiled and held out her hand. "Let me show you the way."

Justin knew the way to the kitchen but made no comment. He took her hand and followed along, his smile wide.

With a hasty glance at the cloudy sky, Reena hurried over to Magnus. "The weather may prove an interference."

Magnus scrambled to choose an area he wished mapped, for he had no particular place in mind. He'd simply wanted her attention diverted away from Justin. And he was feeling foolish, since on closer look he realized Justin seemed interested in Maura, making him feel all the more the fool.

He had never experienced jealousy over a woman before, and it damned annoyed him. "The weather will not matter. I wish you to map the keep." The idea actually would prove fruitful in more ways than he had first imagined. He would spend time with Reena as she mapped, thus learning more about her along with his new home, and he would be able to better determine a defense plan for the keep and the repair work necessary to restore the place. A wise decision, and one he was content with, for it served many purposes.

They walked in silence for a moment as they approached the keep.

Reena stopped and craned her neck to view the entire height of the imposing stone edifice. "A wise choice. You should know your home well; knowledge defends."

Her intelligence often startled him, as did the similarity of their thoughts. "It will also help me to determine the extent of the repair work required."

She continued walking, he slowing to match her steps. She was small, whereas he was large, and yet he felt they were equal in size. And she was thin; he could lift her with one arm, tuck her beneath it and carry her without an ounce of difficulty. *Fragile* had come to mind when he'd first met her, but it had been a deceptive assumption, since Reena possessed an inner strength that surprised him, but which he very much admired.

She was swift and aware of her surroundings. He had watched her in the woods as they'd gathered feathers. She moved with a graceful agility and kept herself alert. She hurried over fallen logs, ducked out of the way of branches, and maneuvered her way through the woods as though she knew its secrets.

She was an intelligent, determined and talented woman who'd captured his interest by surprise, and he intended to see where that surprise would take him.

They entered the keep, and the promised apple tarts, along with a large pitcher of cider, were waiting for them on a table before the burning hearth. With equal speed they rushed to the table like two eager, hungry children and, laughing, plopped down on the benches, each reaching for a tart.

Reena poured the cider after taking a generous bite of the warm tart, and as soon as she did, Horace came racing out of nowhere to plop his plump body down next to her leg. He gave her one solid bark, letting her know he waited for his share.

"You spoil him," Magnus said.

Reena reached down to Horace, a piece of tart in her hand. "I love him."

Her simple words were like a solid blow to his stomach, and for a moment he felt robbed of breath. Why? Why did her love for the small pup hit him so hard? Was he jealous? Did he wish her to say she loved him? A foolish thought. He did not know her well enough to know if they could love. Why then did the thought haunt him?

Reena rubbed a contented Horace behind the ear, gave him a piece of the tart, and continued rubbing him. "Where would you like me to start in the keep?"

Magnus watched the way Reena lovingly stroked the pup, and he actually envied the small animal. Her long, slim fingers ruffled the pup's fur behind his ear, then she rubbed beneath his chin. Finally she stroked his head and told him how wonderful he was, then finished with a hug. The dog lay contentedly at her feet and went fast to sleep.

He felt foolish indeed, that he wished he could feel her hands on him in such a caring and loving manner. The thought lingered.

"Would you walk the battlements with me? We can see the land and the distance it stretches, and any repair work that needs attention."

"A good choice. I will map the battlements with the view of the surrounding land, though I suggest we go now while the storm brews. I can sketch a quick outline and then work on a more formal map later."

Reena disturbed Horace when she stood, and he slowly stretched himself awake, yawned, walked closer to the warm hearth, plopped down and went back to sleep.

Magnus shook his head at the pup.

"I need to collect my charcoal and paper from my room," Reena said. "I can meet you on the battlements."

"We need to pass your room to reach the battlements. I will go with you."

Her room was one floor below his, and when he entered he realized how much it reflected her character. The table held several inkwells and quills. Papers were piled to one side, and five candles lined the front edge, supplying sufficient light for drawing.

Her bed would fit two people, and a chest rested at the foot of the bed, a green wool blanket folded neatly on top. The two pegs on the one wall held a few meager garments, which would soon be replaced by new garments he was having made for her against her objections. She had no choice though;

she was in his service and would dress accordingly.

He watched her hurry to gather her things, and he marveled at her graceful motions. It was as though her body movement was a constant dance, precise and fluid, like the strokes of her quill.

His thoughts instantly took flight, and he imagined how her fluid motion would enhance lovemaking. The easy bend and sway of her hips, the graceful arching of her back, the full thrust of her breasts, the softness of her lips—he shut his eyes.

Their lovemaking would be like creating a work of art, each movement a precise stroke, delicate at times, fast and furious strokes at other times, yet all blending and creating and—

He jumped at her touch, his eyes opening in a flash.

Her hand lay on his arm. "Are you all right?"

He felt the warmth of her hand through his shirt, and her simple touch stirred his blood all the more, making him ache to return the touch, but not in kind. His touch would be intimate, much too intimate.

He reluctantly stepped away from her. "I am fine, lost in my thoughts."

"I often get lost in my thoughts, though I must admit I like where I get lost."

He grinned. "Aye, I like where I get lost as well."

"Perhaps one day we can get lost together and see where it takes us."

Her smile spoke of innocence; his smile spoke of sin, and they left the room both lost in opposite thoughts.

The wind had picked up and the sky had darkened considerably by the time they reached the battlements. Reena knew she had little time to sketch, but if she could hurry and do a few rough views with detailed notes, she would at least have something to transfer to a map. And with this weather change, the mapping would keep her occupied.

She anxiously set to work while Magnus gave the battlements a quick survey.

"Several of the crenel shutters need replacing; I want to make certain my men are well protected during a siege."

She sketched as he spoke and felt the first faint snowflake touch her face. It brought a smile of happiness to her, for the winter would not be one of struggle to survive. Everyone would be warm, and food would be plentiful. Life would be good again.

Reena hurried her sketching and took in all she could with quick glances and mental notes, while the snowflakes swirled around her.

With a sweeping glance Magnus surveyed his land. He was finally here; he had waited and planned, and he was here. He felt a sense of pride and accomplishment, though there was more yet to be done, and he would not rest until all his plans saw fruition.

The snow had grown heavy, the snowflakes fat and beginning to cover the battlement. It would not be long before the land was covered with the fresh white snow.

"This will have to wait," Magnus said and joined Reena.

She had thought the same herself and hastily saw to the safety of her drawings by tucking them away in the inside pocket of her cloak.

Magnus took her arm. "The snow will completely cover the land by nightfall."

"Aye," she said and smiled. "But look at how the snow touches the land with beauty. Nothing stirs in the woods. The sky is still of birds and no footprints mar the freshly fallen snow. Everything is at peace."

She looked up at him. "Do you feel the peace?"

A warmth filled him, a gentleness touched him, and contentment filled his soul, though it was not the snow—it was Reena being there beside him. And he did not stop himself from raising his hand to stroke her cheek and run a finger across her lips.

"You shiver."

"I am cold." Though a lie, she could not admit that his touch filled her with a strange sense of pleasure.

His hand trailed down her arm to slip over her hand, and he laced his fingers with hers. "Let us go seek the heat of the hearth."

"Aye." A single word was all she could manage, the warmth that flooded her having turned to a deeper heat that tingled her senses.

They entered the keep. The stairs being too narrow for two to walk, he released her hand slowly, his fingers whispering across her palm and sending a series of shivers through her that set her legs to trembling.

"Tomorrow we will begin at the top of the keep and work our way down."

Reena remained silent until they reached her bedchamber, where they stopped outside the door. "I will set to work on mapping the view from the battlements."

He stood in silent contemplation, and for a moment she thought he was going to kiss her.

He appeared as if he was about to speak, then

Magnus suddenly shook his head and walked off without a word.

Reena hurried into her room, shut the door behind her, and collapsed against it.

Heaven help her, whatever was she to do?

Chapter 12

Thomas entered Magnus's solar shortly after he did. "Kilkern has men watching."

Magnus did not seem concerned by the news, though he was concerned that he had hesitated when he had desperately wanteded to kiss Reena. "I expected nothing less of him. He does not like being robbed of what is his, though he thinks nothing of doing the same to another." He walked to the stone hearth and added another log to the fire, a sudden chill filling the room. Perhaps it was the memories the name Kilkern invoked in him.

"Our response?"

Magnus watched the flames stretch high and the smoke curl up the chimney, and he allowed his troubled memories to drift away with the smoke. "We do nothing more than what we have been doing. We watch and keep alert to Kilkern's every move. I doubt he plans anything just yet. He probably continues to sulk over being conquered on his own property."

"A sulking man plots."

"As does a wise warrior," Magnus said. "My plans are laid, and he does as I expected. He is predictable."

"How so?"

"He allows his self-importance to interfere with his own strategy, and that, my friend, allows for me to *make* him all the more predictable."

"Traps," Thomas said with glee and rubbed his beefy hands together. "We are setting traps."

"When a prey is cornered he is the most dangerous, and it is the time a warrior must be the most alert. Make certain the men remain vigilant—have them take nothing for granted, not even this storm. There are enemies who strike when least expected, though I doubt Kilkern presently poses any threat. He is a coward at heart and will probably seek outside assistance in this matter."

"Do you think he will seek the king's help even though he knows the king favors you?"

Magnus shrugged. "The king is much like Kilkern; whoever can provide him with what he wants he favors. I trust the king as much as I trust Kilkern. Tell the guards to keep alert and trust no one, and make certain that I am informed of any strangers who enter the village."

"The men keep watchful eyes and know of everyone who leaves or enters the area. Kilkern's men are not discreet and were easily spotted."

"It is the areas I am not fully aware of that concern me," Magnus said and walked over to the table to fill two goblets with ale, handing one to Thomas. "Reena is mapping the view from the battlements, which will help. When this storm passes I intend to investigate the land further with Reena. I want to know every possible avenue of approach. Now tell me if there is anything else that warrants my attention."

"All goes well. Most of the cottages have been adequately repaired to survive the winter, though more extensive repairs will be needed in the spring. The winter food preparation goes well, and the surrounding forest is full of game, so we will not starve."

"How goes Brigid's cottage? I see that you spend much time there." Magnus watched his friend blush.

"She has no one to help her and she is a stubborn one in asking for help," Thomas said and shook his head.

"But you give her no chance to refuse."

Thomas shrugged. "I do what I can for her. I want to be a helpful friend to her."

"No more? Just a friend?"

Thomas looked at him oddly. "What more could I be to her? A woman as beautiful as Brigid could never love a man as ugly as me."

"You love with your heart, not your eyes."

"Brigid's heart belongs to her dead husband, she will love no other ever again," Thomas said with a distinct sadness.

"Her heart needs time to heal."

Thomas shook his head. "She looks for no other man."

"It does not matter, when the time is right she will discover love again."

Reena lost herself in her mapmaking. The evening meal came and went and she gave it no thought. After having gathered her senses, she'd had a logical discussion with herself.

She reminded herself that she was not at all suited

for Magnus, and that he did not in the least favor
her. His touch had been nothing more than him
brushing off the falling snow on her face. And taking her hand? She had laughed at that, realizing the
battlement's walkway was slippery due to the
snow, and holding her hand was a precautionary
measure; in case she lost her footing, he would already have hold of her.

He was her lord and she his mapmaker. Though
she wished to regard him as a friend, she would be
wise to realize her place in his service. And she
would do well to see that he and Brigid spent more
time in each other's company.

She thought to enlist Thomas's help. He'd
seemed to think her idea of bringing Magnus and
Brigid together a good one when she had mentioned Brigid to Magnus on their journey home.

With her thoughts in more sensible order she had
set to work on mapping the view from the battlement. Other maps would be necessary to complete
the entire view, but for now she concentrated on the
area she had hastily outlined before the snow began
to fall in earnest.

She knew the land well, having traveled to the
area on more than one occasion with her father, but
one particular area troubled her. The slope of the
land and the density of the trees did not give a true
picture of the terrain, and she knew closer inspection
was necessary if she was to map the area correctly.

If the snowfall was light she would request permission to investigate the area tomorrow; for now,
however, she painstakingly detailed the view as accurately as possible, knowing more detail would
follow later.

In between her mapping she had seen to the preparation of her new quills, the ones she had gathered just today. She had placed them near the hearth so that they would dry slowly. She did not want them to become brittle and thus unusable, especially with so much mapping to do. She would need extra quills.

She stretched her arms and drew back her shoulders to ease the ache in her neck and back. She often spent long hours at the table creating her maps or simply drawing, detailing an area, a face, a scene, and she loved every minute she spent with quill in hand.

Time being of no importance to her, she remained lost in her work. The knock at her door did not disturb her, and it was not until a solid fist hit her door twice that she jumped and in haste bid entrance to her visitor.

Magnus entered and walked over to the table where she sat.

He looked annoyed, but very handsome and powerful. Aye, very powerful, dressed all in black and intimidating in his confident gait. He could be feared and he could attract in one sweeping glance.

Attract.

The thought upset her, and she chased it from her tired mind, blaming her inappropriate thoughts on fatigue.

"You missed supper."

He sounded as if he scolded, and before she could answer a yawn escaped and she covered her mouth to catch it.

"You have spent too many hours working."

"A bare few," she argued without much strength.

Magnus reached out and took the quill from her

hand and placed it to the side. "Supper has long been finished and most everyone in the keep is asleep." He pointed to Horace, sound asleep in front of the hearth. "He does not stir."

There was no stirring the pup once he fell asleep for the night, though he usually crawled in bed with her. He must have given up waiting for her to retire and fallen asleep.

"I paid no heed to time," she admitted.

"That is obvious. I think it is time for you to retire."

"I have a line or two yet to draw, then I will retire."

Magnus placed his hand over hers. "It can wait."

"In a moment or two," Reena argued.

"Now," Magnus said softly.

Reena chose to remain stubborn. "When I am done."

"What justice can you do your work if you are tired?"

She glanced at the quill, then at him, and her hand stilled. She had expected to see a hardness in his dark eyes and a firmness to his mouth, warning her to obey. Instead his dark eyes held concern.

She nodded and stifled another yawn with her hand. He was right and she was foolish. She needed a clear, crisp mind and a steady hand to map accurately. She stood, about to tell him she agreed, when she lost her balance, her legs more tired than the rest of her.

Magnus was quick to circle the desk and scoop her up in his arms before she fell over. He walked to the bed, though his steps were not taken in haste, and he laid her down gently.

She stared at him for several silent moments, and then her eyes drifted closed; she was fast asleep.

Magnus shook his head. "Stubborn."

He removed her leather boots and slipped the brown wool blanket down from beneath her with little difficulty, she being so light. He then pulled the blanket over her, tucking it in around her to keep her warm.

A tiny whimper beside him let him know that Horace had heard them and wished to join Reena in bed. With another shake of his head he picked up the pup, who looked half asleep, and as soon as he placed him down on the bed he curled up beside Reena and fell right back to sleep.

"A pint-sized lass who thinks herself indestructible and a cowardly plump pup. What am I to do with the two of you?"

Chapter 13

Early morning found the ground barely touched by snow and village activity relatively quiet, though Reena was up early. She woke and slowly stretched herself awake before recalling last night, and a heavy blush rushed to stain her cheeks when she remembered that Magnus had tucked her into bed. She rushed out of bed, dressed, and hastily combed her hair and tied it with a leather strip. Then she grabbed the map from the table and her brown cloak from the peg on the wall, and hurried out of the keep with Horace close on her trail.

Several villagers were busy feeding the animals and attending to outside chores, though they took the time to wave a morning greeting to her.

Knowing that the village thrived once more filled Reena with relief. She had feared another winter under Kilkern's lordship, knowing it would have claimed heavy losses, and any loss would have been one too many. And then there was Brigid.

There was no doubt that Peter Kilkern intended Brigid harm, and with no husband to protect her and a village weak in strength and spirit, what hope did her friend have?

Not so now. Brigid was well protected, and she had a chance to love again, which was why Reena was headed to the familiar cottage. It was time they talked.

Horace bounced happily beside her, and once he realized their destination, he took off barking, running straight for Brigid's cottage.

A shout from Justin caught Reena's attention, and she turned to catch his wave before he hurried toward the kitchen. She smiled. He was going to see Maura, which meant things had gone well between them.

Happiness was fast returning to the villagers. Even her mother and father appeared healthier and more vibrant when she'd last visited them, and the children laughed and ran in play instead of being forced to work the fields.

Reena thought on how good life was, and when she turned and saw Brigid standing in the doorway waving and smiling, her heart swelled with joy. Her smile had vanished with her husband's death, but it had surfaced recently and could be spotted every now and again. Soon it would return permanently.

"Hurry out of the cold," Brigid called. "I have apple biscuits baking."

Reena picked up her pace, and Horace squeezed past Brigid to hurry in the cottage, making certain he was not left out.

Reena and Brigid hugged, and Brigid took her friend's cloak and hung it on the peg near the door.

"I had a feeling you would join me for the morning meal."

Reena walked over to the hearth and sniffed appreciatively. "So you made my favorite, apple biscuits."

"Aye, I saw you wave to Justin. He certainly had a huge smile on his face for so early in the morning. Do you know where he was off to?"

"He had asked me not to speak of it to anyone, but I have no doubt the keep already gossips."

"So tell me," Brigid said eagerly. With a thick folded cloth, she grabbed the pitcher of mulled cider she kept heated near the hearth and poured them each a tankard, leaving the pitcher on the table.

Reena quickly joined Brigid at the table, cupping the full tankard to warm her hands. "Justin favors Maura, the young cook at the keep. He requested my help in meeting her, so yesterday I introduced them."

"It went well?" Brigid's excitement grew.

"Aye," Reena said with a huge smile. "Very well, I would guess, since he was on his way to the kitchen."

"Good, it is about time he found someone to love. And what of you? When do you plan to find a love?"

"We are not discussing me. I am too busy mapping." Reena sounded much too defensive to her own ears. "I have no time for love."

Brigid laid a gentle hand on Reena's arm. "Love finds everyone."

Her response was curt and defensive. "That is nonsense, and I do not wish to discuss me. I want to know what you think of Magnus." She had not intended to be blunt, but now that the words were out, she was relieved.

Brigid took no offense; she knew Reena too well. "What about Magnus?"

"Do you find him appealing?"

Brigid stood and went to the hearth to check the biscuits. "What woman would not? He is a handsome one." With a thick cloth in her hand, she moved the pan of biscuits from the hearth to a wooden board on the table.

"He needs to love—"

Brigid interrupted with a sense of excitement. "Aye, he needs a special woman."

"I thought the same myself." Reena was pleased her friend agreed. "A woman that will understand him—"

"And who he is, for he is no ordinary man himself—he is the Legend."

"Aye, and much is expected of him."

Brigid separated the biscuits with a knife and moved them to a wooden platter. "She would need to have patience and strength."

"Two good traits not every woman possesses, though you do."

Brigid was quick to disagree. "Nonsense, it is you who has the strength, and patience when necessary."

Reena laughed and reached for a biscuit. "Patience is a skill I must learn."

"You have patience. How can you possibly map without patience? The work is tedious at times, and yet I see you sit hour after hour hunched over, quill in hand, finely detailing land, buildings, faces."

"That is different. I love my work and therefore—"

"You are patient and you take your time, no matter how tedious, and it is all because you *love* your work," Brigid finished.

"Of course."

"Then if you love someone, will you not be patient with him?"

"You understand love because you loved," Reena said.

Brigid sighed, and the hint of a smile she wore faded. "Aye, I loved strongly and doubt I will ever find such a love again."

"Do you not want to?"

Tears glistened in Brigid's eyes.

Reena grabbed her friend's hand and gave a comforting squeeze. "I am foolish for asking such a question."

"Nay," Brigid said, letting a tear fall. "You are a good friend, and I cry, for I miss John very much, and I cry because I miss loving him and being loved. And I cry because part of me wishes to love again and part of me is fearful of loving again." She shook her head. "I make no sense."

Reena squeezed her hand again. "You make good sense, and I am glad to hear that you want to love again. You will meet someone special. John would want you to."

"Aye, he was a good man and so unselfish," Brigid said. "I will never find another man like him."

"Nay, you will not, but you will find a good man, and that is what matters." Reena had felt her friend's pain when she had lost her husband, and she felt it now, and it saddened her to know that Brigid continued to hurt. She needed to fill her life with love again; it was the only cure for her empty heart.

"We both need to find good men," Brigid said,

wiping away the stubborn tears that continued to fall. "It is time we both love."

Reena swiped at the last of her own tears.

A knock sounded at the door followed by, "It is me, Thomas."

Brigid called out, "Come in."

The large man had to bow his head and shift his body to fit through the door. His face took on a look of alarm when he glanced at Brigid, and he hurried to her side.

"You shed tears, why?"

"It is nothing. Sit and have apple biscuits with us." She filled a tankard with cider for him.

Thomas turned to Reena, hoping she would offer an explanation. "You shed tears too. What is wrong?"

"Foolishness," Reena said on a laugh.

Brigid laughed as well. "Sit, Thomas, everything is fine, we promise. It is woman nonsense."

Reena saw to changing the subject. "The snowfall was not heavy."

Thomas shook his head. "Your tears made me forget the reason I am here." He turned to Reena. "Magnus looks for you; he waits in the great hall."

Reena grabbed the last of her apple biscuit and stood. "Thank you for this." She held up the half-eaten biscuit. "And for the discussion we both needed. I will see you later."

She walked to the door, leaving the sleeping Horace by the hearth.

Thomas turned to Brigid. "Will you tell me now why you shed tears?"

"Memories," Brigid said on a whisper, and tears rushed once again to fill her eyes. She did not want to cry, least of all in front of Thomas, but the memories had lingered in her thoughts, and she suddenly ached to have her husband's arms around her once again.

The tears ran down her cheeks, and she wiped them away, though they persistently continued to fall. "Please excuse my foolishness."

"You are not foolish," Thomas said softly.

"Aye, I am." A sob rose in her throat, and she fought it back.

Thomas watched her struggle, and it hurt him to see her suffer. He waited and watched and did not know what to do. Finally he could not take any more, and without thought to his actions he scooped her out of her chair and into his beefy arms, where he held her tightly.

Brigid surrendered to her pain, burying her face in Thomas's hard chest, and sobbed.

Reena dusted the biscuit crumbs from her hands before she entered the keep.

Magnus stood near the dais, speaking with two of his men. When he caught sight of her he dismissed them and walked to where she waited by the hearth.

"I want to continue our mapping today."

"That is fine, but there is an area on the map I am working on that puzzles me, and I thought perhaps we could have a look at it today, especially before the snow falls again."

"It is not far?"

"Nay," she said with a shake of her head. She hurried over to grab the map she had tucked in the corner by the hearth before going to visit Brigid. She spread it open on the table. "This is the map I began last night, and that is the area in question."

Magnus looked to where she pointed. "Why do you question it?"

"The hill dips and the trees are dense; unless I can see the terrain up close, I cannot map an accurate lay of the land. And I think this would also prove an advantage point to an approaching enemy."

Magnus studied her work and had to agree. "You have done a fine job, and I can understand your concern."

"Thank you, my father taught me well," she said with pride. "When I was young he would take me with him on his mapping quests and teach me what to pay attention to. It is because of him I am a skillful mapmaker."

"But have no doubt you possess your own unique ability. Now let us go investigate this area of land that intrigues you."

Reena smiled and rolled up the map. "I was hoping you would agree. I much prefer to have a clear outline of a map before I begin another one." She tucked the map away in the corner and waited as a black fur cloak was brought to Magnus.

He resembled a large beast of prey as he descended the keep steps, and those who caught sight of him hurried off, many blessing themselves as they went.

Old Margaret was not one who feared him, but then she had lived long and seen much. Many villagers wondered over her age, for though her face was worn with wrinkles, there was a youthfulness to her that was remarkable. Short and slim, she moved with a graceful slowness that was either forced by age or due to the fact that she was in no hurry. No one knew for sure, but all respected her.

She walked up to Magnus and Reena. "The woods are quiet today; you will learn much." She lowered her voice. "And be careful, someone watches."

"I appreciate your warning," Magnus said. "Do you have all you need?"

"I have all that is necessary," she said with a smile. "Need brings trouble. Go now, for the snow will fall soon enough and this time it will be heavy."

Reena gave her a quick hug and promised to visit with her soon.

Four of Magnus's men joined them as they reached the edge of the woods, two dispersing in opposite directions and the other two, James and Philip, remaining near Magnus and Reena.

The fresh dust of snow made the woods appear magical. Everything in sight sparkled with a white freshness that startled the eyes. With no clear path to follow, they made their own, Magnus's men taking the lead and proceeding with caution.

Reena studied the area well and corrected James when he faltered in direction.

James looked to Magnus. "Reena knows the way, do as she directs," Magnus responded.

Reena was pleased with his confidence in her, but then she knew well of what she spoke. They arrived at the designated spot within no time.

It was a section of land that ran like ripples of small hills and was sheltered by dense trees, a perfect place for launching an unsuspected attack, or shelter from prying eyes.

With a nod from Magnus, his men separated and

disappeared over hills and around trees to see if anyone lurked in the shadows.

Reena stood silent and searched the area with thorough eyes, taking into memory all she could. Magnus remained near when she followed a barely visible path, and the only sound in the crisp air was the crunch of snow-covered leaves beneath their feet.

Magnus did not care for what he saw. This land would need careful watch. In the spring he would order trees cut down, opening the area to a clearer view from the battlements. He had an uneasy feeling about the area, and he heard Old Margaret's words whisper in his head.

Someone watches.

His men returned and reported seeing nothing. Magnus wanted to take immediate leave of the area; it was not safe. With few men to fight and the vulnerability of surprise, protecting Reena could prove difficult, and the thought that she was not safe here increased his unease.

He looked to see her venturing further up a hill. He caught up with her as she stopped on the rise and looked around.

"It is time to go." He took her arm as if to protect.

Reena studied the area with such an intense glare that it gave Magnus the chills.

"Is something wrong?" he asked.

"What do you see?" She kept her sight focused directly in front of her.

A hand signal brought two of his men up the hill behind and to the sides of them. His hand went to the hilt of his sword at his side before he answered her.

He attempted to view the area as intently as she

appeared to be doing. "Fresh snow covers everything, no tracks of any kind, animal or man, and no scent that is foreign to the air."

Reena nodded. "True enough, but look more closely."

Magnus and his men studied the area for several silent minutes, and it was James who spoke first.

"Several thin branches are broken off some trees."

Reena nodded and waited for more.

Magnus was next. "There is an indentation beneath the snow near the large stone."

Philip followed. "There seems to be a piling of sorts, leaves or sticks not far from the indentation."

Again Reena nodded and looked to the men. "Someone has been here."

"Only one person?" James asked.

"Aye," she confirmed.

"How can you be sure?" Philip asked.

"One indentation in the snow, slim branches broken off trees to create a fire sufficient for only one person and small enough so as not to be seen." She turned slightly. "And look in the distance from this hill." She pointed. "Through the opening in the trees."

All the men looked and stared with wide eyes at a perfectly clear view of the keep.

"Gather several men and return here and cut down the trees in this area so that there is no place for anyone to hide," Magnus ordered.

Reena offered her assistance. "A few specific trees will open this area quite nicely."

"Then you will direct the men," Magnus said and took her hand. "Right now we return to the keep to gather more men."

"He is only one man," Reena said, as though there was no reason to fear.

The four men laughed, and it was James who spoke.

"Magnus is but one man, and I watched as he alone conquered fifteen men."

"I have no doubt as to the ability of one man to conquer many, but knowledge and intelligent action can almost guarantee victory," Reena said. "However, I do not think this man means anyone harm right now. He watches, but does he watch for himself or for someone else?"

"So he gathers information now," Philip said.

"Aye," Reena said, "but the question remains—"

Magnus finished for her. "Is it one of Kilkern's men or someone else?"

Chapter 14

Winter set in strong and hard in the following weeks, mostly cold, harsh weather, with one snowstorm that dropped enough snow to linger for a week. A stinging coldness now filled the air, and the villagers remained in their cottages. The animals had been given shelter in a stone and thatched building that needed much repair, but for now it would keep them safe from the inclement weather.

The village folk were also aware that they were being watched, and in return they watched and reported any suspicious movement near the surrounding area. So far, no stranger was spotted, nor did any stranger approach the village for shelter.

Guards were posted along the battlements and surrounding the keep. All was in readiness if there should be an attack, and all felt safe with the Legend's ability to protect them.

Reena and Magnus spent day after day together. She would go over an area of the keep with Magnus in the morning, and in the afternoon she would map, then in the evening they would go over the map she had worked on to see if it needed further detailing.

Conversation flowed easily between them, laughter was plentiful, and even silence between them was comforting. They worked well together, each almost knowing the other's thought or action.

Magnus praised her mapping skills and her drawing talent. He commented on how pretty she looked in the new clothes he had ordered stitched for her, and which she had refused at first to accept. It was only after he had convinced her that the garments were not a gift, that he expected her to wear his colors, that she accepted them without objection.

She favored the deep green and brown underdress and tunics, the wool being soft and gentle against her skin. It was the dark blue underdress with the light blue tunic trimmed in gold that she favored the most, but it did not fit with his colors. Magnus had insisted the garment was for special occasions and she had no choice but to wear it. She'd had no special occasion to wear it yet, but she looked forward to such an event, so soft and beautiful were the garments.

Today she wore a brown underdress and green tunic. She tied her long black hair with a leather strip and gathered charcoal and paper to join Magnus in his solar. Their plan for today was to investigate a room off the tower room. When Magnus had first showed it to her, she'd wondered how he had ever found it. It looked as if it were part of the wall, a room built specially to hide someone or to hide secrets.

Magnus bade her enter when she knocked on his door. She caught her breath at the sight of him, and try as she might, she could not prevent herself from feeling a rush of joy in seeing him. She wondered, and worried, over her recurring enthusiasm with him. Her continuous efforts to bring Brigid and him together were proving fruitless, neither seeming interested, though they were friendly in manner when in each other's company.

Looking at him now had her heart jumping, as it often did. He looked so handsome dressed in dark brown leggings and undershirt, topped by a soft leather tunic in a buttery color. He looked so very appealing.

She blushed at the thought and hurried toward him.

"Are you ready? I look forward to seeing what secrets the room holds." Her words rushed so fast from her mouth that they sounded garbled to her own ears.

Magnus laughed. "There are not many women who would be enthusiastic about searching out secret rooms locked away for years. There will be cobwebs and spiders, you know."

"You mean to frighten me?" she asked, her grin wide. "You will need to use more than cobwebs and spiders to put fear in me."

"Skeletons?" he asked.

"Do you honestly think we may find a skeleton?" she asked excitedly.

"Will you map him if we do?" he teased.

She was serious in her answer. "I often thought it might prove beneficial to map a skeleton—think what one can learn from it."

Magnus shook his head, closing the ledger he had been working on. "Come, let us see if we can find you a skeleton."

She eagerly followed alongside him as they made their way to the tower room. The room was large, the hearth small, and four windows, strategically placed, looked out on spectacular views of Dunhurnal land. A fire had been lit, but it barely warmed the empty room.

"What are your plans here?" Reena asked, turning in a complete circle to view the entire room.

"I have not yet decided, though I have heard told that the tower room is sometimes used to hold a special person prisoner."

Reena took a second glance around the room. "It would be very lonely to remain so close yet so far removed from everyone, and to look out the windows and see the land and be unable to venture out—" She shivered and hugged herself. "How horrible a fate."

"And one that will befall no one in my keep."

His firm yet sad tone chilled her and another shiver raced through her.

"You are cold?"

"Nay, it is the feel of the room that chills."

"I feel it myself," he said. "Let us search the secret room and be done with it."

Reena eagerly followed him over to the room that appeared carved out of the stone wall, a thick chest braced against the open door. It was an ingenious design, the door looking as if it were part of the wall when closed.

"How did you ever find this?" she asked, her hand examining the smooth stone edge of the door.

"By mere accident." Magnus took one of the lighted torches from the wall and entered the room.

Reena followed close behind him, feeling as if she'd stepped into the mouth of darkness.

The chamber was nothing more than a tiny cell, dark and dank, with cobwebs surrounding two trunks that sat one on top of the other in the corner. Nothing else occupied the small space.

Magnus stood frozen for a moment; his eyes were riveted to the far stone wall. She wondered at his thoughts. Did they disturb him? Did he recall a memory of another time and similar room? Lately she found herself wanting to know more about him and his past, and the reason he was called the Legend. But it would not do to ask; she was certain she would discover her answers, given time.

"Let us shed light on what is hidden," he said. "Can you hold this torch?"

Reena took it from him and stood aside while he broke through the cobwebs and moved the two dust-covered trunks out into the tower room. She gave one last look around the small space and was about to leave when something on the far wall caught her eye. She walked the few steps further into the room and held up the torch, casting light on the wall.

She reached out and touched a metal ring secured firmly in the wood. She wondered over its purpose and made a mental note to include it in her drawing of the room.

A last glance yielded no more discoveries, and she left the room to see what Magnus had found in the trunks.

Reena stood, her eyes rounding at the sight of the sparkling gems Magnus held in his hand and the plethora of gems contained in a smaller box in the trunk. Rubies, emeralds, diamonds, and sapphires glittered magnificently.

Magnus dropped the gems back into the small wooden box and took the torch from her, replacing it in the metal wall sconce.

"Secret treasure," Reena said on a whisper, as if no one should hear her. She dropped to her knees and reached out slowly to touch a dark red ruby pendant on a strand of pearls, then stopped and looked to Magnus.

"Touch what you will," he said, a smile defining his handsome features.

Why, then, did she think she saw sadness in his dark eyes?

"The ruby pendant would look lovely with your dark hair."

His suggestion startled her. "Nay, this jewelry is not fit for me; it is meant for a fine lady." She did, however, pick up the necklace, cup it in her hand, and admire its beauty.

Magnus kneeled beside her and reached for a sapphire and diamond necklace. "This one would look nice with your blue dress."

She shook her head and took the sapphire necklace from him. "Though it is beautiful to look upon. Who do you think it belonged to, and why was it hidden away?"

"Someone evidently did not want it to be discovered." He lifted the small wooden box out of the trunk to reveal glass inkwells and several quills.

Reena instantly returned the sapphire necklace to the small box and reached for the quills. "Look," she said with the excitement he would have expected from a woman when she looked upon sparkling gems. "A swan quill and a crow quill, and they look as though they have not had much use."

"Keep them," Magnus said and removed the ledgers.

"Parchment paper," Reena cried out and reached for the roll that had been flattened to the back of the trunk by the ledgers. She carefully uncrinkled and rolled the paper open. "It remains in fine condition."

"They are yours."

"Truly?" she asked, hugging them tightly in her hand.

"I have no use for them, and you will make good use of them."

Reena was so excited over her gifts that she gave no thought to her actions: She only wanted to thank Magnus for his generosity, so she flung herself at him and kissed him on the cheek.

"Thank you, thank you," she repeated, followed by two more kisses.

When she realized what she had done, she slowly moved away to plop down on her bottom, legs folded beneath her. She purposely directed her glance to the gifts in her hand.

Magnus was stunned silent by her spontaneous reaction, but once he realized her unease, he attempted to make light of it.

"Since quills and paper so excite you, I will make certain you are supplied with an abundance of both."

She laughed with relief. "I am sorry, I did not think."

"I like when you do not think."

She raised her head to look at him and found it

difficult to speak, unsure of her response and captured by the tender look in his dark eyes. What was it about his eyes that made her senses tingle? Why did a tiny shiver run through her and settle in the pit of her stomach? And why did she feel the urge to kiss him again?

Magnus leaned nearer. "Continue to look at me with such longing and I will satisfy your desire."

Desire?

Did she look at him with desire? Is that what she felt, or ached? It was an ache, and an unfamiliar one, and she did not quite understand it herself. And did she want to?

"You know little of men and women."

"I watch and see, but understand?" She shook her head. "I cannot say I understand at all."

"Yet you capture the essence in your drawings."

"I see much when I draw."

He leaned even closer. "Then draw me and understand."

Her smile was quick to return. "I would love to draw you."

"Then you will see me for who I truly am."

"Is that a challenge?"

He stared at her for a moment. "A warning."

Again she thought not of her actions and reached out to run her finger down his cheek. "I do not fear you."

His hand grabbed hold of her finger and he brought it near his mouth. His warm breath whispered across the sensitive flesh. "Are you sure of that?" He kissed her finger and then gently suckled the tip.

Her eyes turned wide, her mouth dropped open,

and though she searched for a response all she could do was moan—in pleasure, not in pain.

"Let me taste you," he whispered and captured her lips with his.

She thought to move away, her body already in motion, but his arms were quick and strong, wrapping around her and pulling her toward him. Her hands pushed against his chest, preventing close contact, and the feel of the soft leather over his hard muscled chest tingled her fingers.

His tongue rushed around her mouth and slipped between her traitorous lips. In an instant she was lost in the taste of him. There was no thought, no choice, just response, and she responded without reason. But then it made no sense, how she felt, how she ached, how her body tingled in the strangest places.

There was only a need, and she surrendered to it more completely than she had ever thought possible.

He ended the kiss with a gentle brush of his lips over hers before resting his forehead against hers.

"Think on what we have just shared and then sketch me so that you may understand it all."

She answered breathlessly. "Aye, I will do that."

Heavy footsteps climbing the stone stairs drew them apart, and Thomas soon entered the room with haste.

"A messenger approaches the keep," Thomas said.

Magnus stood. "When you sketch this room, make certain to record the views from each window. Leave the trunks, I will see to them."

"As you wish," she said and watched as Magnus and Thomas hurried out the door.

She returned the items to the trunk except for the

quills and paper Magnus had told her to keep. She refused to allow her mind to linger on their kiss or on the prospect of sketching him, though both thrilled her. She had work to do, and yet not only did her mind drift but her glance drifted as well, to the unopened trunk. She itched to discover what secrets lay in wait.

She attempted to ignore it while she sketched the room, concentrating on the view from each window as Magnus had directed, but her eyes were repeatedly drawn back to the trunk.

After several agonizing moments of fighting with herself, she surrendered to her own curiosity, kneeled in front of the trunk, and opened it.

A small blue wool blanket lay on top, and she gently moved it aside to discover several leather-bound ledgers. She removed one and carefully opened it. The handwriting was neat and small, and the text was French—a familiar name within the lines.

I gave birth to a fine son today after much pain, and though I continue to ache and feel exhausted, I also feel wonderful. He nestles in my arms, his fists tightly clenched, and he snuggles to me for warmth. He has claimed my heart, this tiny son of mine, and I will protect him well. He deserves a fine name and so I have decided to name him after my grandfather, for he was a courageous and fair man. I will call my new son—Magnus.

Chapter 15

Reena stared at the map in front of her, quill in hand. She had retired to her room over an hour ago and had yet to lay quill to paper. Her mind overflowed with all that had transpired in a single day, and she was now trying to make sense of it.

Talk during the evening meal was of the mysterious messenger. Tongues wagged and gossip spread, but no one had an answer as to who could have sent him. But Reena's mind continued to wander to the kiss she and Magnus had shared.

She could not rid her mind of the taste of him. He lingered there and on her lips, warm and pungent, tempting the senses, and she responded to the vivid memories.

Her skin grew warm, her flesh tingled, and she ran her tongue slowly over her lips, reclaiming the taste of him. She shivered, and gooseflesh rushed to prickle her skin.

She shook her head, a firm, hard shake to clear her

thoughts. She was foolish to dwell on a kiss. She had work to do and she was wasting time on nonsense. Magnus was lord of Dunhurnal and she was in his service. She certainly was not the type of woman he would love. He would love and wed a woman who would give him many heirs, tend to him and their children and his keep. She, on the other hand, wished to map, and that would mean travel. She had no time for love, and she did not think she was suited to be a mother. Adventure, travel, mapping was what interested her, and they did not go well with being a wife.

Or were they mere excuses she made for the stark cold fact that the Legend simply would never love a woman such as her?

She turned her troublesome thoughts to the prospect of drawing Magnus. His defined features were made for drawing, and she intended to do as he suggested—draw him.

Would she then understand him better?

There was much to understand, especially the journal she had discovered in the trunk. It had belonged to Magnus's mother, and the trunks seemed to have been hidden away in that small room.

She had had no chance to continue reading the entries. Footsteps had fallen heavy on the stairs, and she had quickly returned the journal to the trunk before closing the lid. Two of Magnus's men had entered the room and removed the trunks, though she knew not where.

Questions gathered like storm clouds in her mind, filling with possibilities and getting ready to burst. Could his mother have lived here at Dunhurnal? Or had the trunks been brought here and hidden? And was there more to the reason why the king had granted Dunhurnal land to Magnus?

She rubbed her forehead, her thoughts a jumble of questions with few answers.

"You work too hard."

Reena jumped, startled by Magnus's sudden presence.

"I did not hear you enter."

"I doubt you would have heard a troop of men enter. You appeared too engrossed in thought." He approached her desk, walking around to where she sat to stand beside her and look over the map she worked on.

"I have not gotten very far."

Magnus disagreed. "You have done more than I expected, and your detail is remarkable." He studied the tower room she had drawn and marveled at the preciseness of her strokes. The windows matched in size, and each window was marked with a Roman numeral and a direction inscribed in Gaelic and Latin, as was a spot on the wall where the door to the small room would be located.

Reena pointed to the Latin inscription. "North, south, east and west so you know where you look upon. The Roman numeral corresponds to another map, which will give you the view from the window. The numeral on the door corresponds to a map of the small chamber, which shows little—a bare, cell-like room with a metal ring secured to thick wood."

"You noticed the metal ring?"

"I make myself aware of all that I see and record

what I see. I know not if it is important, I only know that I see it and therefore record it." She asked one of the questions that troubled her thoughts. "Do you know the metal ring's purpose?"

Magnus remained silent for a moment, and she waited, knowing he would answer after his own thoughts had settled.

"The metal ring is to chain a prisoner."

"The small chamber is a prison?"

"A special prison that no one knows exists."

Reena was appalled. "How horrible. The room is too remote, far removed from the rest of the keep. A person could die in that room and no one would ever know."

Magnus pointed to the tower room. "In this room as well. No cries would be heard even from the windows; they are too far up. The screams would sound like a mere whisper when they reached the ground."

She pointed where he did, her finger touching his. "Will you imprison here?"

There was another moment of silence that had Reena wondering what secrets—or, perhaps, nightmares—haunted him.

"Nay, this room will know no more sorrow."

She thought to comfort him, though from what she did not quite understand; she only knew that the sorrow he spoke of belonged to him. She splayed her hand over his. "Furnishings that lend comfort, tapestries that add color and a larger fireplace that chases away the cold would all welcome anyone who enters the tower room."

He moved his fingers to lock onto hers and held tight. "You have ideas for change, this is good."

As she had extended comfort with her touch, he

extended comfort with his firm grasp, and it was a natural comfort they shared. It took no effort, no thought, no choice; it was a reaction of the heart.

Flutters rushed through her stomach and up to circle her heart and she smiled, knowing there was nothing she could do.

He leaned his face close to hers. "Do what you will to the room."

She shook her head. "The choice belongs to the lord of the keep."

"The lord of the keep is instructing you to see to the changes."

"And if you should not care for them?"

He tucked a wisp of her long dark hair behind her ear, his finger slowly stroking the edge. "I trust you."

A sturdy knock on her door interrupted them and the shiver that raced through her.

"Enter," Magnus called out.

Thomas entered. "You are needed."

Magnus nodded, then turned to Reena. "I will give orders that you are to be helped with the tower room, but the mornings are ours to spend touring the keep, and in the evenings we will discuss our findings." With a kiss of her hand he left, closing the door behind him.

Perplexed by the touch of intimacy, she stared at the closed door. If she gave thought to the time they spent together, she would see that he often reached out to touch her. And while his touch had at first been no more than a helping hand, it had slowly changed without her realizing it—until now.

His hand had often gone to her arm, guiding her along dark passageways. His arm would find her waist when stairwells became steep, and he would stand close beside her when looking over a map, his cheek brushing hers.

Was it on purpose?

Did he find her interesting?

Did he find her appealing?

He would not tend toward intimacy if he did not at least find her appealing.

Or did he favor a mere sexual romp?

Her thoughts were once again a whirlwind of questions, and she shook her head, growing tired of the endless barrage of doubts. She was grateful for the faint knock at her door, the intrusion helping to clear her mind.

"Enter," she said and smiled when Brigid entered. Her grin grew wider when she saw that her friend held a tray filled with tarts and a pitcher of—she sniffed the air. "Old Margaret made her winter brew and you made your fruit tarts." She rubbed her hands together in anticipation and cleared a small table to move in front of the hearth.

Brigid's smile was generous. "Aye, I thought you could use both. You have been busy of late."

She set the tray down while Reena pulled two chairs to the table. The fire snapped and crackled and provided a toasty warmth to the room. The two women sat and were soon enjoying the winter brew and the tarts.

"Your mother tells everyone that while she wishes you would visit with them more often, she knows how busy you are in the service of Lord Dunhurnal." Brigid laughed lightly. "Your father once again tells his tales, though now they are about you. Your parents are proud of you."

Reena's smile was tender. "I am glad to hear this. I had worried so about them."

"You worried about everyone except yourself." Brigid did not accuse: she reminded.

A whimper caught their attention, and it grew louder as Reena walked to the door. She opened it, and Horace ran in, heading straight for the table.

Reena returned to her seat and gave the pup, who had grown considerably over the last few weeks, a generous piece of her tart.

"See," Brigid said on a laugh. "You even put the pup before yourself."

"Can you not see that he grows and needs the sustenance?" Reena laughed herself.

"Horace gets sustenance from everyone."

"Food is plentiful."

"Because of you," Brigid reminded. "The villagers are grateful, though they remain fearful that Kilkern will have his retribution."

"Magnus will see to Kilkern," Reena said with confidence.

"Aye, I agree, but memories of last winter linger, and if by chance Kilkern gains control of this land, he will be harsh in his revenge."

"How could he do that? Magnus's strength far surpasses his."

"Gossip has started that Kilkern will petition the king to return Dunhurnal land to him since it is rightfully his."

"He but *thinks* he deserves it," Reena said. "He has no right to the land, gossip says the king granted it to Magnus in return for his service and the king will see that it remains his. All will go well here."

Brigid nodded. "I believe the same. The sadness

in my heart grows less heavy each day, and with our move to Dunhurnal land, I now look forward to another day."

"You will love again," Reena assured her, but it wounded her heart to think that she might find that love with Magnus.

"I care not about finding another love right now. The pleasures of life are slowly returning to me and I wish to enjoy them." She laughed. "It feels good to cook again and have the food appreciated."

"Thomas?" Reena asked.

"Aye. He has been an enormous help to me and he is so kindhearted. I enjoy his visits. He is a good man and wants only friendship from me. I am at peace with my loss and that is good, and now I go on."

"I am glad to hear this and I am happy for you. It has been too long since we have been happy, though Justin is certainly happy."

Both women smiled wide and leaned closer to share gossip.

"He spends all his time with Maura," Brigid said. "And she with him. They are inseparable."

Reena added her own news. "They are always smiling when I see them, whether they are together or apart. I sometimes wish I had more time to spend with family and friends, but time is something I have little of, though I do not complain, and I doubt many understand my penchant for mapping or drawing."

"No one comments—they accept you for who you are, and besides, they are grateful for your courage."

"I did what was necessary for the good of all." Reena did not wish to discuss herself and quickly changed topics. "I have a favor I need of you. I have ideas for the tower room and would like your help."

"I would love to help you. Tell me your ideas."

The two women discussed the room until several yawns alerted them to the late hour. Brigid bid her goodnight, excited and ready to start the project they had discussed.

Reena was filled with excitement of her own, and though several yawns warned she was not far from slumber, she decided to finish a few details on the map she'd worked on.

A surprising growl from Horace, who lay curled in front of the hearth, alerted her to a late-night visitor. The flickering shadows in the room, the sound of crackling fire, the lateness of the hour and Horace's steady growl gave her a sudden unease.

The knock eased her worry, though she called out, "Who is it?"

"Magnus."

Her concern faded completely at the sound of his strong voice.

She bade him entrance.

"I saw the faint light under your door and could not believe you remained awake at this hour, and still working. And was that a growl I heard from my dog?"

Reena giggled. "I think he grows courageous with age."

"But he growls at his master," Magnus said with a laugh and a shake of his head.

Horace had already returned to his sound slumber, ignoring them both.

"You have worked since I left you?"

"Nay, Brigid visited, I wish only to finish a detail or two."

"Brigid is good?" Magnus approached her desk.

Reena repeated her friend's words. "She is at peace with life."

"I am glad to hear that. She is a good woman."

Reena thought to try once again and see if there was a chance for Magnus and Brigid, though she hesitated for a moment and wondered over her reluctance to speak.

"Do you not look for a good woman to take as a wife?"

"I seek a woman to love to take as my wife."

"Can love not come later in a marriage?" Reena asked.

"It is always possible, but then without a spark of love, a bit of interest or at least an attraction, indifference and hate can also come later."

He walked around the desk, slowly lowered his lips to hers, and kissed her softly. "Goodnight, and while you sleep, think of who *you* wish to love."

Chapter 16

An unusually harsh winter hit the land, and much time was spent indoors by all. Reena visited with her mother and father when she could, though oftentimes when she did, her father was busy entertaining the village children with heroic tales.

Life was good for all right now even though eyes were kept wide and strangers watched carefully. Safety was not taken for granted. Kilkern could not be trusted. He waited and planned, and eventually he would make himself known.

Reena hurried down the stairs to the great hall. She was starving and looking forward to talking with Brigid. They'd made plans to meet this morning and discuss the remaining work that needed finishing in the tower room.

She caught sight of Brigid at a table close to the fireplace. Thomas sat beside her and Magnus stood, his look angry. Something was wrong. She hurried over to the trio.

"What has happened?" Reena asked, a sense of dread descending on her.

Magnus answered. "I received a message from Kilkern that Brigid is to be turned over to him for theft from his property."

"Brigid stole nothing from him," Reena argued.

"He claims otherwise and demands a punishment fitting the crime. He refuses any compensation, insisting the object was invaluable."

"What is it he claims she stole? And why wait until now to accuse?" Reena was furious and stood beside her friend, her hand on her shoulder. She could feel Brigid tremble with fear, and she squeezed her shoulder in reassurance.

Silence hung heavy in the air and Reena wondered over it, glancing from one to another in search of an answer.

Magnus spoke. "He claims he only recently realized he no longer possessed the object and that he was with Brigid when he last saw it."

"And this priceless object is?"

"A map."

Reena shook her head. "A map? A map of what? And why would a map be so important to him?"

"Kilkern claims that this map shows that Dunhurnal land is actually Kilkern land and that it was divided unlawfully and given to one Brian Dunhurnal. Dates and boundaries on the map and the signature of the king would prove his claim. He insists that Brigid stole it for me."

"That is ridiculous," Reena said. "She did not know you until you arrived here with me."

"Kilkern claims otherwise, and if I do not surrender Brigid, he warns that he will petition the king to have her turned over to him, in addition to the return of Dunhurnal land, which he says rightfully belongs to him."

Reena could do nothing but shake her head at the absurdity of Kilkern's claims.

"He but baits me, wanting me to make a foolish move," Magnus said.

"What will you do?" Reena asked, her hand remaining firm on her friend's shoulder.

"First, I will make certain Brigid has extra protection. I would expect Kilkern to make an attempt to abduct her." Magnus looked to Thomas. "You will guard her well."

"Have no doubt of that," Thomas said. "I will not leave her side."

Brigid cast sympathetic eyes on Thomas. "You will tire of seeing my face."

"Beauty never tires the eyes."

"Oh, Thomas," Brigid said. "I am glad it is you who will guard me. I will feel well protected."

"And what of Kilkern?" Reena asked. "What is to be done about him?"

"He will be seen to in time. He will not succeed in taking this land. It belongs to me and will remain mine," Magnus said with a confidence that had none doubting his words. "Until then life goes on as usual. Now let us eat, for I am starving."

Thomas agreed with a strong, "Aye."

Reena added similar sentiments. "I hunger for a good meal."

Brigid laughed. "My stomach tells me the same, and this is good, for if we truly feared Kilkern, none of us would be so hungry."

They laughed along with her, and soon the table

was covered with trays and platters of hot food and pitchers of mulled cider. After they ate Thomas followed Brigid, along with Horace, to the tower room, and Magnus and Reena went off to continue mapping the keep. It was near finished, with only the area beneath the keep, which had served as a prison, to explore.

With torch in hand, Magnus preceded Reena down the narrow stone staircase.

"Watch your step," he cautioned. "A dampness fills this passageway and makes the stones slippery."

The further they descended, the more damp it became, and a stench filled the already musty air. Magnus stopped at the bottom step and held the torch high, the flickering flame casting a ghostly light over his handsome face. "I had the prison cells cleaned as best as possible, but a scent lingers, and I think it always will. If the odor offends you, we can try another day, or I can detail the cells and you can map them from my memory."

"Nay, I need to see the area for myself or else the map will not be as accurate as it should be. The odor is strange and could certainly be obnoxious to the senses, but I will be fine."

"You will tell me if the smell begins to trouble you?"

"Aye," she answered. "Let us start—the sooner I map, the sooner we can leave the foul odor behind us."

Magnus nodded and proceeded down the corridor. "I had several torches lit so that there would be sufficient light for you."

Six torches flamed brightly in metal wall sconces and shed light on an area where darkness had once reigned. Reena stood silent, staring at the cells. The doors were open wide, and complete darkness greeted anyone who entered. The thought of being swallowed by the cavernous black hole ran a shiver through her.

Magnus moved next to her. "Can you do this?"

She took a breath and wished she had not: the odor suddenly turned to a foul stench. "Yes."

"All the cells are the same," Magnus said, raising the torch high after stepping into the first cell, chasing the darkness to crouch in the corners. "Sketch one and you sketch them all."

"Nay," she argued. "That is not so, I wish to see every cell." And she did, her disgust growing as she sketched and thought of the people who had suffered here. A small window set high in the thick wooden door would have been the only source of light in each cell—if the wall torches remained lit. Otherwise, complete darkness engulfed the cells.

The foul odor grew stronger as they reached the end cell, and Reena realized the stench came from the opening beyond the six cells. Magnus blocked the entrance, and when she moved to walk past him, he held out his arm, preventing her from going any further.

"That room needs no mapping."

"If I am to do a thorough map of the keep, all rooms must be included."

"It is not for you to see."

"I must," she insisted.

He was blunt. "It is where prisoners were tortured."

"All the more reason to record it," she said and pushed his arm away to enter the foreboding room.

Reena froze with her first step into the room and then slowly turned in a circle to view the horror in front of her. Metal cages hung from the ceiling and a large cauldron occupied the middle of the room, cold ashes cradling the bottom. A rack with metal cuffs and chains secured to top and bottom stretched out like a bed near the cauldron. Chains with attached metal cuffs hung from metal rings in the wall, and metal implements of torture lay rusted on the ground.

She closed her eyes for a moment and could almost hear the painful screams, the pleas of mercy and the smell of blood and burning flesh.

How could a man inflict such pain on another?

Magnus shoved the torch in the wall sconce and walked up behind her. "Survival has its horrors."

"Nay," Reena said, a tear in her eye. "There is no excuse for man's inhumanity to man."

"Life needs defending at times."

"Defending, aye." She pointed to the various torture devices. "But this is not defending, this is pure horror to humanity. And I will record every speck of it."

She set to work drawing and examining the room in detail so that her recording of this horror prison would be exact. When an hour had passed, Magnus said, "Enough."

"I am almost done." Her hand had not stopped sketching and did not slow down.

"You are done." He stilled her hand with his. "No more, Reena."

She glared at him. "I will finish here, and then I will sketch something of beauty to rid me of this horror."

"Will you be able to recognize beauty after viewing horror?"

Her answer came easily. "Aye, I see beauty every day when I look upon your face."

Magnus stepped closer to her, his hands going to her waist. "You find beauty in the Legend? Some would think you insane."

Her hand dropped to the side, holding on to her piece of charcoal and drawing paper. "They do not know the Legend as I do."

He moved closer. "You know not the Legend, nor do you want to."

She looked in his dark eyes and how they glistened with light from the flaming torches. Light and darkness. Two men in one. "I know he is a fair man."

His laugh was haunting. "Fair? I have seen men tortured—" His silence was sudden, as if he thought better of his words.

She wanted to know more, though her legs trembled. He wore no iron helmet now, but it was the Legend who stood in front of her and who rested his strong hands on her hips.

She found the courage to ask. "Was it difficult to watch?"

His answer sent a cold shiver down her spine. "I was the one who ordered the torture."

This was the Legend, the fearless man who instilled fear in his foe and friend alike. And this was the man she worried that she might be falling in love with? Perhaps she was insane.

His hands tightened at her waist. "You know me not, Reena."

"I would like to know you and understand you, and I will begin by drawing you."

"You still see beauty in me?" He seemed surprised.

She touched his cheek. He had inflicted suffering, but had suffering been inflicted on him? "I see beauty and much more." She traced a finger over his cheekbone. "Pride is obvious."

His fine lips quivered in laughter, though it turned to a smile.

She squeezed his chin. "Stubbornness."

"Strength," he argued on a laugh.

She corrected him with a gentle brush of her finger across his forehead. "Strength." She moved to the corners of his eyes. "Insight." Her finger trailed down to his mouth and slowly traced his lips. "Humor, honesty, gentleness and . . ."

Actions, she decided, would say more than words. She stood on her toes and slowly brushed her lips across his. She traced his lips with her wet tongue and kissed him again. She nipped at his lower lips and kissed him again.

In an instant he pulled her to him, her paper and charcoal falling out of her hand and her arms rushing around his neck. They locked in a fiery kiss, their surroundings ignored, their need a force of raging desire that made them prisoners of passion.

His mouth moved down to claim her neck, and she turned her head, giving him free rein. She gave him mere seconds to enjoy, then returned to claim more kisses from him, hungry for the taste of him.

He stopped her, cupping her face in his hands. "This is not the place for this. I want to kiss you in the sunlight, where I can see the beauty of your face, not in the dark recesses of a room that knew only suffering."

He retrieved her drawings from the ground, handed them to her, and lifted the torch from the sconce. "Let us find a place of light—my solar."

Magnus followed Reena from the room, her lips alive with the taste of him and aching to taste more. It seemed the more she kissed him, the more she wanted to kiss him. And she did not even attempt to dissuade or reason with herself.

Was this nonsensical feeling love?

Or was it foolishness?

Either way she was in trouble, for at the moment she did not care—another effect of love, or foolishness?

And what of the consequences when they entered his solar?

What did he expect from her? What did she expect from herself? Was she ready to face the consequences of her actions? Did she not remember her own intentions? She wished to love and be loved when she chose to share intimacy with a man. No mention of love had passed between them. It was pure passion, nothing more. Is this what she wished for?

Her pace slowed as reality cooled her emotions, and she realized there was more for her to give thought to before she shared any intimacy with him.

Magnus eased a hand to her waist, guiding her up the stairwell and feeling her tension build with each slow step she took. He sought to ease her concern. "You will be able to draw me in the light."

Her step faltered slightly, though his strong hand kept her firmly in place.

"I am eager to draw you." She heard her own relief. Why, then, did disappointment nip at her senses?

He opened the door to his solar and guided her with a firm hand inside. An overcast sky prevented any sunlight from entering through the windows, and the roaring fire in the hearth was the only source of light, leaving shadows to lurk in the corners.

"We will need much more light in here if I am to draw you," Reena said.

"Light no candles," came a raspy, menacing voice from the shadows.

Reena jumped, and Magnus was quick to shove her behind him. His hand went to the hilt of the knife tucked in its leather sheath. "Show yourself."

"Send the woman away."

Reena's hand rested on Magnus's back, and she could feel his muscles tighten at the stern command. He was accustomed to issuing orders, not receiving them.

"I say for the last time, show yourself or suffer the consequences."

A chill ran through Reena. Magnus left no doubt that he was in command. Was she prepared to watch two men battle? And what if Magnus was wounded? She suddenly was ready to defend, not herself but Magnus.

"I remain here."

The strength of her voice radiated throughout the room, and Reena could have sworn she heard the intruder laugh.

Magnus moved his hand off his knife. "Come out of the shadows."

Reena stepped to the side, peeking out from behind Magnus, relieved that he seemed to know the intruder.

A laugh, a shuffle of movement, and from the shadows emerged another shadow. A man draped entirely in black. At first glance one might think him a priest, with his hood pulled down over his head so that no portion of his face was visible. But on a second look it was not a cleric's robe he wore.

In an instant Reena realized who stood before them, and she tensed. Whispered tales were told of him, though no identity or name was known. He was simply called the Dark One.

Chapter 17

"A drink?" Magnus offered, no tension evident in his voice, his body at ease as he moved away to fill three tankards of ale from the pitcher that was kept full on the small table near the window.

It appeared as though Magnus was acquainted with the Dark One. While relieved, Reena remained where she stood, staring at the cloaked figure, her heart beating rapidly and her hands itching to draw his ominous shape. She dared not look too closely, for it was whispered that whoever looked upon his face perished from fright. He blended with the shadows so skillfully that he could be present in a room without anyone's knowledge. And with that skill he was able to accomplish remarkable feats, appearing and disappearing without a trace and taking with him whoever he chose.

It was whispered that kings hired him to rid them of enemies difficult to dispose of and of mistresses no longer in favor. But then there were tales of his exploits in helping the less fortunate, so few knew the truth, and the only truth truly known was that you did not want the Dark One to appear before you, for it meant that you would soon disappear.

"You are the mapmaker."

His voice startled her from her thoughts. It was a harsh whisper, a mask of sorts that concealed his true voice, and Reena wondered why he hid. Was his face as hideous as believed? She suddenly realized he knew of her mapping skills.

"You know of me?" she asked curiously.

His voice rose above a whisper, though the harsh tone remained. "I have heard of your skills and of those who fear you."

"Fear me? Why would I be feared?" She actually laughed asking the question. The thought that anyone would think her a threat was simply laughable.

Magnus laughed along with her. "You are becoming a legend."

The Dark One laughed along with them, though the harsh sound prickled the skin.

"I find it as amusing as you both do, but I do not understand," Reena said.

Magnus handed the tankard to the Dark One and he reached for it, his hand covered in black leather.

Reena trembled, for there was no light to this man; there was only complete darkness.

Magnus explained, handing Reena a tankard. "You open up the land and expand people's knowledge. They can see before their eyes mountains, valleys, rivers and streams that they may have heard existed but never saw for themselves. Suddenly their world is not so small, and many become adventurous, wanting to see for themselves and thinking perhaps they would find a better life elsewhere."

"Leaving those who rule without tenants to work their lands, less men to defend property and the possibility that some other lord or landowner will grow strong with those people who migrate elsewhere," the Dark One finished.

"Knowledge is a powerful weapon," Magnus said, "which is why those who rule keep the populace ignorant of the world."

"How very sad," Reena said. "Knowledge, even a little, could ease much heartache."

Magnus raised his glass. "To three who are feared."

Reena smiled and raised her glass high, adding her own sentiments. "And to three who shed light on the darkness."

The Dark One added his opinion. "Even when it takes darkness to bring light to the world."

For a moment Reena detected gentleness in his voice, and she found her fear of the shadowy figure dissipating and turning to curiosity. Who was this man who seemed friend, not foe, to Magnus?

Magnus confirmed the friendship when he turned to her. "Reena, I need time to speak with my friend alone."

Reena placed her tankard on the table. "Of course, and besides, I have much work to do."

"I will see you later," Magnus said.

She nodded, and as she passed the Dark One, she said, "Good day."

A hooded head bobbed briefly in response.

"Reena." Magnus stopped her as her hand touched the door. "Tell no one of his presence."

"As you wish." She slipped out the door, closing it quietly behind her.

"What are you doing here?" Magnus asked, taking a seat by the fireplace.

The Dark One retreated to the chair in the shadowed corner of the room and slipped his hood off his head. His face could not be seen, and Magnus made no effort to look upon him.

"My skills have been requested by someone, and I am on my way to meet with him, but I was detoured by a request from the earl of Culberry, who appears heartbroken that the woman he loves is being detained by the Legend. He wishes for me to return her to him."

Magnus laughed. "The fool believes he can lie to the Dark One? He is more of an idiot than I first thought."

"Can I assist you in this matter?"

Magnus shook his head. "It is not necessary. Thomas watches over the woman Kilkern speaks of. She is but a piece of bait to him in his foolish trap."

"I can take the woman to a safe place until this matter is settled if you wish."

"Brigid would not go. This is her home and she is happy here and safe. Kilkern plays his game thinking he backs me into a corner, when it is I who maneuvers him into place."

"My offer remains."

"I appreciate your friendship." Magnus leaned forward toward the shadows. "When do you come out of the darkness, my friend?"

Silence followed for several seconds, and a much softer voice spoke. "When the pain in my heart is no more."

"Women and love." Magnus shook his head. "Suffering for sure."

Both men laughed.

"You pick a good woman to love," the Dark One said.

Magnus looked to the shadowy figure in surprise. "Is there nothing that escapes you?"

"Nay," the Dark One admitted. "I see all, but this was easy to see for I know you well, my friend. You never favored the ladies with weak minds or character. You looked for one who would challenge with equal strength, and although the mapmaker is small in size she possesses the strength of a warrior."

Magnus smiled. "She does, and she is as determined as a warrior, though her weapon of choice is a quill, which she wields with skill."

"So I have heard, though beware," the Dark One warned. "There are many who would wish her talent to be theirs. These lands continue to be a mystery to many. A mapmaker would prove a powerful weapon. Then of course there is the fact that you love her."

Magnus shook his head, stood, retrieved the pitcher of ale from the table, and refilled their tankards before returning to his seat and placing the pitcher on the ground beside him.

"She cares for you as well, it is there in her eyes."

"She thinks I better suit her friend, though I believe she is beginning to understand Brigid has no interest in me."

"She would step aside so that her friend could have you when she herself favors you. Friendship like that is rare."

"Reena risked her own life for her entire village by journeying to my home."

"I do not envy you, my friend. A woman with such a caring heart would do anything for the man she loves, even risk her own life."

The thought startled Magnus, and he was quick to respond. "She will do as I command."

The Dark One's laughter sounded more amused than harsh. "You should fast make her your wife, you may then have more control that way." He laughed harder. "Though I doubt it."

"She listens when I command."

"Every time?"

Magnus thought to confirm his query, when he remembered how she had been struck by one of Kilkern's men because she had gone off on her own without his permission.

"Your hesitation is answer enough." His laughter continued.

"You find this amusing. One day you will find a woman such as Reena for yourself, and you will laugh no more."

His laughter subsided. "If I found a woman with the strength, character and honesty of Reena, I would never let her go. I would protect her with my last ounce of strength and gladly give my life for her. But we agree that women like Reena are rare and few. You have found an incomparable gem."

An abrupt shuffle and movement in the shadows caused Magnus to stand.

"I remain too long. I must go."

"You are always welcome in my home."

A black-leather-clad hand emerged from the shadows. "Thank you, my friend."

Magnus held firm to his hand. "If ever you need me—"

"I know where you are." A firm handshake parted them, and Magnus knew not how the Dark One exited the room, he only knew that he disappeared. "Keep safe, my friend."

A winter storm set in hard and fast by midday, and most sought shelter in their homes. With sufficient warmth and food, the villagers were content. Reena draped her warm wool cloak around her and hurried out of the keep to Brigid's cottage, Horace tailing close behind.

She thought to keep her friend company and perhaps ease her worry concerning Kilkern, but when she arrived at the cottage she heard laughter and was surprised upon entering to see Brigid teaching Thomas to make bread. They were laughing because the large man looked quite odd with an apron around his wide girth and his thick fingers buried in dough.

Reena recalled Magnus's words about looking more closely at Brigid's own dreams and desires. Watching the two, she realized the unlikely pair worked well together and, oddly enough, complemented each other.

Thomas looked at Brigid with loving eyes, and she seemed attentive to the large man. Could they be falling in love? It was obvious they wished to be alone, though Brigid insisted she stay and have the evening meal with them. Reena declined, though

Horace remained, the scent of baking bread too tempting to refuse.

Reena returned to the great hall to find it empty, and she realized most would be remaining in their cottages for the night. She felt a sense of loneliness and thought of visiting her parents or Justin. Then she realized that Justin would probably be with Maura and her parents probably were snuggled before the fire enjoying her mother's delicious winter stew, and no doubt the children would gather round her father later and hear his tales.

Where, then, did she belong?

The question disturbed her, for she had always felt a strong sense of belonging and a connection to all in the village. But times had changed and she was no longer the little girl who sat in her father's lap listening to exciting tales. She had actually created her own tales by living her life, and her life was her mapmaking and drawing.

Both filled her days and occupied much of her nights. Why did that thought fill her with a sense of loneliness? Did she suddenly want more? More of what?

Someone to share it with?

Her mother and father had each other. Brigid in a sense had Thomas to protect her and care for her. Justin and Maura spent all their time together, and several of Magnus's men had fallen in love with women in the village.

Why did she think of this now?

And why did her thoughts now take her to Magnus?

He was her lord and she his servant. She mapped

for him; there was much yet to be finished, and here she stood in an empty hall feeling sorry for herself. It would not do.

She hurried off to the cook area, passing through the enclosed passageway that kept the servants safe from the harsh weather when serving meals. She heard Justin's and Maura's voices before she entered the room.

Justin greeted her with a smile and a hug. "Join Maura and me for the meal. Everyone remains home."

Reena saw that the couple was alone, Maura the only cook remaining for the night, the others home with their families. She decided they should have their time alone.

"I would love to, but I have much work to do and thought to fill a tray to take to my chambers."

Maura hurried off the bench, where she sat at a table with Justin. "I will fix a tray for you."

Maura piled freshly cooked venison on a plate, along with fresh baked bread, while Justin and Reena talked about the strides the village had made.

Maura finished the tray with several thick slices of soft cheese. "I can carry this to your chambers for you."

Reena refused her offer with a shake of her head and reached out to take the tray. "That is not necessary. Stay and enjoy your time alone, I assume you both get little of it."

Justin grinned. "Reena always sees what others did not—that is why her maps and drawings are so detailed and accurate."

"I will take my leave now before my head swells

with compliments. Enjoy the evening." With that, Reena took her tray and left the couple cuddled together on the bench as they ate their meal.

Reena climbed the wooden stairs to her chambers. She wondered what was occupying Magnus this eve. They had become close in the last few weeks, working together in mapping the keep. She had come to know him as Magnus, separate from the Legend. He had a caring heart, and yet when necessary, he hardened his heart.

Had she done that when she had decided to seek help from the Legend? Had she put her fears aside and done what was good for the whole? Is that what a great leader did? But she was no great leader. She was a simple peasant lass with no great dreams or aspirations.

She simply wished to map and draw.

But did she not wish to love?

Seeing Justin and Maura, thinking of her father and mother, even seeing Thomas and how he looked at Brigid with such love and concern in his eyes, did she not want someone to care for her?

Magnus.

She shook her head. He was her lord, she in his service, but did they not share interests? Did they not enjoy mapping the keep together? Had they not shared interesting conversation? Had he not kissed her? And had she not wanted him to?

She shook her head again.

She was confused and concerned. Her mapping had occupied a good portion of her time and thoughts, and thoughts of loving Magnus continued to invade her mind. They were hard to ignore, try as she might. And the endless question—Could she be falling in love, and was falling in love with Lord Magnus a wise choice?—haunted her.

A few more steps and she would be in her chamber, where she could lock herself away from the world and think—nay, map. Her thoughts then would be heavily occupied and she would think no more on love and men and all such nonsense.

She opened the door to her bedchamber with a sigh of relief and stopped abruptly.

Magnus sat at a table laden with food. "Where have you been? I have waited for you."

Chapter 18

Reena stood speechless at the open door. Magnus walked over to her, took the tray from her hand, and closed the door behind her.

"Where have you been?" he asked again.

"I thought to visit with Brigid, but she and Thomas are busy baking bread."

He placed the tray on the table with the other foods. "Thomas bakes bread, does he?"

Reena was quick to defend the large man. "He keeps Brigid occupied so she does not overly worry about Kilkern. He is good to her and I see that he cares for her."

He held a chair out for her to take a seat. "I think *Brigid* cares more than she realizes."

Reena hung her cloak on the peg by the door and sat. "Her heart still hurts."

"Thomas heals her heart and she will realize this soon enough. It took you time to see that your friend needed a strong yet gentle man like Thomas. He suits her well, unlike me."

Reena was ready to disagree, but he prevented a reply.

"I have not an ounce of gentleness in me."

Reena thought otherwise and with a hasty tongue let him know her thoughts. "That is not so—"

He would not allow her to finish, and this time his words chilled. "A man who can order the torture of others possesses no gentleness."

Remembering the cold, dark belly of the keep, with its prison cells and torture chamber, gave her reason to pause and consider his words. She could not think of Magnus issuing such horrendous orders, but the Legend could, and the thought set her legs to trembling.

She chose to move away from the subject, giving herself time to reconcile the two men into one, if she ever could. "Your friend took his leave?"

"Aye, and I appreciate your discretion in the matter. Are you hungry?"

His hasty change of topic warned her he did not wish to discuss the Dark One. "I am hungry enough to eat all of this."

He piled her plate high with an assortment of food. "I was thinking that the mapping of the keep is near done. Spring is but a mere three or four weeks away. As soon as the weather clears we should map my property. It may take a few days, but it is important that I am familiar with my land and the land that surrounds me."

Reena felt a thrill of excitement at the prospect of mapping land once again. "A good thought, especially with Kilkern property being so close. It is important you know your boundaries."

Magnus filled his own plate. "It is more important Kilkern knows his boundaries, though he feels he has none."

"His boundaries are defined well enough." Reena paused in taking a bite of her food. "If I may inquire? How did you come by Dunhurnal land? Land is either inherited or—"

"Granted for a favor done," Magnus finished.

She wondered over the favor he had provided to the king to win him land. "If the king himself granted the land, how can Kilkern think to protest?"

"A foolish trick on his part." Magnus poured them more wine.

"Do you know of this Brian Conor, earl of Dunhurnal? This keep was empty when my parents settled as tenants on Culberry land, and it has remained empty since that time. Gossipy tongues spoke of an earl who had taken ill and died leaving no heirs to inherit, so it remained vacant these many years."

He shrugged as if he knew or cared little about the previous occupants, though his voice held conviction as he reached for a thick slice of dark bread. "I know the land is mine and it will remain mine. Kilkern is angry that I robbed him of his tenants and land he feels is his, so he strikes out in blind vengeance. A mistake that will cost him dearly."

"Do you feel he will attack the keep?"

"Nay, it will serve no purpose and only gain him the wrath of the king. He must make it appear that I took what was rightfully his, though my concern does remain for Brigid. He would not hesitate to use her to get revenge."

"You speak as if you know him well."

"I know his kind, but enough of Kilkern. There is a matter I wish to discuss with you."

Reena grew attentive after taking a sip of her wine. She had grown to look forward to their discussions. They often talked well into the night, sitting before the fire in his solar, he talking of faraway lands and she asking for specific details. He had detailed a place so vividly once that she had drawn it for him. He was amazed at her accuracy, so she listened well now, eager to hear what he had to say.

He sat tall in his seat, his chest expanding the dark leather of his tunic and his features growing firm and intent in expression. "I wish you to pay close attention to what I have to say."

The Legend spoke—she detected it in his commanding tone and the way his eyes focused directly on her. Here was the part of him she wished to capture on paper. The warrior intent on command, intimidating in stance and tone, and her drawing would reflect it all.

Her hands itched, her creative passion soared, and she could not contain herself. "Wait a moment."

He looked startled when she jumped up and made a dash for her desk, quickly gathering paper and charcoal and returning with the same haste. She moved platters of food out of her way and positioned her drawing tablet on the table before her. With charcoal in hand and a steady eye on him she said, "You may continue."

Her actions so surprised him that he could do nothing but stare. He had intended to remind her that she was to seek his permission before going anyplace on her own. His friend's words had given him pause to consider that Reena's mapping skills could place her at risk. She would know more of his lands, keeps and surrounding lands than anyone, making her vulnerable to his enemies. If they captured her, they captured a wealth of knowledge about him.

Her small hands flew across the paper, her eyes darting from him back to the tablet. It amazed him how quickly she could produce a drawing, of person or place it did not matter. Her hands and eyes appeared to work in coordination, and the results were a portrait or picture so remarkably detailed it appeared real.

He loved watching her in the throes of creation. She was intent on her task at hand, and she allowed nothing to disturb her. She would sometimes chew at her lower lip or wrinkle her small nose or squint her beautiful eyes as she paid strict heed to her work, leaving room for nothing but her art. Sometimes a strand of her long dark hair would repeatedly fall in her face, and she would tuck it behind her ear again and again, the stubborn strand refusing to stay put, much like Reena herself.

He reiterated his words. "You are to pay attention."

"I can listen while I work," she assured him, her hand busy creating sweeping lines and curves.

Magnus thought to argue, but it would do little good. He would have his say and make certain she understood, then he would look at her drawing, for he wished to see for himself how she viewed him.

"I wish you to remain close to the keep—"

Before he could finish, Reena spoke up, her drawing hand slowing until it stilled. "Why do you fear for my safety?"

He should have realized she would question him. She was the only one in his service who did and the only one he would tolerate doing so. When he issued a command, it was to be obeyed, not questioned. Not so Reena, but he had come to accept that about her. Her spark of challenge and adventure intrigued him and made her all the more appealing.

He was honest with her; he could be no other way, for she would haunt him with questions until she discovered the answers. "You are my mapmaker and therefore you hold certain knowledge that could benefit my enemies. It is wise of me to protect you."

She borrowed his habit of a moment's silent thought while considering the matter at hand. "That makes much sense and I understand your concern. I will make you aware of my whereabouts so you need not worry, and I will not foolishly venture off on my own."

He'd thought she would argue with him, but then she was sensible. At least in certain matters she was sensible.

Her hand immediately returned to drawing, her eyes squinted, she chewed at her bottom lip, and Magnus knew she was lost in her work. He watched her engrossed in her drawing. He noticed a small beauty mark near her right ear and a faint scar at her hairline above her left eye. Her blue eyes reminded him of the sky on a crisp, clear day, and her lips did not quite match in size.

But what amazed him the most was the intensity she put into her drawings. He wondered if she even realized she possessed such a passion, such a driving force to create. Would that passion extend to lovemaking? Would she find it a work of art and pour her passion into it as much as she did with her drawings?

Of late he had thought much of intimacy with Reena. The innocent touches, the few shared kisses had made it necessary for him to address the emotions that were stirring in him. While sex had always been a driving force within him, a need, a want he could satisfy with any willing woman, now he found he wanted something different with Reena.

Did his need to protect her rise from that? Was love nipping heavily at his heels? The thought that she would suffer needlessly because she was his mapmaker did not sit well with him. Visions of the keep's torture chamber weighed heavily on his mind and the mere thought that Reena would suffer for what knowledge she knew angered him.

"You will surrender any and all information asked of you concerning me if you are ever taken captive," he said with a sudden firmness that startled Reena.

"I would not betray you." Her own response was firm, yet soft.

"It is not about betrayal; it is about survival, and I wish you to survive."

She stared at him, his words haunting her thoughts. Did he care for her? Did he worry over her safety? Or was she merely a servant worth more alive to him than dead?

"You will do as I say and not suffer because of me."

She lowered her glance to the paper where she had sketched his face. She felt tears rush up to wet her eyes. She fought them like a warrior bent on pushing back advancing enemy troops, and she held them at bay.

"You suffer." She barely whispered the words.

He looked confused and was about to shake his head when she held up the drawing tablet for him to see.

He was stunned silent, for there in his face she had captured not only his strength but also his weakness. While his features were cold and hard and portrayed him capable of any command, she had captured in his dark eyes the heaviness of his heart when difficult decisions needed to be made. There was his suffering, his anguish of doing what was necessary but not necessarily right. There was the war he fought within himself. Good and evil. He possessed both traits, and they warred within him like vengeful enemies.

He could not take his eyes off the drawing. It was as if he was able to see the two men in one that he had become.

The troubled look in his eyes and the unease with which he shifted in his seat had Reena reaching out to him. She placed her hand over his, and he instantly threaded his fingers with hers and clung tightly.

"You are a good man and help many."

"For a price," he reminded her. The feel of her warm, soft skin against his was more comforting than he cared to acknowledge—or was it the thought that she cared enough to offer comfort? He had known such caring once and had desperately missed it when it had been taken from him.

She moved her hand off his, and though she remained close he felt an empty ache fill his heart.

"And what price have you paid?" she asked.

He stared at her strangely.

"You have suffered, have you not?"

His anguish was his own, and he never spoke of it to anyone. Yet she knew. She had captured it in his eyes, and he could see it clearly in his portrait. It was as if she could look into his soul.

Someone dear to his heart had borne a heavy burden for him, and he would not see her do the same. He took hold of her arms, his fingers firm in her flesh. "You will not suffer for me. If captured you will give whatever information is asked of you."

"Why? So those who impose the torture can torture me more? If I were to do as you say, your enemy would not believe I tell him all. I would be tortured regardless of what information I willingly or unwillingly gave."

He shook his head, then rested his forehead on hers. "What am I to do with you? You are much too intelligent for your own good."

Her answer came easily. "You are to trust me as I trust you, for I would not betray you, as I know you would not betray me."

"You are so sure?" Magnus whispered.

"Aye, I have come to know you these many winter weeks we have shared mapping the keep, though I honestly admit it is *you*, Magnus, I have come to know. The Legend remains a mystery to me. I have had but a brief glance of him on occasion, and I know not of him what I know of you, and I wonder if he allows anyone to know him."

He softened his hold on her. "It is best the Legend remains a mystery."

"Why? Does he not feel lonely at times?"

"The Legend was born out of necessity and he does what he must."

She moved away from him, his hands falling off her, but just before she moved out of his reach Magnus grabbed hold of her hand.

"Do you fear the Legend?"

Her nod was gentle as she approached him. "At times."

"He would never hurt you."

"Yet he has hurt others." Her voice trembled in a whisper.

"When necessary." He stood and drew her to him. "Do not fear me."

"I do not fear you, Magnus, but the Legend?" She shivered. "He puts the fear of the devil in men and women alike, and the cold dark metal of his helmet does not help, for it makes him appear unapproachable, impenetrable and emotionless."

"He is a warrior."

"He is a man," she reminded.

"Aye, that he is," Magnus agreed and slowly brought his lips down on hers to capture a much wanted kiss. He savored the taste of her and while he wanted, very much wanted, to feel her against him, he kept a safe distance. He did not trust himself, and she had just mentioned how she trusted him. He would not betray that trust. When they made love—and he was certain they would—it would be her choice.

He did, however, allow his hand to roam down her back, along her slim waist and over her hips, narrow but with a curve of definition that appealed to his male senses and caused him to swell with desire.

When finally their lips parted, she sighed and rubbed her cheek to his. "I am confused."

"Why?" The simple act of her placing her cheek to his soared his passion, but he kept tight rein on it. How could such a simple and innocent gesture bring him so much pleasure? He had shared the gesture time and time again with many women, but never had he felt the rush of warmth and the hasty beating of his heart that he did when Reena so casually put her cheek to his.

"I thought you perfect for Brigid, then you began to—" She stared up at him, almost reluctant to admit her thought.

"What did I do, Reena?" he encouraged softly.

Her hesitation was brief. "You touched me and then kissed me and—"

"Made you feel." He finished what she could not.

She nodded, then shook her head. "I do not even know what I feel."

He took her chin in his hand and held it firm so that she would have to look at him. "Let yourself feel. Do not fight it."

"I cannot fight it. It is there more often than not."

He cupped her face in his hands. "I am glad to hear that."

"Why?" Her look remained confused.

He smiled. "For it could mean you are falling in love with me."

Chapter 19

Reena was lost in her thoughts as she and Brigid sat at a table before the hearth in the great hall, a roaring fire keeping them warm. It was late afternoon, and Reena had not seen Magnus since early morning, when he'd left the keep to scout his borders with a troop of men.

His words from the night before echoed in her mind.

Could mean you are falling in love with me.

She had been considering the possibility since last night, the exciting and frightening prospect having haunted her before Magnus had made mention of it. Could it be true? Could she actually be falling in love with the Legend? But did he feel the same toward her? Was love nipping persistently at her heels?

Brigid sighed and sat in silence beside her friend, her hands hugging the goblet of hot cider in front of her, though she had not taken a sip, nor had she touched the small cakes on the platter in front of her.

Reena sensed something troubled her friend. She waited, but she remained silent. She raised her goblet and finished the last of her cider. When she reached for a small cake from the platter, Horace immediately raised his head from where he lay curled by her feet. He yawned, stretched and sat up to stare directly at her.

He had grown considerably in the last few months and would grow even more before the season's end. He was already a good size, with large paws, a body to match, a big head, and loveable eyes and droopy ears. And he had grown more attentive and protective than anyone expected.

Reena, as was her way with him, gave him half of her cake. He took it and, satisfied with the one bite, returned to snuggle at her feet.

Brigid finally broke her silence. "He is a good dog."

Reena shook her head and looked at her friend. "Are you going to tell me what troubles you? I have been waiting patiently since we sat down."

Brigid sighed. "You know me too well."

"It is plain on your face for anyone to see."

"No one looks as closely as you do."

"More fools them." Reena reached out and placed a gentle hand on her friend's arm. "Tell me."

Brigid looked around the great hall. Servants scurried about in preparation for the evening meal several hours away, while the Legend's warriors wandered in and out to talk and drink. Those guarding the posts ate when time allowed. With the constant activity, there was little privacy.

"We could go to my bedchamber," Reena suggested, realizing the reason for Brigid's hesitation.

"Why not the tower room?" Brigid asked, and a slow smile warmed her face.

Reena had to agree. Brigid had worked hard to convert the empty, cold room into one of warmth and welcome. Magnus had even been stunned when he had first seen the results of Brigid's efforts. The task had served her well, for it had kept her busy, leaving little time to think of Kilkern. Thomas had remained a constant at her side and had helped her with the work in the room.

Together, along with Horace, Reena and Brigid climbed the stairs to the tower room and settled in the comfortable wooden chairs with plush dark green velvet seats that were grouped in front of the small fireplace. Wooden chests, a table and chairs, tapestries covering the walls and windows to help block the cold, and a plethora of candles had turned the barren room into a comfortable sanctuary.

"Tell me," Reena urged, eager to help set her friend's mind at ease.

Horace gave one loud bark, then settled himself in front of the hearth, his attention on Brigid as though he waited to hear her words as well.

Brigid laughed and rubbed his head, then turned her glance on Reena. "I loved my husband very much."

"Everyone knows that."

Brigid rubbed her hands together in worry. "I thought with a love that strong I could never possibly love another."

Reena suddenly realized what troubled Brigid. She remained silent, allowing her to voice her concerns.

"John invaded my every waking thought and often my sleep as well. I could think of nothing but him, the love we shared, the plans we had made, the children that I would never have, but recently—" She stopped and shook her head, tears beginning to fall from her eyes. "I have not thought of him; I think of another."

"This is good," Reena said, leaning forward to comfort and encourage her friend with a squeeze of her arm.

"Nay," Brigid snapped. "How could it be good? If I truly loved my husband, how could I so soon love another?"

"Do you not see," Reena said. "It is because you loved John so strongly that you can love another. You learned what true love really is and would not dare settle for anything less. You know it and feel it in your heart. John had a good, loving soul as you do, and two loving souls cannot help but love deeply. Thomas has a good, loving soul, and that is why you have fallen in love with him."

Brigid gasped. "You know?"

Reena grinned. "I have watched you both fall in love in front of my eyes."

"You think Thomas loves me?"

Reena looked at her oddly. "Has he not told you of his love?"

"Nay, he has made no mention of it. He has not even kissed me, though his touch is gentle, but that is only when he offers help. And then I think perhaps that is why I feel this way about him, he protects me and is good to me."

"Like your husband was to you."

Brigid smiled through her tears. "Thomas is actually more tolerant of me than John was. He bakes bread with me and enjoys it. John would never have helped with women's work." Tears ran down her face. "But that made no difference, for I loved John."

"You loved him for who he was, and Thomas loves you for who you are, just as you love him for who he is." She thought of the advice she offered her friend and thought it was good advice for herself in dealing with the Legend side of Magnus. If she was falling in love with Magnus, then she was falling in love with the Legend as well, and she would need to accept him for who he was.

"He is not big and ugly as some whisper," Brigid said adamantly in defense of Thomas. She wiped at her tears and giggled. "I like that I can step behind him and no one can see me, and he lifts me with but one arm, yet he is gentle in his enormous strength."

Reena sat back in her chair, bringing her legs up to tuck beneath her. "I am happy for you and Thomas. You are both good people and deserve to love."

Brigid shook her head slowly. "But he has made no mention of love to me. I have only realized my feelings toward him and—"

Reena waited, knowing her friend had difficulties with her feelings because she felt she betrayed her dead husband.

With gained courage, Brigid spoke. "I find my feelings growing no matter how hard I try to ignore them. I look forward to seeing him and I do not grow bored of our time together. We always find things to discuss or laugh about, and even silence is comfortable with him."

"Then love him and be done with it."

"I feel—"

Reena wasted not a moment; she finished voicing

what her friend could not. "Guilty for loving him, when you should not. John would want you to be happy, as you would want the same for him. Do not waste time in doubt and guilt. Love Thomas, Brigid, love him with all your heart."

"How?" Brigid asked. "He has shown no sign of loving me."

Reena laughed. "It is obvious."

"Again you see what others do not."

"Magnus sees it."

Brigid brightened. "Perhaps Thomas has made mention of his feelings to him."

"Would you feel more comfortable with your own feelings toward him if I found out how he felt toward you?"

"Aye, I would. You would not mind inquiring, discreetly of course?" Brigid asked with a grin.

"If I do, what then will you do about it?"

"You challenge me," Brigid said.

"Aye," Reena admitted. "Thomas is a shy man with women. He thinks himself ugly, and while he loves you, I think he finds it difficult to believe that you could feel the same for him. So it will be up to you to make your feelings known to him."

"Find out how he feels toward me, and then I will gather the courage and speak with him. But what of you?" Brigid returned the challenge.

Reena acted as if she did not understand. "What do you mean?"

Brigid laughed and shook her head. "I know you as well as you know me, Reena. We have grown up together and have known things about each other before a word was spoken. As you have seen my love for Thomas bud and grow, I have seen the same with you and Magnus, though I must say, his love for you has been evident."

"You speak nonsense," Reena said.

Brigid laughed again. "You know it is not nonsense. Magnus keeps you forever at his side."

Reena sighed and slumped back in her seat. "I am confused."

"Sounds like love," Brigid teased.

"I had thought love was more simple and more defined."

"If only it were," Brigid said and relaxed back in her seat.

"The ache in my stomach—"

"Is part of love."

"The constant thought of him—"

"Is love," Brigid repeated.

"I tingle when he is near," Reena whispered.

"Love."

Reena grew silent, staring at the flickering flames in the hearth.

"Why do you fight your love for him?"

Reena turned to her friend. "I ask myself that question. How can the Legend love me?"

"Why would he not?"

"Gossip says the Legend knows not of love, and look at me." Reena held out her arms as if offering herself for inspection. "I am not exactly the type of woman the Legend would find appealing."

"You never did pay attention to gossip, nor cared about it. Foolish tongues make for foolish minds, you would say." Brigid's tone turned adamant. "And why would the Legend not find you appealing? You are truly beautiful."

"True enough about gossip," Reena agreed. "But me appealing to the Legend?" She shook her head.

"You have come to know the Legend—"

"Nay," Reena corrected. "I have come to know Magnus."

"They are the same."

Reena shook her head. "They are not."

"Then you do not look close enough."

Brigid's words startled Reena, and she stared wide-eyed at her friend. "I look *too* closely?"

"What is in front of our eyes is usually what is the most difficult to see."

Reena turned away to stare at the flames and think on her friend's words. The Legend was not in front of her long enough for her to know him—or was he? Was she failing to see what was in front of her? And if she did, was she failing to see the possibility of love? She turned her eyes to her friend, when suddenly she remembered something, and her gaze shifted quickly to the concealed door in the wall.

"I had forgotten."

Brigid looked at her strangely.

"I have been so busy mapping the keep that I forgot about the chests in the concealed room."

"Of what do you speak?"

"Secrets," Reena answered and sat forward. "There is a concealed room here, and when first I saw the tower room the door to the concealed room was ajar. Inside were two chests. One of the chests contained journals."

Her voice lowered to a whisper, and Brigid sat forward, the better to hear her.

"One journal was written in French by a woman

who wrote, 'Today I gave birth to a son and I named him Magnus.' "

Brigid gasped. "Magnus's mother?"

"I had the same thought."

"Could Magnus have brought the chests here?"

"And placed them in a concealed room in the tower?" Reena shook her head. "That would not make sense. Besides, the room looked as though it had not been opened in some time."

"Unless he did not want anyone to know about them."

"Or the chests had been here all this time."

Both women grew silent in thought.

Brigid broke the silence. "Thomas has made mention that Magnus does not allow anyone to take from him what is his. Could this land, this keep, be rightfully his?"

"The king granted him this land for a favor well done."

"But why this land?" Brigid asked.

Reena shook her head. "I do not know. And what of this map Kilkern claims was stolen from him. Could it actually exist? Would it show the two lands as one?"

"If the two lands were actually one property, then who does the land rightfully belong to? Is it Kilkern property or Dunhurnal property? And why was the land divided?"

Reena had her own questions. "And how is Magnus's mother part of it all?"

"Where are the chests with the journals? Reading them would help solve the mystery."

"If only I had paid heed to the chests. I grew busy mapping the keep and gave no thought to the journals. When I recalled reading the brief passage, I went in search of the journals, but the chests were already removed from the tower room."

"What of the concealed room?" Brigid asked with excitement.

"It has been closed each time I have visited this room."

Both women stood.

"Do you know where the concealed room is located?" Brigid asked.

Reena nodded and hurried over, Brigid close behind her, to the section of the wall she knew contained the concealed room.

She ran her fingers over the seam of the door. "It is here, but I do not know how it opens."

Brigid felt where Reena's hand touched. "A lever or something must work the door, otherwise the door would be too heavy to move."

Reena looked about, Brigid joining her in the search.

"It would be close by," Brigid said.

Reena nodded, running her hand over the stones near the door so as not to overlook anything.

"The peg," Brigid said, her excitement growing. She hurried to a section of the wall where a metal peg protruded. She pulled on it, pushed up, attempted to twist and turn it, but the sturdy peg remained solid in the wall.

"Here, I found it," Reena said, barely above a whisper. "Come feel this in the wall."

Brigid hurried over and let Reena take her hand and guide it over the wall. She felt a slim, long piece of cold metal hidden between the stones.

"Amazing," Brigid said. "It cannot be seen and barely felt if one did not know to look for it."

"Someone certainly wanted something kept hidden." Reena yanked on the metal lever, and Brigid's hand joined hers as they both struggled to move the lever. It finally gave way, and a section of the wall creaked slowly open.

Reena was quick to collect two candles from the table, and the two women, hugging close beside each other, entered the room. They looked about, Reena holding her candle high to cast light over the dark, dank, cell-like space.

Brigid gave a small gasp and pointed to the back wall. "An iron ring to chain a prisoner. A cell for sure."

"But why up here in the tower room when a dungeon exists below the keep?"

Brigid voiced her thought. "Someone did not want anyone to know who was kept here?"

"I would say that might be so."

"There are no chests here." Brigid shivered. "It is cold and damp and would be so terribly dark without the candles. I cannot imagine someone chained to the wall and left in such darkness. The darkness alone would frighten me."

"A torturous thought for sure," Reena agreed. "And one I cannot help but wonder over."

At that moment the two heard a creak. When they both turned toward the sound, the door began to close quickly.

"Hurry," Reena urged Brigid and pushed her through the opening, which had become considerably narrower.

Brigid gave a yell and barely managed to clear the closing door. She turned to help Reena, and both women realized there was not sufficient space for her to squeeze through.

"I will get help," Brigid said as the door closed completely shut, and she shivered as she raced from the room, hearing Reena's final word as her candle flickered out.

"Hurry!"

Magnus entered the great hall after a day of riding his borders and making certain his land was well guarded. He had traveled over hills and meadows, though the weather was anything but cooperative. A cold wind and snow flurries certainly did not announce that spring was but a week or so away.

His warriors did well in guarding his holdings. They were alert to their surroundings and aware of any intruders, except, of course, the Dark One. But then no one seemed to be able to prevent his entrance anywhere, and he was a friend who was welcome anytime at the keep.

His men were aware of every stranger that traveled his land, some proving harmless, others proving suspicious, but all were watched and their actions reported to Magnus. He knew Kilkern kept a watchful eye on Dunhurnal land, and he could almost predict Kilkern's next move. Right now the man gathered force behind him, hoping to sway the king to his cause, as well as those lords whose lands surrounded Kilkern land. But Magnus was patient and his plan was to take no action, at least not yet.

Magnus sat on a bench before the hearth, stretching his legs out to warm his chilled bones. A pitcher of ale was quickly brought to the table. He was filling a tankard when Thomas entered the great hall.

Thomas joined Magnus at the table and appreciated the warmth of the hearth and the taste of the ale.

"We are well protected," Thomas said, reaching for the full tankard.

"From what we see, but it is what we do not see that needs our attention."

"Kilkern works on the king."

"Of that I have no doubt," Magnus said.

"You sound as if you worry not about it."

"Kilkern's complaints will benefit us."

"How so?" Thomas asked.

"It never helps when too many know too much, and Kilkern has a loose tongue and thinks it benefits him."

Thomas scratched his bald head. "You sound as though you wait for the truth to reveal itself."

Magnus grinned and raised his tankard. "Kilkern is bound to slip up somewhere, and we will be waiting."

Thomas stood suddenly, causing Magnus to do the same, and they both cast a suspicious glance around the hall.

"Do you hear that?" Thomas asked and tilted his head as if straining to hear.

"What—"

"Help! Thomas, help!" Brigid flew down the stone steps screaming. She burst into the great hall to see Thomas and Magnus rushing toward her and servants scurrying in to see what was amiss.

Brigid flung herself at Thomas; his large arms wrapped around her and held her firm.

"What is wrong?" Magnus asked, a sinking feeling in his gut warning him that Reena was in trouble.

Brigid remained in the safety of Thomas's strong arms. "Reena is—" She needed to pause and gasp for breath. "—stuck." Her breath left her again.

"Where?" Magnus urged.

"Tower room," she rushed out before her breath failed her again.

Magnus dashed out of the room, Thomas close behind, along with Brigid.

He rushed into the tower room to see Horace scratching and growling by the stone wall. He found the lever to open the door and watched as the door creaked slowly open, wishing he could force it open more quickly.

Thomas hurried into the room, torch in hand, Brigid slipping out from behind him to race to the door, which was barely ajar.

"Reena, I have returned. I have Magnus and Thomas with me."

"Reena," Magnus called out and reached for the torch Thomas held.

"I need light," Reena called out.

Magnus shoved the torch through the slim opening and felt it yanked away.

"Hurry," Reena said.

Her trembling voice tore at his heart. She was frightened, and he was angry that he could do nothing but wait for the door to open enough for him to squeeze through. He wanted to tear the door down. When this ordeal was done, that was exactly his intention. The door would be permanently removed.

The opening was finally wide enough for him to squeeze through, and he had to order Horace to sit and stay, the dog anxious to rescue Reena. His glance rushed over the room, his heart stilled, his stomach rolled like a pitching sea, and he silently swore as he hurried to where Reena sat huddled on the floor, her knees bent almost to her chest.

Magnus quickly bent to comfort her and alleviate her fears.

"You must see this, Magnus."

Her words slowed his descent as he noticed she studied something in her hand. She was not at all frightened; she was intrigued with the object she held.

He kneeled beside her, his interest more in her than the object. "Were you not fearful being locked away?"

"Nay," she said with a sense of excitement. "I knew you would come for me."

"Not another would come for you, Thomas or a guard? You expected me?"

"Of course," she said confidently. "You will always rescue me, of that I have no doubt. Now you must see what I have found."

He wanted to know why she felt so confident about his ability to rescue her no matter the circumstances, but she was excited about her discovery and eager to share it with him.

"What have you found?" he asked, moving closer.

Reena held her hand up. "It is a piece of broken metal that looks as if it has been sharpened from use." She placed it in his hand and fumbled to get to her feet.

Magnus held on to the piece of metal and helped her up with one hand. "How did you find this?" He examined it as she answered.

"The light from my candle reflected off the metal just before the flame went out. It took me a few minutes to locate the object in the dark, but I did." Reena held the torch up around the area where the metal ring was attached to the wall. "It only took me a moment to realize that the sharp object had to be an implement used by whoever was imprisoned here."

Magnus studied the sharp-tipped object, then looked to Reena, who held the torch up high while examining the stones around the metal ring. "Trapped in the dark you concerned yourself with a piece of sharp metal?"

"A piece of metal that had no place here." Reena turned to see Thomas and Brigid standing in the open doorway. "Remain by the open door. It is either old or has been fashioned to close on its own after an allotted period of time."

Brigid took Thomas's hand and urged him back away from the inside of the room. "Reena is brave, I am not," she whispered to him.

"You are more brave than you know," Thomas said and gently squeezed her hand.

"Here is what I look for," Reena said with joy. "Just as I thought. Someone used the piece of metal to write in the stone."

"But what of freedom?" Thomas asked. "Why not attempt to free himself? Dig the metal ring from the wall and then attack the guard when he enters."

"A practical plan and one a man would think of, but I do not think a man was imprisoned here. I think a woman was held here."

"Why a woman?" Brigid asked.

"A man would think of escape, overpowering the guards once he freed himself from the confines of this cell. A woman would not have the strength to overpower guards, so she would free herself in a different way."

"By writing?" Thomas asked. "Writing would not free her."

"Aye, but it would," Reena said. "It would keep her mind free."

"What does she write of?" Brigid asked.

"She writes in Latin of love and hope: 'Remembrance of love keeps hope in my heart. Will not forget. Never.'"

"She must have been a woman of wealth to speak the Latin tongue. Few if any women know the language, it is meant for the tongues of the clergy. How did you learn it?" Thomas asked.

"My mother taught me. She has a thirst for knowledge and taught herself many tongues."

"How sad it must have been for her, being locked away and writing of love and hope," Brigid said. "I do hope she escaped and found love."

"Enough," Magnus said, annoyed. "Thomas, go and bring enough men to dismantle the door. This room remains locked away no more. Brigid, go with him and see that drink and food is readied and brought here for the men to enjoy."

The couple left, and no sooner had the door to the room closed behind them than the stone door began to shut, the heavy strength of it shoving the wooden chest that attempted to brace it out of the way. Magnus grabbed Reena by the arm and hurried her out.

It was not until the door was fully closed that Reena turned to Magnus. "It was your mother who was imprisoned there, was it not?"

Chapter 20

Magnus stood silent for several minutes, staring at Reena. He needed the few moments
to form his answer and to keep remembrances at
bay. His return to Dunhurnal had not been easy for
him. Memories had flooded his mind with each
step he had taken inside the keep, bitter memories
mixed with tender ones. No one knew of them, and
he chose to keep them locked away. One day he
planned on releasing the hurt and pain of the past,
but Reena's discovery now forced that day upon
him sooner than he had planned.

"How did you know my mother was imprisoned
here? Did she engrave her name in the stones?"

"I read one of the journals in the chest when you
first showed me the room," she confessed. "The en-
try spoke of giving birth to a son and naming him
Magnus. I simply made an assumption."

A commotion outside the door prevented Magnus
from answering, and the door soon opened. Thomas

entered in a rush, followed by several men.

He stopped abruptly when he saw Magnus and Reena standing in the middle of the room. "I thought you may be trapped in the room, so I rushed."

"We made certain to exit the room before it imprisoned us," Magnus said, then turned to Reena. "Wait for me in my solar. I wish to talk with you."

She nodded and left, hoping Magnus would share his childhood days with her. She could only imagine the pain he must have suffered over his mother's imprisonment and what the woman herself had been forced to endure. She prayed that his mother was safe and free from harm; but then, the Legend was her son, and by now she must be free. How long had his mother actually been imprisoned there? This was only one of many questions she hoped Magnus would answer.

Her curiosity also had her wondering about his connection with Dunhurnal land. He had known all along it sat adjacent to Kilkern land, yet he'd made no mention of it to her when she had approached him about protecting her village.

And why then did the king grant him the land? Was it a favor? Or did the land actually belong to Magnus by birthright?

Reena ran into Brigid, who was rushing up the steps, as she turned the spiral staircase to go down a few levels to Magnus's solar.

"You are all right?" Brigid asked through labored breaths.

"I am fine," she said and wished she could tell Brigid of her discovery, but that would not be fair to Magnus. He had kept the secret of the keep to himself, and perhaps for a good reason. She would not betray his trust and share his secret.

"You were not fearful of the dark and being trapped?"

"Nay, I knew you would return with Magnus and, of course, Thomas."

"Was it not completely dark in the room?"

"The darkness was more thick than I thought possible," Reena said.

"And this did not frighten you?"

Reena gave her question a quick thought. Recalling the door closing, the light flickering out, and the glint of metal made her realize she had been too curious about the mysterious object to worry about her predicament. "My thoughts were elsewhere—besides, I knew you would be returning in a short time."

Brigid shivered. "Being trapped in the darkness is not a fate I wish to experience. It must have been terrifying for the woman who was chained in the small room. And why chain her if she could not escape, that was even more cruel."

"I agree, and I hope she now has her freedom."

"I must go," Brigid said. "Maura needs help in the kitchen with the extra preparation for the men. I wanted to make certain you were all right."

One last firm hug and the women parted, Thomas coming around the curve just as Brigid disappeared from sight.

"You are well?" Thomas asked, stopping beside her.

Reena was grateful for caring friends. "Aye, I am fine. It is Brigid who worries more than I."

"She worries over you, though she need not, but

then memories haunt her. Time will help heal her pain."

"Love will help heal her pain."

Thomas nodded, and a touch of sadness filled his voice. "Aye, she will find someone to love her, and she will be happy." He raised a beefy fist. "And he best be good to her or else."

Reena smiled. "Oh, I have a feeling that the man who captures her heart will treat her like a princess. Would you not treat her such?"

Thomas lowered his fist and his voice. "I would treat her like a queen and love her with all my heart and be forever grateful she was mine. And I would allow no one—no one—to hurt her."

Reena had no time to comment, as a shout for Thomas's help from the tower room had him fast turning around and rushing up the steps. She would make certain Brigid learned of how Thomas felt, and she continued down the steps to Magnus's solar.

She did not go far when she ran into Brigid, who had tears streaming down her cheeks. "Thomas does care for me."

"You heard," Reena said with joy. It was better she heard from Thomas himself than from someone else. His own words would have more impact, and they certainly had.

Brigid wiped at her wet cheeks. "He cares for me, I cannot believe it."

Reena shook her head. "He more than cares for you; he loves you. Did you not hear him say he would treat you like a queen and love you with all his heart?"

Footsteps on the stone staircase caught their attention, and they could detect from the raised voices that it was Magnus and Thomas who approached. A bark alerted them that Horace followed.

Brigid attempted to wipe away her tears, but she was not fast enough. Thomas immediately saw that she was upset and hurried to her side. Reena had to brace herself against the stone wall to allow the large man to pass by in a rush.

"What is wrong?" he asked, his arm going instinctively and protectively around her. Horace snuggled against her leg as if he understood she needed loving.

Brigid attempted a smile, and it settled naturally on her lovely face. "Nothing, I was merely concerned with Reena's well-being."

"She is fine," Thomas assured her.

He looked to Reena to confirm his words and ease Brigid's worry, and her heart went out to the large man with the many scars. He had a big heart, and he had given it to her dearest friend.

"I feel wonderful," Reena said and threw her arms wide, though when she caught the look on Magnus's face she wondered how long her wonderful feeling would last.

"I go to bring the food for the men," Brigid said, her glance set on Thomas.

The couple left without a word to Reena or Magnus, Horace close behind, the word *food* having caught his attention.

"Tell me," Magnus said, walking over to Reena and bracing his hand on the wall beside her head. "Do you ever get to your destination without a challenge arising?"

She turned a smile on him that stunned his heart. "Challenges make life interesting."

He pointed down the steps. "To my solar, where

challenges will definitely prove to be interesting."

She took the steps without trepidation. Magnus would tell her of his mother or he would not. The choice was his, though she knew that a secret long kept carried burdens that often needed lifting. He could trust her with any secret, for she would take it to her grave if he asked.

She went to the hearth, bright with flames, and reached her hands out to warm them. Magnus closed the door and walked up behind her. To her surprise, he slipped his arms around her waist.

He would touch her in ways that surprised and pleased her, a simple touch to her arm, holding her hand, a hug that brought them close, a gentle kiss, a brush of his cheek against hers and a kiss that stole her breath. And it had her growing all the more confused with him and her own emotions. What developed between them? Was this mix of confusing emotions love? Was the indecisiveness of how to handle it all part of love, or were her own doubts interfering? And was now the time to be thinking of such matters when she was eager to hear about his mother?

"Silence is not something I often find you practicing."

"I wait for you to speak." She placed a warm hand on his arm, more out of instinct, since of late she reached out to him without thought to her action. "Though I do offer my apologies for reading a page from your mother's journal. Had I known it belonged to her I would have respected her privacy."

"And what if I confide in you? Will you keep the information private?"

"Have no doubt of it. I would breathe a word to no one."

He moved away from her, though he grasped her hand for a moment before walking past her and bracing his hand on the mantel. He gazed at the fire, the flames casting a soft glow on his handsome features. His hesitation spoke louder than words. Did he trust her? Or did the secret remain his?

Reena watched him and saw the hurt in his eyes grow and spread, and she felt when anger took over and consumed him, followed by regret. Memories could prove powerful allies or horrific adversaries, and at the moment Magnus struggled with both. Reena wanted to rush over to him and hug and kiss him and tell him that everything was all right. She refrained; he was, after all, her lord, but then he was also the man she believed herself falling in love with.

"My mother kept journals from when she first learned to write." He kept his gaze steady on the flames. "An uncle who was a cleric who fell from grace with the church taught her to read and write just before she wed my father. She told me often that she feared if she did not continue to read and write she would lose the skills.

"My father died when I was barely two years, an enemy's arrow to his heart took his life quickly and left my mother heartbroken."

Reena remained silent and listened, seeing reflected in his dark eyes the pain and hurt of those memories.

"Her family wasted not a moment in arranging another marriage for her. She pleaded with them to allow her to remain home and raise her son, but her father turned a deaf ear to her pleas. She would wed the man of his choice, and in so doing her father condemned her to a living hell."

Reena shuddered and said a silent prayer for the woman.

Magnus raised his head. "My stepfather was a man of little feeling and even less morals. He wed my mother for the simple fact that he needed a wife to produce heirs, and of course my mother came with my father's inheritance."

"Dunhurnal land," Reena said sadly.

"Aye, Brian Conor, earl of Dunhurnal, was my father and this is my home. Everything changed when my mother was forced to remarry. My stepfather brutalized her. At times I think I can hear the awful names he called her or hear the sound of his hand across her face or feel the sting of his hand upon me."

He grew silent with his memories.

Reena walked over to him and took his hand in hers. It felt cold though he stood close to the hearth. She hugged it against her chest and held tightly.

"He would sit me in front of the secret room in the tower and make me watch as he chained my mother to the wall. My mother showed not an ounce of fear, and I knew her bravery was for me, for I knew she was terrified of the dark. He would force me to sit and watch as the door began to close, then suddenly it would close completely, and she was shut away from me, left alone in the dark to tremble with fear. If I made any attempt to help her, he would retaliate by beating her. I had often wondered how my mother endured her imprisonment, and today, with your discovery, I finally understood."

"I also found writing on the lower part of the wall."

Magnus nodded. "There were times he would simply throw her into the room and leave her there.

I would sit outside the door for hours and wait for him to free her. Other times during her confinement he would torment me."

"Her family knew nothing of her plight? Was there no one to help her?"

"Her husband owned her, and she gave him a son after several miscarriages. Her own father died, leaving my mother with no one to turn to, so there was no escape. She was wed to a beast until death."

She hugged his hand tighter. "I fear to ask what happened to her."

His wide smile suggested a happy ending, and she listened closely.

"My mother was strong and could endure much, but she could not bear seeing me suffer, the son of the man she loved with all her heart. She was patient and managed to hide coins from him and a few pieces of jewelry.

"One night when I was ten and the keep was asleep and the winter wind blew cold and hard, she came to my room, woke me, made me dress in most of my clothes so that I had several layers of garments to protect me from the frigid night, and then together we snuck out of the keep and away into the darkness.

"We came upon a band of people with less than we had, and we remained with them, traveling together until we found a place in the woods far from Dunhurnal land. There my mother raised me, and it is there she met a man who she came to love."

"She is well, then?" Reena asked, feeling near tears for a woman much more brave than she could ever be.

"Aye, my mother is well, and her husband, James, is good to her. It was he who taught me my warrior skills. They live on my land now and are well protected."

"Did your stepfather search for your mother and you?"

"His search proved useless. My mother was more intelligent than him and knew his ways too well. We heard talk of his furious search for her and his fury when she could not be found. But her wise ways and her strength kept us safe."

Reena could not hold her tongue. "And your step-father's fate?"

Magnus hesitated, his eyes narrowed, and his jaw tensed. "He tasted his own dungeons and met his demise as he lived—a coward."

There was no hesitation in Reena's actions; it was a natural response for her to step up to him, keeping his hand close to her chest. She stood on her tiptoes so that her lips reached his—and she kissed him.

Chapter 21

Magnus grew as rigid as a stone statue, his heart turning cold, his soul locked stubbornly away. Reena kissed him out of pity. He wanted none of her pity; he wanted her love.

But her tender fumbling began to warm his heart. She barely knew how to kiss, yet here she was, attempting to kiss his troubles away with soft, sweet lips that reminded him of warm honey. And she tried hard to keep herself steady on her tiptoes, so determined was she to kiss him.

Nay, not merely kiss, but comfort and ease his painful memories. He admonished himself for his foolish thoughts. Reena would not pity herself, therefore she would not pity another. She was different, special, and damned if he was not falling in love with the pint-size lass.

So why, then, did he feel angry instead of happy?

Her mouth whispered across his again, only this time the tip of her tongue faintly touched his lips and sent him into a spin. His heart crumbled and his soul rejoiced and his body responded in quick succession.

Angry.

The answer was simple, he thought, as his arms wrapped around her and pulled her up against him.

He wanted her love and he wanted it now. It mattered not why he found the slim wisp of a lass appealing; he simply did. They had worked side by side these winter months and had grown to learn more and more about each other and they had touched and kissed—and now?

He wanted her more than he ever thought possible.

"Damn, Reena, you tempt my soul," he whispered and kissed her with a passion that stole her breath and warmed *her* soul.

He took charge of the kiss, and soon they tasted each other like two starving souls needing nourishment. While they feasted, Magnus grabbed hold of her small waist, lifted her so that her feet no longer touched the floor, and walked toward the table.

He let her stand on her feet a mere few seconds while he shoved things aside, then he grabbed hold of her, dropped her back on the table, slipped over her, and braced his hands flat on the table at the sides of her head.

He then proceeded to nibble at her soft, delicious neck. "Damn, but I want you, Reena," he claimed over and over in between succulent nibbles.

She moaned, enjoying his sensuous nibbles and the feel of his body so strong and hard against her. And he was not the only one who wanted. She could think of nothing else but him, the feel, the taste and the passion; it overwhelmed her.

His hand found her small breasts, and he gave each a loving squeeze before running a gentle hand along her waist, over her stomach. When he rested his hand firmly between her legs she lost all sense and reason.

Her eager response fired his loins, and he captured her hungry moans with his own hungry lips.

"Magnus, Magnus." His name was a litany on her lips, and it grew in intensity as her hands reached out and touched him.

What brought him to his senses he did not know—perhaps it was the urgent passion of his name on her lips, or the way her small hands eagerly ran over his body, or how her own body responded so willingly to his touch. Whatever it was, it mattered not. What mattered was this: The first time they made love would not be on a table in his solar.

He eased himself off her with great reluctance, especially when her small hands grabbed for him. He held them tight in his, and their heated eyes settled on each other.

She saw the passion in his eyes, and yet he stopped without saying a word, and she wondered. When he touched her did he find her unappealing: were her breasts too small, her body too slim? Why, when it seemed they were on the brink of joining, did he stop? She wished she had the courage to ask him, but she could not, for she worried over his answer. She suddenly felt the need for solitude, or was it escape from her concern and doubt?

Magnus helped her off the table.

She was relieved when a knock sounded at the door and a servant advised he was needed in the tower room.

He was annoyed, wanting time to discuss his intentions with her, but then his lingering passion would probably interfere with sound reason, and nothing would be accomplished. At least that was what he attempted to tell himself, but the ache in his groin was adamantly disagreeing. "We will speak later," he said and left the room.

She was glad for his departure. She needed time alone. Her feelings for Magnus were growing in leaps and bounds. She missed him when he was not near, and she felt his hurt when she saw it in his eyes. She was becoming a part of him, or was he becoming a part of her? Or was there a difference?

And yet there was a part of her that doubted all of it and attempted to convince her that she was a foolish young woman who believed that her lord wanted more than just a lover's tryst.

With her mind in turmoil she decided the best thing for her would be to get away from the keep, if only for an hour or so. With a brief stop at her bedchamber to grab her cloak, as well as a quick message to Brigid informing her of her whereabouts should Magnus ask, she was off to see her parents.

She pulled up her hood and hugged her cloak around her. Dusk bathed the village with its gray skies, a chill wind blew, and smoke curled from cottage chimneys. From the cottages came the echoes of laughter, children's voices raised in song, and scents so delicious they made one lick one's lips in anticipation.

Reena smiled. This was how she remembered her village; she was home at last.

She heard her father's voice, crisp and clear in storytelling, when she approached her parents' cottage. She opened the door slowly so as not to disturb, and entered. Her father sat not far from the hearth, a small group of children circling him. His dramatic voice would grow in pitch and their eyes would widen, then narrow as his voice softened.

He acknowledged her with a brief nod and continued telling his tale. Her mother rose from the chair next to the hearth and walked over to her and took her hand.

"I am glad you have come to visit." Whispering was not necessary; her tone was already gentle. "Come. We will sit where we will not disturb anyone."

Reena moved her mother's chair from the hearth to the corner of the room beside another chair. A small table with a lone candle sat between the chairs and provided a faint light. Reena removed her cloak, as the room was comfortably warm.

"I am sorry I have neglected you and father," Reena said, feeling guilty that she had not spent enough time with her parents of late.

"Nonsense," her mother said. "You have important work to do for Lord Dunhurnal. Everyone in the village talks of your importance and your skills. Your service to him is greatly respected."

She needed no praise nor wanted it. "I am who I have always been."

Her mother patted Reena's hand, which rested in her lap. "The villagers need their gossip, and what better gossip than their own hero. They are proud of you and rightfully so. Let them talk"—her mother stopped abruptly and smiled—"and make you a legend."

Reena laughed quietly. "There is only one legend."

"Aye, and he earned the title." Her mother shivered.

"What tales have you heard?"

"Not tales, the truth."

"How do you know it is the truth?" Reena asked. "If tongues wag in gossip about me, then most certainly they wag about the Legend."

Her mother easily switched to French so that if anyone overheard them, they would not understand their conversation. "This is not gossip, it is hushed words whispered in awe and respect, and I think fear."

Reena was quick to defend the Legend. "Magnus is a good man."

"Aye, all agree he is a good man—to us. His enemies, or those to whom he poses a threat, are a different matter."

"As is the way with most warriors."

"He is not like most warriors," her mother said. "He is the Legend—"

"And legends are often created by wagging tongues."

Her mother did not agree. "Legends are made by deeds done, and not always good deeds. Kate, the cook, and her helper Maura tell Justin many tales about the Legend, but it is different tales he hears from the men who come and seek his tanner skills. He shares the tales with your father in whispered voices, though they think me asleep."

"And your hearing is good," Reena said with a laugh.

"When you listen, you learn," her mother reminded her.

"What did you learn?"

Her mother leaned closer. "Villagers desert their homes when they hear the Legend is near, men beg at his feet to spare their lives, he tortures without provocation and lives hold no meaning to him, whether man, woman or child."

"That is pure nonsense," Reena said, her voice harsh. "Look at what he has done for our village."

"His village," her mother corrected. "And glad I am to be part of it, for his reputation alone protects us and keeps us safe, and besides—" Her mother sighed. "I feel sorry for him. He must make decisions that affect many lives, and in the end someone will suffer. That is the way of battle and war. And I see that he cares for what is his and does what he must to protect; it cannot be easy for him."

"Yet you sound as though you also fear him."

"I would be a fool not to. The villagers speak of your return to the village with him. He was a fearful sight sitting astride that huge black beast of a horse, his face concealed by his helmet and his garments all black." Her mother shivered at the memory. "I do not care to see him in that helmet; he intimidates."

"He is the Legend."

"Aye," her mother readily agreed. "Without it he is Magnus, lord of Dunhurnal, a fair and protective lord."

"But yet he is truly one man."

Her mother shook her head. "Two men in one, and only the good Lord"—her mother crossed herself—"above knows how one can live with the other. We are all lucky we deal with Magnus. We all watched in shock as the Legend struck at Kilkern's men without an ounce of fear and without hesitation when he saw that one of the men had injured you."

Reena remembered how he had struck fast and hard, surprising everyone. His swift blows had sent three men to the ground in quick succession before anyone had thought to respond.

Her mother continued in French, a gentle smile surfacing. "I see how good Magnus is to you, and I am grateful you serve a protective lord. He will let nothing happen to you."

"He treats all who serve him well."

Her mother nodded slowly. "True, but I think Lord Dunhurnal treats *you* extra special."

Reena sighed. "You have heard gossip."

"Nay, you are my daughter, and I have watched and listened to you talk of him."

Reena stared at her mother, speechless.

Her mother laughed softly. "This surprises you? Do you not realize your own feelings?"

"I am not sure what I feel."

"That is a sure sign of love," her mother said. "I was uncertain of my feelings toward your father after we met."

"How then did you know you loved him?"

"I did not." Her mother laughed. "I only knew that I did not want to live without him. He made me smile and laugh often. He always had kind words for me, and he never failed to let me know how beautiful he thought I was, even to this day."

"What you are saying is that I will never be sure."

"No one can be sure of love," her mother said. "It is best that we follow our hearts, especially when it is obvious that a good, strong man cares for you. Let yourself feel, Reena, the rest will follow. Do not dwell on it, for it will serve no purpose. Now tell me, does your mapping go well? And what of your drawings?"

Conversation turned light, though Reena's thoughts remained heavy. She could not help but dwell on her mother's words and her feelings toward Magnus. While he was a fair and caring man, there remained that fear of the Legend. Or was it the fact that she knew so little of the Legend? She had learned much about Magnus but knew almost nothing of the Legend—but then perhaps Magnus preferred it that way.

The children around her father's chair insisted on another tale when he claimed he was finished. He looked to Reena, torn between visiting with her and entertaining the children.

Reena understood and made his choice easy. "Have my father tell you the tale of the fairy king."

The children's eyes widened, and one little boy tugged at her father's legging. "You truly met the fairy king?"

Her father grinned, sent her a wink, and was soon lost in a tale that had all the children mesmerized.

After promising her mother she would visit soon, she returned to the keep. Her first thought was to speak with Brigid, but she realized she would rather be alone with her thoughts. She needed some solitude to think over her concerns.

And her first was, if what existed between Magnus and her gave her concern, then how could she think of it as love? She shook her head at her own doubts and climbed the staircase slowly.

Once in her room, the door closed behind her and she went to her table, lit the many candles, and reached at a small wooden bowl for a well-used piece of charcoal. She began to draw. She did not want to think at the moment, she had thought enough and had solved nothing, nor had she reached any conclusions or made any decisions. Her mind needed clearing so that her thoughts would make more sense, and the only way to achieve a clear mind was to draw.

Time stood still when she took charcoal in hand; nothing mattered but what she was creating on paper. Sometimes she did not even consider what she would draw—she allowed her mind and hand free rein. She always appreciated the results and was even surprised at times.

The knock on her door went unheard and unanswered, and she did not hear when the door opened and Magnus entered. He closed the door quietly and watched her work from where he stood.

The flickers of light from the candles caused shadows and light to dance as equal partners across her lovely features. Her hands flowed like a perfect melody across her paper. She was lost in her drawing. He had seen her time and time again just like this. He had entered her room without her knowing, so engrossed had she been in her drawings. He would watch her draw, watch the way she chewed at her bottom lip in thought, how she rubbed her chin when deciding where to go next, how her chin or nose forever wore a smudge of charcoal.

The familiar scene warmed his heart. He could sit content by the hearth for hours watching her just as she was, and with a nod to his own thoughts he sat in the chair next to the fireplace.

Reena stared at the drawing, the piece of charcoal

a mere stub. She had worked diligently for hours and had produced a stunning piece of work that completely surprised her and produced heartfelt emotions.

She studied every line and stroke, amazed by her own skills, yet grateful. What she recorded would live on long after she was gone, and it would be there for many to see and enjoy and learn.

A strange sound interrupted her thoughts, and she quickly looked about the room. She was stunned to see Magnus asleep in the chair near the hearth.

Asleep and snoring.

With drawing in hand she walked over to him and quietly kneeled in front of him. His head rested to the side, his one arm was draped over the arm of the chair, his other arm rested on his leg. He wore all dark garments as usual, though he wore no leather tunic and his long hair looked alive with bursts of sunlight, the fire's glow highlighting the sun-colored strands.

He was a handsome man even when he slept and far from a legend, since he snored like the common man. It was not a heavy snore, but deep and steady, almost rhythmic in nature.

She listened to the delightful melody, giggling when it reached a crescendo then slowed before it began again. She should wake him, but he appeared so very content. The thought that he had not disturbed her when he had entered her bedchamber and seen her drawing but had sat beside her hearth to wait warmed her heart and endeared him to her all the more.

His snoring crested once again, only this time more loudly than before. He woke himself up.

Reena giggled as he sat up with a start.

"I do not snore," he said.

"I did not say that you did, though I did hear a strange sound." She bit her lip to prevent a giggle.

"Horace," Magnus accused and looked around for the pup. "He is never around when I need him."

Reena could not stifle a giggle.

"You find this funny?" he asked with a smile.

"Your snoring is like a melody, I do not mind it."

"Many women whose husbands snore would adamantly disagree."

"I suppose many would," she said. "But I would be grateful to hear my husband snore night after night, for that would mean we were safe beside each other."

Magnus leaned forward and stroked her soft cheek with the back of his fingers. "You look at things differently than most women."

His gentle touch sent gooseflesh rushing over her, and a soft sigh followed suit.

Magnus had not intended to kiss her, but he could not help himself, she looked so appealing with that smudge of charcoal on her chin.

He leaned forward and caught her lips with his. He was about to taste more of her when his eyes caught sight of her drawing and he pulled back away from her, his hand reaching for the paper.

He was struck by the detail. Reena had captured the scene as if she had been there and had seen it with her own eyes. It took him back to when he was a little boy, and that little boy's emotions came pouring forth. His heart pounded in his chest and he fought the urge to weep.

Reena watched his emotions war in his eyes and

on his face. "I do not know why I draw what I draw sometimes. I had not planned on this drawing."

Magnus shook his head slowly. "I cannot believe the accuracy in it. It was as if you saw it clearly with your own eyes and that you felt—my God, you actually captured her pain."

Reena and he looked upon the drawing. Magnus's mother stood chained to the wall of the secret room, her wrists tight in the shackles, her fingers holding firm a piece of metal she used to scrape words on the stone wall. Her long hair hung down her back and her head rested to the side on her arm. She resembled Magnus, though her beautiful face portrayed a woman deep in sorrow, strong in strength and fighting her fear.

Magnus kissed her cheek. "Thank you. I shall cherish this drawing forever."

"But it makes you sad," Reena said, her own heart as heavy as his, for the drawing invoked deep emotions.

"I cannot deny it brings back difficult memories, but your drawing proves to me what I thought as a child but now I know as an adult—my mother faced her ordeal with strength and courage, and no one, absolutely no one, could take them from her. So thank you again, you gave a little boy what he needed badly. You gave me the truth."

Chapter 22

Spring rushed in, forcing winter away. The days turned sunny and bright, the air lost its chill, the skies seemed bluer, the birds hurried to build nests for their expected young, and the trees were budding.

The village was also a buzz of activities. Repairs were started on the cottages, the land was being prepared for planting, and the healthy farm animals were near to giving birth, along with several women in the village.

Life was good, though on closer inspection guards had been doubled around Dunhurnal land, people kept a watchful eye on strangers who requested to stop and rest before traveling on, and Thomas remained forever near Brigid's side.

Spring had brought beautiful weather, and along with it a better chance for Peter Kilkern to make a move.

Reena hurried out of the keep, Horace close behind her. She did not have much time. She had already bade her parents and Justin farewell, and she had to see Brigid before she left. Early that morning Magnus had announced that they would take a few days to travel to parts of his land he wished mapped with more detail and that they would leave by midmorning.

She'd barely had time to pack a small satchel and say her good-byes. Brigid was the last one left to see, and then she would be ready to go.

Magnus and she would have collided had he not seen her rushing out the door. He braced himself and grabbed firm hold of her as she rushed into him, though Horace collapsed with a start against Reena's legs. She was forever rushing. She was a small bundle of exuberant passion that simply could not be contained, and he found he did not wish to contain her; he wished her to remain free of heart and spirit.

"Are you ready?" he asked and frowned at the now sizeable Horace, who cautiously peeked out from behind Reena. "Still a coward."

"I must bid Brigid farewell and then I am ready, and Horace is not a coward, he is a loving, thoughtful and true friend."

"Do not take long, I wish to leave shortly, and Horace the cowardly dog will not be going with us," he said and released her reluctantly. He watched her rush off, the dog taking a wide berth around him as he hurried along beside Reena. As usual, Magnus felt a sense of emptiness fill him. He had thought his pursuit of Reena would be easy. She was, after all, a woman, and women were not that difficult to understand. Show her interest, comment on her beauty, and a woman would respond. However, the more

time he spent with Reena, the more he realized she
was not like other women. Comments on her work
meant more to her than comments about her lovely
features. She grew thrilled when offered quills and
paper but was less enthusiastic when offered fine
gems. If the land needed scouting, she was quick to
request permission to go so that she could accurately
map the area.

She would forage in the woods for feathers to
make her quills while other women busied themselves making candles or stitching. People interested her, and she watched them speak, walk, bend,
move about, and she would reproduce their movements on paper, making them appear alive.

And her mind flowed as creatively as her hand,
conversation with her never being boring. The more
time spent with her, the more time he wished to
spend with her, and he was surprised that by winter's end he had not yet made love to her. It was not
that he had not thought about it; she was constantly
on his mind, and he constantly thought of her naked
in his arms.

Nay, it was that he wanted more than sex; he
wanted Reena to *love* him, now and always. He
wanted her as his wife. He wanted to spend all the
rest of their days together, have children and grow
old together. He wanted her forever by his side.

He loved her that much. He could not say when
he had come to fully realize his love. It had developed naturally, starting from a mere interest in a
small wisp of a woman and growing into a love he
would forever cherish.

How he would proceed from here he was not certain. That they would wed he had no doubt. She would love him; he would have it no other way.

He laughed to himself as he entered the keep. He knew full well that Reena felt the same toward him as he did toward her. He felt it when she melted in his arms or when she was left breathless from his kisses or the way she responded to his intimate touch.

They would wed; it was simple. After they returned from this short excursion he would see to speaking with her father and settling the matter. He entered the great hall feeling pleased with himself and issuing orders that departure time was within the hour.

Reena was breathless by the time she reached Brigid's cottage. Horace raced forward, jumping up and down around Brigid, who attempted to pet the bouncing dog.

"I heard you are leaving for a few days," Brigid said, giving Reena time to catch her breath. "And aye, I will look after Horace and your parents and be watchful and careful."

Reena laughed. "You know me too well, though you did miss one."

Brigid gave it thought and shook her head. "I can think of no other."

"Thomas perhaps?"

Brigid gave a hasty twist of her head toward the cottage roof. "Shhh, he will hear you. He works on repairs to the backside of the cottage roof."

Reena stepped closer to her friend. "Have you not made mention of your feelings to him?"

Brigid kept her voice to a whisper. "I know not what to do or how I feel. One moment I feel myself in love with him, the next I feel guilty for even thinking I could love anyone other than John, and then sometimes. . . ." She sighed heavily.

"You want him to hold you in his big arms."

Brigid stared at her friend. "How did you know that?" Her eyes widened in realization. "You feel the same toward Magnus."

"Minus guilt, add confusion."

"And he toward you?"

"I think he loves me, but then I know nothing of love." Reena sighed in frustration. "There are times when we have come close to—" She stopped, not certain whether to share the intimate details, then realizing she would learn nothing if she did not discuss it with Brigid, who was certainly more knowledgeable than she.

"Being intimate?" Brigid asked bluntly, making it less difficult for her friend to share.

"Aye, intimate, but love is never mentioned, and I know not what to do."

"Do you love the Legend?"

Reena shivered and hugged herself. "That is another problem. I know Magnus well, but the Legend remains a mystery to me. I know they are one, and yet they appear to be two different men. While I feel comfortable with Magnus, I cannot help but feel a sense of unease, perhaps even a twinge of fear, when the Legend steps forth."

"And who do you go with on this mapping quest?"

"Magnus."

"Are you certain?" Brigid asked, her glance going

past Reena, and her eyes rounding as she looked in the distance.

"The Legend waits for me?" Reena barely whispered.

"Aye, that he does in all his glory." Brigid shivered. "I can understand your apprehension. His clothes are as black as the night, as is his helmet. I can understand how his enemies would think him a vengeful demon." She lowered her voice to a hushed whisper. "I think it is time you get to know the Legend. Only then will you truly come to know Magnus."

Reena nodded her head slowly, not certain if she actually agreed with her friend, but having no other recourse. Of course Horace peeking from behind Brigid and whining at what he saw did not help the situation.

"He waits," Brigid said and gave Reena a slight push.

Reena caught sight of Thomas's head near the peak of the roof and cast a glance his way. "He waits also."

The two women hugged and reluctantly parted, neither ready to deal with men and love.

Reena hurried her steps, her legs trembling after catching sight of the Legend. His appearance certainly intimidated. He looked larger, broader, stronger and much more unforgiving. He seemed opposite of Magnus, and yet they were one.

He spoke not a word to her when she walked up to him; he simply grabbed her around the waist, lifted her up on her horse, handed her the reins, then mounted his own black steed. With his hand firm on his reins, he gave the signal to depart.

Two men led and two men followed.

Villagers waved farewells, children trailed along the side smiling and waving exuberantly, dogs chased at their feet, and laughter drifted in the crisp spring air. Reena then noticed the double guards at the barbican and that the portcullis remained descended a quarter of the way, reminding her that the keep was on alert, ready and waiting.

"You do not worry that Kilkern may cause us harm?" she asked.

The Legend kept his glance straight ahead. "We remain on my land and he knows better than to attack a lord on his own soil. He would have much to explain to the king. Besides, there are more of my men about than you know. Our protection is not in question."

His imposing tone and arrogant confidence sent a shiver racing through her. Who was this man she rode beside? He sounded nothing like the Magnus she knew who treated his tenants fairly and was patient with a cowardly but loveable pup.

He was the Legend.

The man she had learned about listening to tales when she was young. The tale of the Legend had been the one that had caused her to huddle beneath the blanket in fright. She had promised her young self that she would keep her distance from the Legend, and here she was riding next to him and falling in love with him.

But what did she really know of the Legend?

His infamous exploits had earned him his name, but how had it all begun? He had not set out to become the Legend. Had life circumstances forced the roll upon him?

She suddenly became quite curious. "How did you become a warrior?"

He kept his eyes on the road ahead of him and answered, "Out of necessity."

She waited for further explanation. When none was forthcoming, she continued her query. "What necessity?"

"Survival."

His short answers gave the impression that he did not wish to discuss the topic, but Reena was persistent. "For yourself or others." She purposely did not mention his mother, but she felt that perhaps the woman had helped determine her son's fate.

He turned to look at her, and she swallowed the nervous lump that rose in her throat. His dark eyes glared, and his helmet concealed, and his lips, which she often thought tasted like warm honey when he kissed her senseless, were set tight.

She had asked a question that appeared not to please him, and she thought perhaps he would not answer her.

After several silent moments he spoke. "Are you certain you wish this discussion now?"

He had warned her about learning about the Legend. Was she ready? Or did she really have a choice? Was it not time she knew all about the man she felt she loved?

"Aye."

Another moment of silence was followed by a frustrated sigh, and then he began. "Life was difficult after my mother and I made our escape. Our coins went quickly, especially since my mother had a tender heart. The group of people we joined was accepting and generous with what little they had, but one woman in particular was ill and required much care and what healing potions could be found. Though we had traveled as far from Dunhurnal land as we could, my mother could not take the chance and be seen. She remained at the campsite while others went out and scavenged for food and things we needed, as well as going to purchase potions for Lena, at least until our coins ran out.

"Stealing food at times was the only way we did not starve. I did well, being young and lightweight and quick on my feet, until one day I stole from the wrong person."

Memories silenced him momentarily, and Reena waited for him to continue.

"I attempted a theft from a wealthy man protected by four guards who had just left an inn. I was caught and they were beating me rather badly when a warrior happened upon the scene and rescued me. I knew when I watched him effortlessly defend himself against the four men that I wanted to be as powerful a warrior as he.

"His name was James, and he returned me to my campsite bruised and bloodied. When my mother rushed to my side to care for me, he grabbed her arm and ordered her to leave me be, that I was a man and would lick my own wounds for being so foolish.

"That was the beginning of my warrior's training. When James learned of our plight, he took me aside and told me that it was my duty to see that my stepfather paid for what he did to my mother and to my honor as a man."

"He taught you then?" Reena asked.

"He taught me well and all I thought would be necessary to know to become a great warrior."

"Not so?"

He shook his head. "Not near enough. He told me that patience and gratitude were the most important attributes a warrior could possess. I did not understand him, but I was soon to find out. He sent me away to learn from his friends, and that is when I became a true warrior. I learned combat skills I never knew existed, and I learned just how patience could save not only my own life but also the lives of many, and how gratitude for all that I had learned could greatly benefit me, that taking nothing for granted would win me wars and wealth, and my reputation grew."

"Until?"

He hesitated. "Do you really wish to hear this, Reena?"

"You have told me nothing that makes me think differently of you. You did what was necessary to survive. There is nothing wrong with that. You learned skills that proved beneficial to you and others. You are a warrior."

"I am the Legend." He sounded as if he admitted to a heinous crime. "And the legend began far from here and followed me over sea and land and grew after my return."

"Are you telling me there is more to the Legend than I have heard?"

He simply stared at her with pain-filled eyes.

"Tell me." She fought down the nervous lump that tried to rush up in her throat. "Tell me how the Legend was given birth."

His somber laugh sent a chill through Reena.

"I know you have heard many tales of me. Now you hear the truth."

She nodded, as if reaffirming she was ready to hear whatever it was he had to tell her. And she wanted to hear every word, she wanted to know all she could about the Legend and understand all she could about him. The Legend was, after all, Magnus.

He hesitated a moment as if weighing the wisdom of his choice.

She smiled and reached out to rest her hand on his arm, the gesture one of comfort and support, letting him know she cared for him no matter his words.

He glanced down at her hand on his arm and raised troubled eyes to hers. "The legend began when I killed one of my teachers and his entire family."

Chapter 23

Her hand fell away and she was stunned silent.
One of his men called to him, letting him
know they approached an area he had designated
for mapping.

The Legend turned to Reena. "I expect your duties as my mapmaker to be carried out no matter the
circumstances. This episode will then put your abili-
ties to the test."

"I will map," Reena said firmly. She was actually
grateful for the interruption, for she needed time to
think on what he had just told her. He had been
blunt, offering no excuse for his actions, and his
words seemed to defy her to understand. Or did
they beg her to understand?

The horses were brought to a halt and Reena dismounted before the Legend could assist her. At the
moment she wanted no one's assistance; she preferred relying on herself and she preferred solitude. Solitude to draw and to think.

She walked around her horse to the Legend. He stood where he was, a glint of anger in his dark eyes. She assumed he was annoyed with her for dismounting on her own. Her actions did give the impression she did not wish him to touch her, but she would deal with that later. Now she needed time to herself. "What do you wish mapped?"

He pointed. "The area seen from the crest of that hill."

She nodded, took her charcoal and paper from the satchel strapped across the back of her horse, and walked to the crest of the hill. She stood silent, staring at the land spread out before her. It looked as empty as she felt, and she forced herself to take a closer look. Her mind rebelled, noticing none of the new spring growth about ready to blossom or the way the land rolled like a gentle green wave cresting over each hill, nor did she see the birds busy foraging for material to build suitable nests in which to lay their eggs. She heard only the Legend's words repeated over and over in her head.

What would cause a man to kill an entire family?

And not any man but his teacher, who had willingly shared his wisdom with his student.

She feared that he could provide no justifiable answer. If not, what then would she do?

Her mind needed settling. She could do nothing now, but later she would question him, and she would expect an answer. She began to draw, and in no time her hands flew fast and furiously and her mind numbed; she was lost in her mapping.

They rode on to another area, little conversation passing between them, and stopped for a light midday fare. They rested near a stream, spreading out a cloth that held meat and bread. The Legend had walked off, leaving Reena with his men. She did not share in their conversation but listened to humorous tales of their adventures.

An elderly man and woman looking worn from traveling on foot approached them cautiously. The woman appeared ready to collapse, and Reena was quick to stand and offer them rest and sustenance.

The man repeatedly thanked Reena for her generosity, and the woman looked ready to weep as they eagerly walked over to Reena. But a sudden abruptness halted their steps and fear filled their eyes, and Reena knew that the Legend had walked up behind her.

The man slipped his arm around the trembling woman, and with a courteous bow of his head he whispered, "My lord."

A strong command left no doubt as to what they should do. "Join us."

Reena thought about making conversation with the pair to help alleviate their fear, but the two ate as if they had not eaten in weeks and kept their eyes lowered, though they did remain huddled close to each other.

"Your destination?" Magnus more demanded than asked.

Reena admired the way the man met Magnus eye to eye, though his voice trembled some.

"My wife Beth and I search for a home. Being older and my hands—" He stopped and looked at his wrinkled and gnarled hands as if he did not recognize them. He shook his head. "I cannot create the fine bows and arrows I once did, so I am useless."

"A skill is never useless," Magnus said.

"A skill is only good if you can make use of it," the man said with disgust.

"Then use your skill the one way you can."

"How?" the elderly man asked, sounding hopeful that perhaps he was of some use after all.

"Teach what you know." Magnus sent a signal to one of his men, who walked off into the woods without a word.

The man shook his head. "To who? Most villagers and lords have a bowman."

"Skilled or not, there is always something to learn. I would be honored to have you share your knowledge with my bowman and do whatever you can to assist him. A cottage and food is included in the offer if you are interested."

His wife cried softly, and the elderly man stood a little prouder. "I am John, and I accept your generous offer. I will do my share and serve you well, my lord."

"I have no doubt you will. We must be on our way, but you are to wait here. Two of my men will return shortly and escort you to my keep. Once there, Thomas will see to your needs."

"Bless you, Legend," the woman said, her tears falling hard.

Magnus acknowledged her gratitude with a brief nod, then walked to his horse, ordering his men to mount.

Reena went to her horse realizing he'd left the food for the elderly couple to take with them. He lifted her to her horse, and as two of the Legend's men walked out of the woods, the Legend, Reena and his men rode off.

She smiled, thinking of what a good man he was.

Then she recalled his confession of murder, and she shivered.

"You are cold?" he asked. "A chill still clings to the air, spring has yet to fully blossom."

"A slight chill, nothing more."

"I have a heavy cloak if you need it," he offered.

She looked over at him where he rode beside her, so large and terrifying all in black, his face mostly concealed by the helmet. Yet he was concerned for her well-being.

He cared for her and she cared for him. She could not be foolish and allow her doubts to cloud her emotions. She needed to seek her answers and understand. So her question was asked not out of curiosity but from a loving heart.

"Tell me about your teacher and his family."

He stared at her for a silent moment, an indication he was deep in thought. Part of him wished he could remain there, in his mind.

Few knew the true story behind the tale that had earned him the title of the Legend. It was not something he wished to discuss or remember, and it certainly was not a tale he wished were true. By the time the story had traveled to his homeland it had grown into a legend—a legend that was far from the truth.

Could he trust Reena with the truth?

She had spoken not a word to anyone of his mother being the woman kept prisoner in the secret room. If she had he would have known, for the news would have run rampant through the keep, gossip being a way of life. But not a word was made mention; she had kept her word, keeping his secret.

Reena waited patiently, knowing he would speak

when he was ready. And though he looked as if he warred with his own decision, she felt confident he would choose to share the past with her and free his tormented heart and soul.

He spoke low, his words for their ears alone. "William was a good man and was a master in understanding instinct. He explained that it was an important part of who we are and what we amount to. Instinct allows us to live with less fear and more hope. It allows for understanding and less ignorance. Instinct is an essential part of us all that is rarely acknowledged and barely used.

"He taught me that all creatures except man use their instincts to survive, for man's arrogance causes him to ignore his instincts. At first his lessons seemed trivial and of no real importance to me until I began to realize the depth of his teachings. I spent a year with him, and it was a year I will never forget or regret.

"His thoughts and ideas were foreign to many, and he had moved his family several times to keep them from being persecuted, since there were many who believed he practiced dark magic. I asked him once why he did not keep his tongue silent so that he did not have to run and hide in fear. He laughed at me and told me that I should think about what I asked of him and when I had my answer I would need him to teach me no more."

"Did you discover the answer?"

"Not until the very end."

Reena felt her breath catch, and tears gathered in her eyes. This was difficult for him, she could see the way he warred with his memories and the hurt that surfaced and grabbed hold of him.

"Friends of William warned him that officials were on their way to accuse and persecute him and his family. His wife, Bella, believed as he did, as did their daughter Mary, a young lass of barely ten years with a voice sweeter than the heavens. When she raised it in song, all quieted and listened, for it was a sound so lovely it mesmerized.

"The warning came too late. Officials arrived and began to question William and his family. He understood immediately his situation and the danger he and his family were in. There was no longer anyplace for them to hide. He was quickly accused of heresy and imprisoned in a nearby keep's dungeon, his wife was imprisoned shortly after him, and William feared that his daughter would suffer a horrible fate, left on her own.

"He knew it was only a matter of time before he and his wife would be put to death by fire. He asked that I spare them the suffering. . . ."

Magnus stopped and took a breath.

Reena fought a losing battle with her tears.

"He also asked that I made certain Mary did not suffer. He believed that together, they would all be happy in the afterlife. He asked as a good friend that I do this for him. I had to tend to the matter immediately and then leave and return to my own land. He told me to take the night to think on the matter for there was little time, and he told me to tell Mary how much she was loved and that they would unite with her soon, that she would understand."

Magnus shook his head. "I could not do what he asked of me, not until I returned to the dungeon the next night, having bribed the same guard with a bag of coins to let me in. William and Bella had been tortured and lay in horrendous pain from their horrible ordeal. William begged me to end their suffering and see to Mary. I did not think twice."

He paused, shutting his eyes for a moment. "I will spare you the details and tell you their deaths were swift and painless. Bella felt nothing, she simply smiled and whispered her thanks just before the end. Before William died he asked me if I had the answer to why he did not keep his tongue silent so that he did not have to run and hide in fear. I gave him the answer, and he smiled and told me that I needed him no more. I laid them side by side, went and took care of Mary, then left."

Tears ran down Reena's cheeks. "When did you discover the answer?"

"That moment before he was to die. I realized that he was not the one who ran and hid in fear. It was those who hunted him that were running and hiding in fear."

"You tell me the true tale; what is the gossip that preceded you home?"

"It was said I confronted evil and without fear destroyed it and that only a man of strong conviction and honor, a legend, could do what I did. The tale traveled far and wide and I was hired by many monarchs to deal with their battles and wars, and I was substantially rewarded."

"And all feared you because they thought you capable of turning on a friend and killing him without thought or remorse."

"Aye. I was the Legend, a warrior without a heart or soul, a formidable commodity to those looking for protection from their enemies."

"You told no one the truth?"

"No one would believe it, and I would place myself in danger if it were known I did it to save them from suffering. And my teacher would have expected no less from me, for instinctively he realized what would happen after his death, and that would mean his death was not in vain."

"You would live to help others, while those in power thought you helped them."

"Helping those in power allowed me to help others who were less fortunate, and it helped me to grow in my own strength and power until I became a force of my own."

"I will tell no one the true tale, but . . ." She lowered her voice to a whisper. "I wish you to teach me the understanding of instinct."

He stared at her for a moment. She was so very different than the women he had known. Her interests were more similar to his, wanting to understand all that she could.

"You practice much of it already."

"Do I?" she asked, surprised.

"Aye, you do. The first part of understanding instinct is awareness. You must be aware of your surroundings and see all. You do that when you sketch."

"I see everything and keep it clear and strong in my mind," Reena said with pride.

"That is a good beginning in understanding instinct."

They remained in discussion until they reached their destination.

Reena immediately understood why the area was important to him. "Guards could be posted here without being noticed, and the rise in the distance would give a clear view to anyone who approached."

"I thought the same when we first passed through here, but I wanted a more thorough mapping of the area."

"We should investigate the areas heavy with foliage." She pointed out one or two. "The information may prove useful."

A couple of hours were spent walking the surrounding area. Magnus and Reena remained by each other's side, each sharing their opinions and thoughts about the land. His strong hand was there every time the terrain became more demanding with hills and ruts and fallen trees. He made sure of her footing and her safety.

Reena talked continuously even as Magnus lifted her about the waist to assist her in mounting her horse. She offered excellent suggestions to him and he listened carefully, though he could not ignore his growing need for her.

What surprised him the most was that while he desired her and wanted very much to make love to her, his need for her sprang more from the fact that she filled his life with joy and love. He could not think of what a day would be like without her. She was so very much a part of him now that he could not imagine her *not* being in his life.

The thought frightened him, a man who supposedly knew no fear. Yet he feared *not* having Reena by his side. He was hopelessly in love, and it was time he did something about it.

They camped for the night in a small clearing. They enjoyed a meal of roasted rabbit and good conversation. It was not long after that Reena found herself alone with Magnus. They sat by the fire, next to each other, and Reena wondered if their solitude was intentional.

Today she had come to understand the Legend more than she'd ever thought possible, and she had realized that Magnus and the Legend were truly one and the same. His dark and imposing helmet instilled fear in many, but it was actually meant to conceal his caring nature. While many believed the Legend brought harm and suffering, others thought of him as a savior. He had saved her village from further suffering, he had saved the elderly couple from certain suffering, and he had saved his teacher and his family from a horrible suffering.

The Legend was a man with a tender heart and soul, and she loved him more than she ever thought possible. She loved him for his strength and courage, and she loved him for his tenderness, and she was annoyed at herself for not realizing his true nature the very first time they met. A man who could love and protect a small cowardly pup had to have a tender heart.

The question was, what now?

While she had no difficulty with patience for mapping and drawing, patience itself was not one of her stronger virtues. So she thought it was best to speak her mind.

She reached her hand out to him as he reached for her.

Chapter 24

Their hands locked, and it was Magnus who said, "We have things to discuss."

"Aye," she agreed with a nod. "I thought the same myself."

"We often think much the same."

"I have noticed," she said and smiled softly.

Her smile hit his gut hard and sent a silent groan rippling through him. He could not stop himself from reaching for Reena, and in one swift swoop he had her in his lap and his cheek next to hers, soft, silky and kissed by the fire's warmth.

Were her lips that warm?

His groan was not silent this time, and he whispered against her cheek, "I am going to kiss you."

"Please." Her murmur was urgent, and it sent his blood rushing through him like a raging river.

Their lips touched like hungry souls reaching out for sustenance, and they tasted long and hard of each other until finally they broke apart for much needed breaths.

Foreheads rested against each other, breathing was heavy, and love filled both hearts. Neither spoke, but then neither could, and thoughts made no sense. The only sense was that they were in each other's arms safe and secure and in love and wanting to make love.

She cupped his face in her hands and with a quieted breath she whispered, "I love you."

If he thought her smile punched his gut, he was mistaken. Her words devastated and thrilled all at once, and he needed to speak from his heart as she had done. "As I said, we often think the same, you and I, for I love you too."

She smiled, joy filling her heart, and she gave him a quick kiss. "You are sure?"

His own joy caused him to tease. "I must have a moment to reconsider, for you can be stubborn at times."

She kissed him again before continuing. "And you are demanding."

He feigned shock. "Me demanding? Never!" His teasing turned to loving and he gazed in her blue eyes. "I demand but one thing of you."

"Tell me," she murmured.

He tightened his arms around her waist, pulling her closer to him. "I demand you love me forever, for that is how long I shall love you."

They kissed slowly and lovingly, and when their lips parted, they rested cheek to cheek.

Reena took a moment to gather her thoughts, and after carefully considering her decision, she spoke up. "There is something I ask, not demand, of you."

Her serious tone had him paying close attention. "Tell me."

"I have thought much on love of late, and I realize the enormous responsibility that comes with it. It cannot be taken for granted or expressed on a whim. Love is born in the heart and soul of two people and it is to be cherished, nourished and protected. I love you with all my heart and I wish to love you forever—" She paused. "But the love I speak of is the love I wish to give to my husband."

"Are you asking me to marry you?" he asked with a grin.

She eased away from him and held her chin up high, ready to defend herself. "Do you wish to marry me?"

He eased her to him. "Since forever."

Her heart thudded in her chest and her stomach quivered. "Truly?"

"Truly," he said and nibbled at her lips.

"It matters not that I am your mapmaker?"

"It matters not to you that I am the Legend?"

She giggled softly. "Why would that matter?"

He shrugged. "Why would it matter that I wed my mapmaker? We wed because we love. What better reason?"

She cuddled close to him. "This day ends in much joy. I would have never thought it so."

"This day will end in much more joy," he teased and nuzzled her neck.

She playfully pushed at his chest. "We are not yet wed."

"The heavens heard us confess our love; we are bonded, you and I, and nothing, absolutely nothing, will keep us apart."

His words sounded like a proclamation for all to hear and with no objections allowed.

The crunch of leaves and steady footsteps caught their attention, and Reena attempted to move away, but his strong hands held firm to her waist.

Philip, one of Magnus's men, stepped out of the woods and looked to Magnus, unmoved by the intimacy of his lord and his mapmaker. "All is set, I sleep now until my shift."

Magnus nodded, and the man took the rolled bedding tucked beneath his arm and spread it on the ground not far from the fire. He turned his back to them to sleep.

"We are as good as wed, Reena," Magnus whispered and moved her so that they could stretch out beside each other, placing Reena closer to the fire's heat. He cuddled against her back and draped a possessive arm over her.

She felt the length of him, and the heat of his body penetrated her slowly and steadily, unlike the rush of heat from the fire's flames. She rested her hand on his arm, glad that they'd made their love known to each other, glad that they would wed and eager for her husband's touch.

Life was good, so very good, and she was grateful, and she fell asleep with happiness filling her heart.

It dawned sunny, the air less chilled. After a quick morning meal the small group was off for a day of mapping. They stopped at a section of land thick with trees. Magnus stood talking with Philip, while Reena was busy surveying the area. It was soon evident that she did not have a good view for mapping, and she turned in a slow circle to determine the best position.

After several slow turns, she tilted her head back, staring up at the tall tree not far from her. "Perfect."

She fashioned a satchel of cloth from her shawl to carry her sketching items and draped it around her neck to rest to the side. She then proceeded to grab at the lower branch of the tree and pull herself up.

Magnus caught her antics out of the corner of his eye and turned to watch her attempt to hoist herself up on the branch. Her feet swung wildly and her small hands looked as though they could barely hold onto the thick branch. She was going nowhere and tiring herself out fast, but she persisted.

He walked over to her. "Whatever are you doing?"

After a huff and puff or two she managed to answer. "Need a better view."

He shook his head and with ease hoisted himself up onto the branch from where she dangled.

She cricked her neck and stared up at him. He did not wear his helmet; his handsome face was fully exposed down to his sinful smile, and the morning sun shone through the branches just budding with spring leaves to kiss the warm honey-colored streaks in his brown hair.

A handsome one he was, and he belonged to her.

"You smile as you dangle from the tree."

"I smile at the man I love."

He leaned over, grabbed her arms, and pulled her up, steadying her as her feet found their footing on the thick branch. "You are foolishly—"

"In love," she finished and kissed him, almost sending them both toppling off the branch, were it not for Magnus's quick reaction.

He steadied them and then braced her to rest

against the thick trunk of the tree. "Is this tree climbing necessary?"

Reena looked up at the next branch.

"Absolutely not," Magnus said, shaking his head firmly.

"I need a better view of the surrounding area. With the trees not fully in bloom I can see far and wide and produce a more accurate map. Then you will know all approaches to your land, for one map will follow the other and you will have a clear and concise drawing of your property."

Magnus gave thought.

Reena suddenly looked alarmed.

"What is wrong?" Magnus asked and quickly surveyed the surrounding area. Seeing nothing to warrant concern, he turned his attention to Reena.

She immediately voiced her apprehension. "I will remain your mapmaker when we wed, will I not?"

Magnus took careful steps over to her side and placed a gentle hand to her cheek. "I would never deprive you of your work. I will provide you with paper, charcoal, quill and ink for as long as you wish, and you may map until your dying day if you so choose."

Reena sighed in relief and kissed the palm of his hand.

Her moist lips tingled his flesh and jolted his senses, his male senses. "If only we were not in a tree."

"Are you not the Legend?" she teased. "A man of many talents and skills?"

His hand grabbed hold of her cheeks, puckering her lips. "You will learn well of my talents and skills." He smiled. "And I will teach you some of your own."

She spoke between puckered lips, but her response was clear. "Good, I love to learn new things."

Magnus groaned deep and harsh and kissed her puckered lips. "Damn, Ree, but you excite me in a most unusual way."

She eased his hand off her face. "I am glad, for I feel myself eager to be with you."

He ran a tender finger over her lips. "I promise you that our joining will be a time you long remember."

She kissed his finger. "I have no doubt of that."

"Map," he ordered, and she understood. If she did not soon tend to her work, they would be tending to something much more intimate.

Reena made fast work of the temporary map, asking him relevant questions and giving him pause to reflect on answers that would serve him well in protecting his land.

When they were ready to climb down from the tree, Magnus ordered her to remain as she was and not to move an inch. She gave her word, and he grasped the branch and easily swung himself down to the ground. He then walked with haste to his horse, mounted, and returned, stopping the large steed beneath the tree.

"Drop me your satchel."

She did as he said.

"Walk out carefully on the branch to where I can reach you."

It was a bare few steps she needed to take, and she took them without trepidation. She had climbed enough trees with Brigid not to worry about one with a thick and sturdy branch.

"Careful," he warned with a snap, startling her.

She lost her footing and swung her arms to steady herself, but she could not hold her balance, and she toppled off the branch.

Magnus reacted instinctively, his arms reaching out, and she landed with a solid plop right in them. His heart thudded in fright and his breath raced out in a sigh. She simply smiled.

He shook his head. "You smile when you fall from a tree?"

"I smile because I knew you would catch me."

"You had no doubt?"

"Nay, not an ounce of doubt. I knew you would be there for me. You never fail to help those you love or those your heart will not let you ignore, no matter the price to you."

One of his men hurried out from the dense tree covering to the small clearing and shouted to him that strangers were spotted in the distance.

"See what they are about," Magnus ordered and gave a quick glance at the sky. The sun had suddenly disappeared behind a flurry of gray skies and the distant sky did not look promising; a spring storm seemed probable. "The hills just west of here would be a good place to make camp for the night. There are several small caves where we can seek shelter if it rains. Meet me there when you are done with the strangers."

The man nodded and disappeared after taking only a few steps into the woods.

"You think a spring storm brews?" Reena asked, glancing at the gray sky.

"I do not wish to take the chance, and besides"— he gave her a hasty kiss—"I wish to be alone with you this night."

The thought his remark invoked caused her to shiver, and she cuddled against him.

"I will keep you warm," he whispered in her ear and sent gooseflesh racing down her arms.

"And what of mapping?" she asked, attempting to keep her senses rational, to ignore the rush of tingles that nestled between her legs. She wished to be alone with him and get to know him intimately as much as he wished for them to be alone, but fear mingled with her desire. What if she disappointed him? She was thin and small and not as shapely as most women. And that doubt lingered and nagged at her. But since he loved her it should not make a difference. Still, there would be that moment when she would stand in front of him naked, completely vulnerable. Would he still want her? Or were her doubts her own insecurities?

"Do not fear, there is much for you to map, but *right now* is for you and me."

He helped her onto her horse and they rode off toward the hills in the distance, the gray clouds thickening and a chilled wind swirling down around them.

It was not long before a sprinkle of rain began to fall and Reena was glad that the hills were not as far as she'd first thought, for the rain turned hard and steady. When finally they reached the hills, they were both soaked through, their skin wet and their bones chilled.

Magnus's men arrived only minutes later, and they exchanged hasty words before two men and Magnus hurried off in search of sufficient shelter and the other two saw to the care of the horses. Reena waited under a large tree, which kept her protected from the heavy rain, though a fine and steady drizzle kept her wet.

Shelter was located in mere minutes, and the men hurried her and the horses into a cave large enough for them all. A small fire burned and she hurried to warm herself, shivering from her wet clothes and the chill in her bones.

Try as she might, she could not get warm. Her wet clothes continued to keep her cold no matter how close she got to the fire. The men tended the horses while one took bow and arrow and left the shelter in search of food.

Reena shivered and rubbed her hands together. It would be a long night, though not the night she had in mind. Not wanting to feel any sorrier for herself than she already did, she went to her horse, grabbed her satchel, and returned to the fire. She wanted to make certain none of the maps were disturbed by the weather. She always made certain to protect her maps with leather wrappings. Her father had taught her to do so, explaining that he'd lost several maps before he was wise enough to keep them from being destroyed by the elements.

A shiver continued to run through her every now and then, and just as she finished tucking her maps back into the satchel, Magnus entered the cave.

He walked over to her and took her arm. "Come with me."

She had no time to respond or to pick her satchel up off the ground: his hold was firm, and she was forced to follow him. With rushed steps and rain pouring down on them they made their way a few feet past the cave and entered another cave.

Reena wiped the raindrops from her face and

glanced around the cave. It was small but high enough to stand and move about. A campfire burned in the middle of the earth floor, and wool blankets were spread out on one side. A bird of some kind roasted on the wooden spit over the fire and was just beginning to scent the cave with a delicious aroma.

She turned to Magnus, smiled, and shivered.

His hands instantly went to the ties on her cloak. "I want you out of these wet garments now."

Chapter 25

Reena placed her hand on his and stilled it. "I do not know if I am ready for this." The thought of standing naked in front of him chilled her more than her wet garments and filled her with apprehension.

He slipped his hand from beneath hers. "You are not ready to rid yourself of wet clothing and seek the warmth of a blanket and the heat of the fire?" He let her cloak fall to the ground. "For at this moment that is what I offer you."

She felt foolish and expressed her misgivings. "I will disappoint you for sure—"

His brisk laugh interrupted, and his hands went to the cloth belt around her waist. "It is not possible for you to disappoint me."

"I most certainly can," she insisted. "When first I drew my maps they were not at all good, though my father told me I had talent. It took time and much practice."

Magnus laughed again. "Then we will practice as much as you like."

"You will not mind if at first I disappoint you?"

His hands grasped the sides of her tunic and drew it up and over her head, leaving her wearing only her shift, the wet garment clinging to her chilled skin. After letting the tunic fall to join the cloak, he took hold of her arms. "I love you, Reena, you could never disappointment me. Besides, you have a passion in you that cannot be denied. It is in everything you do, from your drawings to your love of others to your joy of mapping. It is who you are, a woman full of passion and life."

"You make me sound more than I truly am."

"Nay, you simply need to learn who you truly are." He kissed the tip of her nose. "Now finish undressing while I see to the food."

He walked to the fire, squatted down, and slowly turned the stick so that the roasting bird would cook evenly and not burn. He kept his back to her, giving her privacy to rid herself of her remaining wet garment, but as she did she could not help but judge herself. What womanly qualities did she truly possess? Her breasts were barely a handful and her hips were narrow, though they had rounded some since food was no longer scarce and her appetite heartier. Many of the village women commented on how birthing would be difficult for her, and then there was her height, a mere two inches, no more, over five feet.

Whatever did he find attractive about her?

She was who she was, not beautiful, small in size and a mapmaker, certainly not the makings of a good wife. Or was there something she failed to see about herself? Was there something for her to learn?

She stared at his back, broad and strong and carrying the weight of far too many, and yet he remained caring and honorable. He had even turned his back so that she might undress in private.

The Legend certainly was a man of honor; she could see that clearly. Why, then, could she not see herself as clearly?

She quickly finished the task he had started, wrapping a soft brown wool blanket around herself once she stood naked. Then she spread her wet garments out on a large boulder to dry and sat herself down by the fire, adjusting the blanket around her and leaving her shoulders bare. Her long dark hair hung down her back, rainwater dripping from the ends of her hair onto the blanket.

He stood after hearing her sit and quickly shed his tunic and shirt, and her breath caught when he turned to face her. Muscles rippled over his chest and down his stomach. They filled his arms, and the firelight glistened off his damp skin, making him appear as though the fire had kissed it.

"Unlike you, I have no problem standing naked before you, so if it disturbs you to see me naked—" His hands went to the ties at his waist, and Reena closed her eyes in a flash.

She heard his laugh and felt like a coward.

"In time, Ree," he said quietly and sat down beside her, a blanket wrapped around his waist. "You will not be able to get enough of me naked."

It was her turn to laugh. "You are so sure of yourself?"

"Nay," he whispered in her ear. "I am sure of you."

She opened her eyes and turned her head, their lips brushed once, twice, three times, and then he kissed her.

A sudden crash of thunder rocked the ground and startled them apart.

"Do you think the heavens warn us?" she asked.

"Aye, they do, the heavens grow tired of us delaying our union as man and wife. We are meant to be together, for I think we are the only ones who understand each other."

"You jest with me," she said and teasingly poked him in the arm. It was a solid wall of muscle and warm flesh, and it sent a tingle running down her spine. "Though I do agree that we understand each other better than most."

The scent of the cooking bird grew heavy in the air, and Reena sniffed it appreciatively and gave a small yawn.

"Hungry and tired?" he asked with concern.

She wiped away a small spot of rain that had settled on his chest from the wet ends of his hair. "You care so very much."

"Of course I care, I love you."

She shook her head slowly. "Nay, I do not mean only me."

"Be careful," he whispered. "You may ruin my reputation if word spread that—"

"The Legend has a caring heart," Reena finished.

He turned away from her, but she caught the troubled look in his eyes. "None would believe you. I am the Legend and I earned my name."

She reached out to him, her hand resting on his shoulder. "You are—"

She stopped suddenly, and he turned to see her eyes wide and her mouth open, as if she were about to speak, then froze.

He grew concerned. "What is wrong?"

"You have a caring heart." Her blue eyes shone brightly, and she looked excited, as though she had made a discovery.

"So you say, do you think otherwise now?"

"Nay, nay, you care, and because you care you could not have killed Mary, your teacher's young daughter. You did not kill her, you protect her." She did not let him answer. "And I realize now that your teacher never meant for his daughter to die, and you understood this. He knew you would make certain she was cared for, he understood you as I do."

"I am not that complex, but Mary's situation is such that I must ask you to give me your word that you will repeat none of what you know."

"You have my word, I will say nothing."

"And I will tell you no more, for there are those who search for her, and I will not have your life endangered by knowledge of her whereabouts."

"As you wish," Reena said, "but if there should ever come a time—"

"I will seek your help," Magnus assured her. "I do not know about you, but that bird smells delicious, and I am starving."

Reena rubbed her hands together, part in anticipation of the feast and part in knowing The Legend had earned his title because of love. "Let us feast."

They talked about many things while they ate,

and they laughed often, until finally words drifted away and they looked upon each other in silence.

Tingles ran over Reena, mixed with a loving warmth; a strange and pleasurable sensation and one she would never grow tired of feeling. She wanted to reach out and touch him and let him know she was content here with him, just the two of them.

She looked at her hands, which needed cleaning from their meal, and with a smile she stood and hurried over to the opening of the cave. She stuck her hands outside to let the rainwater wash them clear.

She heard Magnus approach from behind and his arms slipped past her, his hands joining hers to cleanse them. They rubbed each other's hands slowly, the chilled rain feeling good on their warm skin.

And then he stepped closer, his body pressing against hers. He lifted her up with one arm to rest against him, while he rested his cheek to hers.

"I am too small in height for—"

"You are perfect," he whispered.

"Nay," she said with a soft laugh. "Love blinds you."

"Beauty blinds." He kissed her cheek and then her neck.

His tender kisses sent gooseflesh rushing over her, and she shivered.

He turned her in his arms. "I want to make love to you. I want to touch and kiss every part of your beautiful body and make you mine and mine alone."

This time she shivered from his words.

"The choice is yours; I will not force you. I want

our joining to be one of love, our marriage to be one of love, our life together to be one of love. I will have it no other way."

He placed her on the ground, and her eyes filled with tears.

"You are truly a man of honor."

"Without honor a man is nothing." He raised his hand to wipe away the single tear that slipped slowly down her cheek.

She kissed the palm of his hand. "My tear falls out of love, not shame or regret or doubt, but pure love."

He leaned down and brushed his lips over hers. "Then let me love you."

She hesitated but a brief moment, then her hand went to the blanket at his waist. "Let us both love."

His blanket fell away as his hand reached for the fold of her blanket and released it to fall at her feet. They stood naked in the mouth of the cave.

"You are beautiful," Magnus said softly, then scooped her up into his arms and walked to the campfire, lowering them both to the blankets.

He stretched out alongside her, ran his fingers though her hair, and smiled as her arms reached out to wrap around him and draw him near.

His body felt deliciously good against hers, warm and hard and soft all at once, and the taste of him— she did not want to stop tasting him. The more she tasted, the more she hungered for him. She could not get enough of him.

His hands explored her, touching and titillating her senses beyond reason.

"Your skin is like silk," he whispered and nibbled her ear. "And your breasts—" He cupped her breast in his hand. "A perfect size for me to hold and enjoy." His mouth descended on her nipple, and with slow licks it disappeared into his mouth.

She moaned and grasped his arms, holding tight while he took his pleasure and gave her pleasure.

His mouth drifted down, and he rained soft kisses on her belly. He did not stop and continued to taste every part of her, making her squirm and moan with pleasure.

She soon lost complete control of her senses. Nothing mattered but his touch, his kiss, his loving. She wanted to scream, laugh and cry all at once, and she wanted him never to stop loving her as he did this night.

He moved over her, rubbing his heated body against hers, and she felt the length and hardness of him.

"I need to touch you," she said, her words an urgency that spilled hastily from her lips. She pushed at his chest to force him onto his back so that she could have her way.

He did not argue, and when her hand slipped around him in slow curiosity, he grew harder.

"You feel like silk," she said, surprised, and ran her finger up and down the length of him before her hand completely encircled him. Once again she tested the feel of him.

He moaned before speaking with haste. "If you continue to excite me with your touch, this night will end quickly."

"But you feel so very good." Her hand moved down to cup him delicately, and she moaned herself. "I do so want you."

To his surprise she climbed on top of him.

"This is permitted?"

He laughed and groaned. "Aye, very permitted." Then he took a breath and grabbed hold of her slim hips to hold her steadfast. "But this is your first time and it may be painful for you this way, and I want you to suffer no pain."

"I will feel no pain," she insisted, moving against him in a motion that was instinctive and natural.

He groaned, his own body joining hers in the rhythm. "You will tell me if you do?"

"Aye," she said on a moan and moved to slowly settle herself down on him.

He reached out and touched her intimately, firing her passion even more. She groaned and flung her head back, arching her body as she descended down on him. Then she leaned forward, her long dark hair tickling his face, her hands pressing firm on his shoulders.

His hands went to her waist, and he attempted to assist her, hoping to ease her slowly down on the full length of him so that she would feel nothing but pleasure. But she was lost in her passion and she was intent on feeling all of him.

"Easy," he warned.

"Nay," she said on a cry. "I need to feel all of you."

"You will hurt."

"You will never hurt me," she said on a rushed breath, kissed him soundly, then forced him completely into her in one solid thrust. She let out a sigh of absolute pleasure, and her smile was wide as she moved and swayed like a woman born to love.

Magnus groaned at the feel of her so tight and hot around him, and he lost his senses.

They mated in a frenzied love, their movements natural, demanding, tender and forceful.

Reena loved the freedom of loving him as she chose, and he loved allowing her that freedom, and their powerful climaxes reflected their unselfish love. It was something Magnus had never experienced before and Reena had never known. They lingered against each other, Reena spent, her damp body stretched out over him, Magnus content with her there on top of him.

They eventually slipped beneath the blankets and cuddled in each other's arms, drifting off to sleep—but not before they both at the same time turned and whispered, "I love you."

Chapter 26

The days that followed were made for lovers. The sun shone bright, the birds chirped in song, the buds on the trees began to blossom, along with Magnus and Reena's love.

They hugged, they touched, and they kissed and spent much time off on their own. Sunsets were a favorite time of theirs, and sunrises, and they watched both wrapped in each other's arms, safe and very much in love.

Reena learned more about her soon-to-be husband, and what she learned often moved her to tears. His dark helmet was certainly a mask, for it hid his true nature from the world. She understood why he so often wore it. His caring heart had difficulty accepting what was necessary to his warrior side, and the helmet hid his true self.

They finished their mapping in four days' time, both Reena and Magnus eager to return to the keep and have time to themselves. The weather remained dry so cave dwelling was not necessary, and the loving couple found little chance to be alone.

And with the improving weather Magnus wondered over Kilkern's intentions. He sent word ahead to the keep informing them of their imminent return, and after several private discussions with his men, Reena demanded to know what was being kept from her.

"I cannot protect myself if I do not even know I need to protect myself," she said to Magnus after he returned from a discussion with his men that obviously appeared worrisome.

"I protect you, that is all you need to know," he said after mounting his horse.

"Nay, it is not," she insisted, holding tight to the reins of her horse and her temper. "I am not some meek-minded, weak-willed woman who quivers in fear when threatened. I will defend myself when necessary and be aware when necessary."

"You are more of a woman than I counted on." He smiled. "In more ways than one."

She grinned wide, and her annoyance faded. "Aye, that I am. Now stop attempting to misdirect me, and tell me what goes on."

Magnus knew it was useless to argue with her. She would see to having her way one way or the other, and the thought filled him with a sense of peace. He loved a strong and courageous woman, whom he was proud of and would love until his dying day and beyond.

"Kilkern's men have been seen near the keep."

Brigid was busy kneading dough for her bread when Thomas entered her cottage. His somber expression warned her that there was a problem, and her hands stopped.

"Are Reena and Magnus all right?"

Thomas walked over to her and laid a comforting hand on her shoulder. "They are fine and should return to the keep before nightfall."

"Then what is wrong?" she asked, nervous to hear his answer.

"Kilkern's men are near the keep."

She immediately wrapped her arms around him as far as she could get them and buried her head in his massive chest.

"Do not worry, no one will touch you. You are safe with me."

She drew a deep breath and stepped away from him, though he was reluctant to let her go. "I cannot understand why Kilkern does this to me."

"It is simple. You are beautiful and he wants you."

Brigid's eyes filled with tears. "He will use me and discard me at his whim."

Thomas's face turned red with anger. "I will not let him. He will not hurt the woman I love."

Brigid was stunned silent, as was Thomas, who turned a deeper shade of red after realizing he'd blurted out what he had kept hidden in his heart since the first moment he'd met her.

"Oh, Thomas," she said and wept.

Her tears alarmed him. "It is all right, Brigid, you need not love me in return. I am not foolish enough to think a woman as beautiful as you could love a man as ugly as me."

Brigid wiped at her tears. "You most certainly are not ugly."

Thomas took a step away from her and stretched

his arms out from his sides. "Look at me, Brigid, I am ugly."

Brigid walked up to him and ran a flour-covered finger down his nose and over his cheeks, leaving a powdered trail. "You are a handsome man with a huge heart."

He blushed and could not look at her. "My heart belongs only to you."

She sighed and cupped his big face in her hands, forcing him to meet her eyes. "I would take care of your heart, Thomas."

It took a moment for him to comprehend her words—or perhaps it was that he did not believe his own ears. "You like me?"

"I more than like you, Thomas."

"But you do not—"

"I still heal from the loss of my husband and feel guilty that I should care for another man."

Thomas placed his hands on her slim waist. "I know you will always love your husband John and rightfully so. If you but love me half as much as you loved him, I would be a happy man."

"And if I love you more?"

His breath quickened and he thought for a moment he could not breathe. "I would be honored."

"Oh, Thomas," she said. Tears once again spilling down her cheeks, she kissed him.

He held her with gentle hands, fearful he would hurt her, and kissed her just as gently.

"I will not break," she said when they parted.

Thomas hung his head. "I am not well versed in the ways of love."

Brigid smiled softly and took his hand. "Then let me show you."

* * *

Magnus and Reena arrived well after sunset, the sky dark and filled with ominous clouds that drifted in haste past the full moon—not a good omen, and one that had many crossing themselves as they hurried along to their cottages.

Reena was eager to see Brigid and how she fared, though she knew Thomas would keep her safe. She wondered how Justin and Maura were, and her parents. She felt excited to be home, really home, for Dunhurnal land would truly be hers once she wed Magnus.

She hurried off her horse and headed to Brigid's cottage.

"Wait," Magnus called out. "I will go with you, for I am sure to find Thomas there."

Reena slowed her step, allowing Magnus to catch up with her, and they both hurried on to the cottage. Calling out her friend's name, Reena opened the cottage door with a sound knock. Once inside, she stood frozen in shock.

There, in bed, were Brigid and Thomas, naked beneath the covers and wrapped in each other's arms.

Magnus smiled as he walked up behind Reena. "Time for a wedding."

"Only if Brigid agrees," Thomas said, his arm firm around Brigid. "I will not have her marry me if she does not wish to."

Reena continued to stare in silence.

"My only objection would be"—Brigid looked to Thomas, and the large man held his breath—"is if Thomas does not love me, then I wish not to wed."

Thomas let out a whoosh of relieved breath. "No

one will love you as deeply and strongly as I do, Brigid."

"I know this," she said, snuggling against him. "I but wanted to hear you admit it."

"I will shout it if you wish," he said seriously.

"I do not think that necessary," Magnus said and reached for Reena's hand. "We will leave you now, and I will speak with you in the morning, Thomas."

Reena was almost out the door when she stopped and looked to Brigid. "You are happy?"

"More than I thought possible."

Reena smiled, and before she could respond, she was yanked out the door.

"They need time alone," Magnus said. "As do we."

"But you have things to see to."

"All will wait till morning." He sounded as though he insisted and would have it no other way.

But it was not to be, for when they entered the great hall, several of his men were waiting, and they appeared concerned. After speaking with them, Magnus told her that there were things needing his attention and that he would see her later in the evening.

Reena understood. Though she wished he would confide in her what was amiss, perhaps later tonight, when they shared his bed, he would speak of his concerns.

She retired to her bedchamber and set her sketches out on the desk. She thought of mapping, but her mind was too cluttered and her room too confining. She grabbed her cloak from where she'd dropped it on the bed, swung it around her shoulders, and headed out the door.

The great hall was busy with warriors gathered

around Magnus. Maps were spread out on several tables, and she was pleased that her mapping would assist him in protecting his home. She did not stop to speak to him, intending to return before he finished with his men, which looked to be several hours.

She slipped out the doors without being noticed and turned in the direction of her parents' cottage. She hoped her father was free to speak with her. It had been some time since they'd had a chance to talk, and he would enjoy hearing about her mapping experiences.

"Mapmaker."

Reena froze, not certain if she'd heard the whisper or imagined it. The night shadows made it impossible to see clearly, and heavy clouds had moved in to conceal the full moon's light. Was it her imagination? Did she hear a voice?

"Listen well, mapmaker."

Her breath caught and her heart raced at the sound of the Dark One's harsh voice. He blended with the night shadows so well that Reena had no idea where he was, and she did not care to look upon him and his ominous dark garb.

"Tell Magnus that he must look closer."

"What do you mean?" she asked, curious and eager to help the man she loved.

"Tell him." His response was harsh and firm and expected obedience.

She expected further explanation. "I cannot tell him what I do not comprehend."

"It is not for you to comprehend, you are merely the messenger."

She was fast to argue. "I will deliver no message I myself do not understand."

"You refuse to do as I say?"

Reena thought for a moment, a mere moment, since it did not take her long to disagree. "You comprehend me clearly, now what say you? Do you explain, or do I continue on my way?"

A moment of silence was followed by a low rumbling laughter. "He will have his hands full with you."

"Aye, and I will love him and understand him as no other can." She raised her head in pride.

"He is lucky to have found you."

"I intend to remind him of that often."

He laughed again.

"Tell me of what you speak," she urged, "so that I may help him."

The Dark One obliged her, the harshness gone from his tone. "What is it that Kilkern seeks?"

"A map," Reena replied, "to support his claim that Dunhurnal land is actually Kilkern land and that Magnus has no claim to this property."

"So then if he seeks a map to prove his claim, who better than to provide him with one?"

"A mapmaker," she said in a hushed whisper. "Kilkern needs a mapmaker to map the land for him, proving his claim." It took a moment for her to digest the information and realize that she was in danger. "My friend Brigid has no need to worry?"

"Kilkern seeks Brigid for a different reason. He is a man that intends to get what he wants at any cost."

"So he seeks Brigid for pleasure and me for mapping."

"Aye, but at the moment the map is more important. He can find another woman to satisfy his lust;

he cannot find another mapmaker with your knowledge of Kilkern and Dunhurnal land."

"I am valuable to him."

"More than you realize. Be careful and share this information with Magnus, for I am not certain he is aware of it."

Reena remained silent.

"You hesitate."

"Magnus will keep me confined once he learns of what you say."

"For your own safety," he assured her.

"He will worry over me."

"He loves you and will worry regardless."

She sighed. "Something does not make sense to me."

"What do you mean?"

"I do not know." She shook her head. "All this talk of the land and who has rightful claim to it." She shook her head again. "Something is amiss."

Magnus's men began spilling out of the great hall, disrupting their solitude.

"Go speak with him now," the Dark One warned her.

"I will tell him."

"*Now*," he reiterated firmly.

"As you say," she said with a resigned sigh. "Can I offer you food and shelter for the night?"

"I have all I need, but thank you for your generosity."

"Be well," she said in a soft whisper, but she knew that the Dark One had blended further into the shadows of the night and probably did not hear her.

She changed her direction and returned to the

keep. She did not find Magnus in the great hall and went in search of him. She did not find him in his solar and decided to drop her cloak in her bedchamber before proceeding to his chambers. She was surprised to see him standing in the middle of her room looking perplexed and perturbed.

"Where have you been?"

"I thought to visit my parents."

Magnus was beside her in two strides, his hands grasping her face. "Tell me when you leave the keep."

"I was not going far." She placed her hands over his to soothe him.

"If I do not know where you are, then it is too far." He leaned down and kissed her, and the soft, gentle touch of his lips soon turned ravenous, along with his hands. It was as though he had to touch her, had to feel her warm, soft body and be assured that she was there with him, alive and well.

He stopped to take a breath and rested his forehead to hers. "I am a warrior used to fear, and yet when I am uncertain of your whereabouts fear rises in me like I have never known before. Damn, Reena, I love you so very much."

Her heart swelled with joy. "I will do my best to not cause you fear."

He laughed softly. "Why do I think that will be a problem?"

"I am adventurous; I cannot help it."

He scooped her up into his arms. "Then you shall be adventurous with only me."

She slipped her arms around his neck and placed her small nose to his. "Promise me?"

"You have my word," he said and captured her lips.

They were on the bed in seconds, their garments discarded just as fast and entwined in each other's arms with the same speed. He intended to linger in their lovemaking: she intended the same, but their passion took hold and they were soon fast in the throes of lustful sex.

He touched, she nipped, he tormented, she teased, she moaned, he groaned and they joined in a fiery union that had their naked bodies perspiring, their hearts beating wildly, and their climaxes exploding, leaving them completely breathless and thoroughly satiated.

They lay beside each other, catching their breath and cooling their heated bodies.

When common sense returned, Reena remembered the Dark One's message. While now did not seem an appropriate time, she thought it best she deliver the information as she had promised. *Now.*

She turned on her side to face him. "I have something to tell you."

Magnus turned his head. "This sounds important."

"The Dark One spoke with me this evening when I was on my way to my parents' cottage. He told me that Kilkern looks to substantiate his claim on Dunhurnal land and to do so he must produce a map designating the land as his. To do this he needs the assistance of a—"

"Mapmaker," Magnus finished.

Reena looked at him oddly. "You were aware of this?"

"I have known from the start that Kilkern needs you more than anyone."

She frowned. "From the start?"

Magnus stroked her hip, his tender touch meant to soothe.

"From when we first met?" she asked before he could answer.

Magnus gripped her hip as if he feared her leaving his side. "The day you arrived, my people were packed and ready to leave the next day for Dunhurnal land."

"My mapping made no difference in your decision, then?"

"Your mapping made a large difference in my choice."

Reena sprang up and turned wide eyes on him. "Your arrival here and my association with you would force Kilkern's hand in claiming what he believed is his land." She shook her head, doubting her own explanation. "He could have had me map for him any time since his arrival. It makes no sense."

Magnus took her hand. "A map was not necessary until now."

"Why?" She more demanded than asked, hurt by the truth that it had not been her skills at all that had brought him here but his own intentions.

"Because he needs one now."

"Why?" she demanded again.

"To prove a false claim."

"You know it is false." Her stomach ached from what she might hear.

"Aye." He gripped her hand tightly.

"How do you know?"

"I possess the map that shows Kilkern land was originally Dunhurnal land and was falsely divided by Robert Kilkern to give to his brother."

Her heart thudded in her chest, and she waited.

"Philip Kilkern was Robert Kilkern's brother, and Robert Kilkern was my stepfather."

Reena closed her eyes for a brief moment. "Making Peter Kilkern your—"

"Half brother."

Chapter 27

Reena sat in bed, shocked, a chill racing through her. Magnus was quick to wrap a blanket around her, and he hugged her shoulders tightly.

"Let me explain," he said, his voice apologetic, though firm in his resolve.

He rested his hands over hers where they lay in her lap. "Peter Kilkern is the son my mother had by Robert Kilkern. My stepfather barely let my mother see her own son, so therefore Peter cared little for my mother. I, on the other hand, saw Peter quite often and watched as my stepfather showered him with attention and adoration, giving him whatever he wished from a very young age, and making certain that Peter knew I was insignificant and entitled to nothing."

"Is Peter the reason your stepfather divided the land?"

"Aye, he thought to protect his son, since Dunhurnal land belonged to my father's family for generations. My father served the king well and so his land was protected, until my father died and my mother married Robert Kilkern."

"Against her wishes," she reminded him.

"I remember her pleading with her father not to force the marriage upon her, but he paid her no mind. He was determined she would have a husband to protect the land."

He looked away for a moment, as if the memories were too painful, and she slipped her hand from under his and squeezed his hand gently.

Magnus continued. "Robert was a sly man, and he agreed to wed my mother only if he was granted a portion of the land."

"But the land was legally his once he wed your mother."

"My grandfather was a sly and determined man. He intended to make certain that I inherited what was rightfully mine, since there was a good chance that the union would produce more children who could very well inherit the property, something my grandfather had no intentions of happening. Dunhurnal land would remain intact for me to inherit. Kilkern would control it until I reached my majority, then he would have to make due with the small section of land agreed upon in the marriage contract."

Reena shivered and rubbed her arms. "Kilkern would have never let you reach manhood, would he?"

"Nay, he would not, and my mother understood that, especially when my grandfather died. My mother knew it was not an accident that took his life; Kilkern had something to do with it.

"She knew all too well that our lives were in danger and that we had to flee. She told me of the crude map my father had of his land and how Robert Kilkern had hidden it away along with their wedding agreement; both would prove my ownership of Dunhurnal land."

Reena closed her eyes for a moment and took a deep breath. "You tortured Robert Kilkern to find the whereabouts of the map?"

Magnus nodded. "I could not have what was rightfully mine if I did not have the map and the wedding agreement to present to the king. My stepfather refused to tell me where they were, and he laughed at me, telling me that I was as weak as my mother and that Dunhurnal land was no more, that it was Kilkern land and would forever remain in Kilkern hands."

"He underestimated you."

"He underestimated my love for my mother and father and my honor to my name and land. He paid dearly for his mistake."

"But why did you not claim the land immediately? You had your proof. You could have easily taken the land from Philip Kilkern; he was a fair man, far different from his brother—" She halted abruptly, understanding dawning. "You *wanted* to take the land from Peter Kilkern."

"He has prepared for this confrontation as long as I have, and besides, I was busy reclaiming my grandfather's land, Kilkern having made attempts to lay claim to it: otherwise I would have returned to claim my land sooner. I would never have allowed Kilkern to starve tenants that actually belonged to me."

"This all makes sense, but what of me? Why did you make me map for you? Why did you not tell me the truth from the beginning?"

"Your arrival at my keep simplified things for me. I needed to make your acquaintance and learn just how skillful you were. The men I sent to scout and spy on Kilkern land informed me of your talents. If what they had learned was true, then I had no doubt that Peter Kilkern would be after your services with no intentions of compensating you for them."

"So you had me map."

He nodded. "I needed to see for myself how fast and accurately you could produce a map, and being under duress as you were made it better for me. If you could map under those circumstances, then Kilkern would certainly be able to use your talents. Making you my mapmaker served two purposes— it afforded you protection from Kilkern, and I acquired a truly gifted mapmaker."

"Aye, that you did," she said with a teasing poke to his side. "But why did Kilkern not seek my skill when he first arrived? Why wait? And why did his father not destroy the map so that no proof existed?"

"If by chance I did resume control of Dunhurnal land, Kilkern would still have been entitled to a small portion of the land. Without that paper he would get nothing, and he was not foolish enough to lose everything by destroying the agreement."

"Why then did Peter Kilkern wait and not have a map drawn when he first arrived?"

"Arrogance, perhaps foolishness to think that his father would not betray him and divulge the location of the original map to me." He shook his head. "I do not know. I do know that my stepfather never ex-

pected my return or that I would see that he paid for
what he had done to my mother and my grandfather."

"So when you returned you claimed Dunhurnal
land but left Philip Kilkern alone on purpose. You
waited for Peter to become earl of Culberry, which
could have taken forever if Philip had not taken ill
and died."

Magnus raised a brow.

Reena gasped in understanding. "Peter killed his
uncle?"

"Do you think he intended on waiting to become
earl of Culberry? His family history was one of
killing and stealing to obtain land—why should he
be any different than his ancestors?"

Reena sat back against the bed with a sigh. "I but
innocently stumbled on a devious plot dating back
many years and unknowingly became a pawn. You
had it all planned, every step of the way, my arrival
making it easier for you."

He moved next to her and in a flash scooped her
up to sit on his lap. "You made it more difficult."

Surprised by his unexpected actions but content
in his lap—and curious about his remark—she
asked, "How could I have made it more difficult? I
delivered my mapping services to you at your door.
It was not necessary to seek me out, you had me exactly where you wanted me."

He kissed her. "Aye, but I never expected to fall in
love with you. I never expected to fear when I did
not know of your whereabouts. I did not expect to
desire you with a passion beyond reason or to feel
such joy when with you. You stole my heart, mind
and soul."

She sighed and nibbled at his lips. "I did not steal

them, you gave them to me freely, for love can only be given freely. It cannot be forced or manipulated. It cannot be stolen or imprisoned. It is simply given freely from the heart—"

"Mind and soul," Magnus finished with a kiss.

"Now I have all of you," she said and laid her head on his naked chest.

"And I you." He wrapped his arms around her.

"What now, Magnus?" she asked, hoping there was some way this all would end peaceably, yet knowing that was not possible.

"We wait. I have proof Kilkern land is and always has been Dunhurnal land. It is up to Peter Kilkern to make known this map that he claims will show the land as belonging to him."

"He sounds so sure of his ability to produce this map. Perhaps he will find another mapmaker to accommodate him."

"There is only one skilled enough to produce such a map."

Reena tensed.

"What is wrong?" he asked, holding her more tightly.

"My father is a skilled mapmaker."

"But he does not know the land as well as you, and time is of the essence for Kilkern. He requires someone who knows well Kilkern and Dunhurnal land and can produce a map quickly."

"How does he think to get me when I am so well protected? It seems a foolish thought on his part."

"That is one of the reasons he seeks Brigid."

Reena grew indignant. "He intends to use my friend to get me?"

"He knows well of your friendship with her. Remember, he will count on that friendship to misdirect you. Or when he discovers that we love and will wed, he may use that to force your compliance."

"He would attempt to hurt you?"

"Kilkern will attempt anything, and that is what I want you to remember. He lies and thieves to have his way and cares naught for anyone." He took hold of her chin. "Listen well, Reena. If by chance you should find yourself having to map for Kilkern, you will do so without any thought of betrayal to me."

Reena was about to let him know what she thought of his warning, but he held her chin firm so she could not respond.

"I will not have you suffer for me: in this you will obey me." He released her chin and waited for the only answer he would accept.

She thought she saw fear in his eyes, and the idea that the Legend feared for her touched her heart. "I will do as you say."

His worry faded, replaced by a smile. "Then I say we sleep, for it has been a long day and the night late. And tomorrow will be busy."

She slipped off his lap and rested on her side, Magnus moving up against her, his arm draped over her waist, his hand resting on her breast.

"Why will tomorrow be so busy?" she asked on a yawn.

"Two weddings need to be planned."

"Should we not wait until this is all settled?"

"I will not wait upon Kilkern." He was adamant.

"You are right; he cannot dictate our lives, and besides, the village would love a celebration. But still, it will take a couple of weeks or more so that we may do it properly and the flowers will be in bloom, and there will be time to stitch wedding dresses, and—"

He nuzzled her neck. "Enough, take what time is necessary, and you and Brigid enjoy making plans for the weddings. I will go speak with your father about wedding his daughter. Now sleep and know that I love you."

"And I love you," she said, only to feel his arm grow heavy on her waist and his breath steady in her ear. He was sound asleep.

She smiled and closed her eyes, content in his arms and content that though there were difficulties to face, they would face them together.

A few minutes later she opened her eyes, wide awake, her thoughts much too chaotic for sleep to claim her. Try as she might, she could not stop thinking of the circumstances that had brought them together.

She turned, dislodging Magnus from her, and he turned onto his back to snore lightly. She smiled at the light, easy rhythm, happy to hear it and know he was there safe beside her.

When she realized that sleep would not come quickly, she slipped from beneath the blanket and reached for his shirt on the floor, dropping it over her head as she walked to the hearth. A fire burned brightly, keeping the chill from the room.

She was grateful for the fire's warmth, and she sat on the small bench before the hearth, pulling the large shirt down over her bent knees so that only her toes were visible. She hugged her legs and gave her thoughts free rein.

What troubled her the most was how much Magnus and his mother had suffered and how difficult it must have been for his mother, married to a man that cared naught for her or her son.

His mother had spent much of her time imprisoned in a small room, alone with her thoughts and fears and concerns for her son. She had written to keep her sanity and she had planned, planned her escape. She had written in Latin, a language not all could speak or understand.

Had she done so for a reason?

Reena stood suddenly and looked to where Magnus slept soundly, still snoring lightly. She did not waste a moment; she rushed out of the room, closing the door quietly behind her. She grabbed a torch from one of the many metal wall sconces and hurried up the spiral stairway to the tower room.

Her feet and legs grew chilled, and when she entered the room, the total darkness made her pause momentarily in fear. She shook it off, determined to read the message Magnus's mother had left on the wall. She hurried into the darkness.

The torchlight chased the darkness to the corners, where it lurked in flickering shadows, waiting for her to leave. She entered the secret room without fear of being locked in, for the door had been removed.

Once at the wall she bent down and ran her fingers over the words etched into the stone. It had to have been difficult and painstakingly slow to write in the stone, but then all Magnus's mother had had was time.

She ran her fingers over the writing, stopping here

and there to make certain she understood what the woman had written. She shook her head and read again a passage near the bottom of the wall.

Could she be wrong in her translation?

She read it again and wept.

Chapter 28

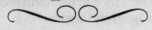

Reena woke alone the next morning. She had felt Magnus stir earlier, his warm fingers gliding over her naked flesh ever so lightly, stirring her senses. He had pulled the blanket down to taste her hard nipple, and while her body had tingled with pleasure, she had just been too tired to respond with interest. She had not fallen asleep until just before dawn, and her body and mind had been exhausted and ready for slumber.

Magnus had whispered, "I love you" in her ear and kissed her cheek before leaving the bed, and she had fallen into a deep slumber, only waking now because of the heavy rain pounding the windows.

The information she had discovered late last night continued to disturb her. What should she do? Did Magnus know what his mother had written on the stone wall? And if he did, should she wait for him to tell her? And what if he did not know? Should she be the one to tell him? The information would prove painful to him, and she did not want to see him suffer any more than he already had. She would bide her time and see if he confided in her what she already knew. If not? She did not wish to think on it, for it would grieve her to deliver such startling news to him.

She hurried to dress, choosing a shift and tunic in shades of green and plaiting her long, dark hair so that it would stay out of her face—not that several silky strands did not fall lose and frame her visage.

Her cheeks held a faint blush, and her blue eyes shone bright as she entered the great hall. Magnus sat in discussion with Thomas at a table near the hearth, Horace at his feet, gnawing on a sizeable bone.

Her heart filled with joy at the sight of him, and she smiled as she hurried to him. He was dressed all in black but the darkness did not disturb her, for she knew that beneath lay a person filled with light and love.

He turned and saw her, and his joyful smile matched hers as he stood, stepped over Horace, and opened his arms to her.

She raced into his embrace, and he lifted her up off the floor and hugged her tightly to him.

"I missed having you beside me at the morning meal," he whispered in her ear before nibbling the lobe.

Her arms circled his neck and she laughed softly, rubbing her cheek to his. "I was lazy this morning."

"You had difficulty sleeping?"

She did not want him to worry or discover her little escapade last night. "Nothing of importance."

"You should have woken me." He lowered his

voice to a mere whisper. "I would have made certain you grew tired enough to sleep."

She laughed and kissed him. "I will remember that and make certain to wake you the next time I have trouble sleeping."

He kissed her before lowering her to the floor.

She turned to Thomas. "Good morning . . ." He did not look happy, and she grew alarmed. "What is wrong?" She looked to Magnus. His smile had faded.

"A message from the king."

Reena braced herself for the news.

"The king orders Brigid to produce the map that Kilkern has accused her of stealing, and if she does not, then the king's men will journey here to question her and determine who speaks the truth."

"They will torture her," Reena said on a whisper.

"They will not touch her," Thomas said, his large fist pounding the table.

Horace jumped, whimpered, and attempted to bury his head under Reena's dress.

She soothed him with a pat on the head and a few soft words, but still he kept his snout under her dress.

"What can we do?" she asked. "And does Brigid know of this?"

"Nay," Thomas said quickly, his voice low. "And she will not know. She is happy planning our wedding, and I will not see her robbed of her happiness. Magnus and I discuss now what can be done."

"Then I join this discussion," Reena said and walked around Magnus to take a seat on the bench next to where he had been sitting. Horace was quick to trail her, bone in mouth. He slipped beneath the table for added protection, lying beside her.

Magnus returned to his seat.

"You have the map to show the king's men," Thomas said. "Will that not satisfy them?"

Magnus shook his head. "Unfortunately not, since Kilkern claims another map exists that disputes my claim."

"And by claiming that Brigid holds the map he puts pressure on us."

"Aye," Magnus agreed. "He knows I cannot prevent the king's men from speaking with Brigid, for then I defy the king and make myself appear guilty. All will think that I had Brigid steal the map for me."

"But you did not know Brigid, you only met her when you arrived at the village," Reena said.

"It is for me to prove otherwise. Until then it is assumed she acted on my behalf."

Thomas rubbed his chin, the look of concern heavy on his face. "Kilkern believes he has you in a chokehold."

"Nay, not me—Reena."

"I don't understand," Thomas said.

"Kilkern believes that I will come to him and willingly agree to map the land in exchange for Brigid's safety," Reena explained, then turned to Magnus. "He wishes to use me against you, and when he discovers we are in love and will wed he will be doubly pleased. Who knows of our intention to wed?"

"Thomas," Magnus said with a nod toward his friend. "I thought that you would prefer to tell Brigid, so I have said nothing, and now I see that it would be better if it remained a secret."

"Aye, our wedding must wait."

"Nay," Magnus said adamantly. "It will not wait. We wed in a few weeks' time. Brigid can be trusted to keep the plans a secret, and I expect this matter to be settled by then."

"I agree she can keep a secret, but what of the present problem? What happens when the king's men arrive?" Her voice was filled with concern. She would not have her friend suffer; she would do whatever was necessary to prevent it, even if it meant mapping for Kilkern.

"I know your thoughts, Reena, and do not even think it," Magnus warned. "No map, no proof that this land is his, and he discredits himself in front of the king when he cannot produce the map. He is shamed before all and stripped of any possessions, even the small piece of land granted the Kilkern name in the wedding agreement."

"Then your revenge is complete?" she asked.

"Aye, for he will have nothing and can do nothing but beg for even a morsel of food."

"As you did?"

"I want him to have a taste of the life he and his father forced on my mother and me. Perhaps in the end I will be merciful and let him die with a full belly."

There was not an ounce of compassion in his words, and Reena realized he must know what she had discovered last night. She shivered at the thought.

"For now our concern is Brigid. Kilkern will more than likely attempt to abduct her in hopes that Reena will barter for her safety. He had also made mention to the king that he would be lenient with

Brigid if she returned the map to him, having her serve her punishment as service in his keep."

Thomas snorted. "Service him is what he means."

"True enough," Magnus agreed, "but his leniency makes him appear a better man to the king. After all, she was a mere tenant on his land. Her punishment could be death for stealing from him."

"But she is your tenant now and under your protection," Reena said.

"But she is accused of stealing from one lord for the sake of another. That makes it another matter—the king's matter, which Kilkern knew it would come down to in the end. I would present my map and wedding agreement to the king and my land would be returned to me. He approaches the king first with false accusations that allow him time to formulate a plan and produce a map that will dispute mine and in the end have Brigid for himself."

"Where is Brigid now?" Reena asked.

"In the kitchen with Maura happily discussing food for our wedding," Thomas said. "Two guards watch over her, though she does not know it. And all guards are on full alert to strangers or strange happenings."

"Kilkern seems self-assured of victory," Reena said with a brief shake of her head. "Almost as if he knows something we don't."

"He will prove himself a fool," Magnus said with assurance.

"What of the king's men?" Reena asked, worried.

"Kilkern will not allow it to go that far, for then Brigid would be useless to him after torture, and she will not be able to confess the location of the map, proving that no map ever existed. He wants us to snap at his bait so that he may hook his catch and feast off the victory." Magnus grew silent a moment. "That will never happen. He will pay, pay as dearly as his father paid."

"For now we wait?" Thomas asked.

"Why?" Reena said before Magnus could answer. "Waiting places Brigid in danger. Why not—"

Magnus turned angry eyes on her. "Do not say what I think you intend to say."

"But I can end this simply by producing a map that in the end will be his downfall."

"How is that?" Thomas asked.

"Do not encourage her," Magnus said, his anger mounting.

Reena ignored him and explained. "Magnus remarked that his father's map was crude, as it should be, since it was done many years ago. I would map as I map today, detailing the land that has changed since Magnus's father possessed it. Once the two maps were shown to the king, he would realize the difference."

Thomas turned to Magnus. "She makes sense."

Magnus tempered his anger. "She would need to spend time alone with Kilkern."

Reena was quick to interrupt. "Kilkern is not interested in me."

"So say you," Magnus said, "but I am not willing to take that chance."

"I agree," Thomas said. "Kilkern cannot be trusted."

"Then we wait for what?" Reena asked, throwing her hands up in frustration.

"We wait for Kilkern to grow as impatient as you," Magnus said with a playful tug of her hair.

"Then he will make a mistake and I will be there to correct him."

"You are certain?" she asked, his confidence truly that of a strong warrior.

"Aye, are you that certain?" Thomas asked. "I will not see her suffer in any way."

"Nothing will happen to Brigid," Magnus said adamantly.

"She needs to know," Reena said. "This concerns her, and she has a right to know and be prepared for whatever may happen."

Magnus turned to Thomas. "I will leave the decision to you. She is your woman, and the choice should be yours."

"I will think on it."

It was over an hour later that Reena finally returned to her room to map. Brigid had been busy with Maura, talking of her wedding celebration, and she had flung herself at Reena when she'd entered the kitchen. Reena had not seen Brigid that happy in a long time, and she thought about what Thomas had said. She realized he was right: Brigid should not be deprived of her happiness.

Reena made no mention of Magnus and her intention to wed; she did not feel it an appropriate time. She had much too much on her mind to spare talk on flowers, wedding finery and such, and she longed for the solitude of her bedchamber and the peace of mind she received from her mapping.

Unfortunately, her mind would not allow her peace. Her thoughts continued to drift to the secret room and the writing on the stone wall. Had she seen it clearly? Had she translated it correctly? But then with Magnus's obvious hatred of the Kilkerns, he must know the truth.

Tormented by uncertainty, Reena decided the only way to settle it was to read the passage again. With torch in hand she climbed the stairs to the tower room and entered. Surprisingly, a fire was burning in the hearth, chasing the chill from the room. Reena shivered anyway, perhaps from the shadow of memories that haunted the place or from her own misgivings about what she had read.

She walked into the cell-sized room and kneeled on the wooden floor, positioning the torch so that the light was sufficient for her to read the troublesome passage. She brushed at the stone to make certain the lettering was clear, and she read the words etched there.

Time and again she read it, and time and again it read the same. She was not wrong; what she had read was correct.

"I like you as you are, but not here in this room."

Magnus so startled her that she fell on her backside as she scrambled to stand. He went quickly to her side, helping her up and taking the torch from her hand to place it in the lone metal sconce in the room.

"Are you all right?" he asked, his arms circling her small waist.

"I did not expect you." She sighed as if in relief.

"And I did not expect to find you here. I thought you to be in your bedchamber, mapping."

"My intentions," she admitted, "but I wished to read more of what your mother wrote."

"I do not speak Latin. Someday you will tell me some of what she wrote, but not now." He leaned down and captured her lips in a heartwarming kiss. "Now I want to make love to you. I have wanted to make love to you since this morning, when I woke to feel you warm and soft beside me, but you had little interest in loving."

"Not true." She moved her body against his, her need for him turning to a pleasurable ache. "You stirred my passion, but my body and mind wanted nothing more than to sleep."

Magnus enjoyed the feel of her against him, his thoughts on the lovemaking they would soon share. "I promise you will have no trouble sleeping tonight."

Lost in desire, she gave no thought to her response. "Good, then tonight I remain in bed."

He was about to kiss her senseless when he stopped and asked, "Remain in bed? You left our bed last night?"

Her passion cooled instantly when she realized her mistake, and she silently chastised herself for being so foolish.

When she did not answer, Magnus asked, "Where did you go?"

"A brief walk in the keep to clear my mind," she said, not looking directly at him.

He raised her chin with the tip of his finger. "That is no answer, and I do not intend to repeat the question. I want no secrets between us, Reena. I want us to trust enough to share all—after all, you did trust me enough to fall from a tree into my arms."

She did trust him, and she knew that she would

not be sharing something with him that he did not already know.

"I came up here to this room to read more of your mother's writings. It must have torn at your heart when you learned that it was Robert Kilkern who shot the arrow that pierced your father's heart."

Chapter 29

"What did you say?" Magnus asked, his dark eyes narrowed, his nostrils flared. His deep voice was much too calm and in control.

Reena held her breath for a moment, her mistake all too obvious: *he had not known.* "I am sorry," was all she could think to say, feeling the pain that twisted at his heart.

He grabbed her arm and shoved her toward the wall. "Read me the passage."

"Magnus—"

"Read it to me now," he demanded through gritted teeth.

"I must kneel to read it," she said, attempting to free herself.

He would not let her go: he kept a firm grip on her and lowered her to the floor so that she may read it to him, and Reena for a moment felt the fear of being shackled and imprisoned. She shook the disturbing thought off, reminding herself it was Magnus, the

317

man who loved her, who had hold of her. He would never hurt her.

"Read it," he demanded once more.

She knew that what she read would only bring him more pain, but she had no choice. "Your mother writes sparsely, since it was extremely difficult to etch in stone."

He nodded. "Read it as she wrote it."

She read with a tremble on her lips. "My heart hurts. Discovered Robert killed my beloved Brian. Land. Wants land."

Dead silence followed, Magnus's breathing grew heavy. He bared his teeth, and then he released a cry of torment that tore at the soul. When he finished, he reached down to yank Reena up against him.

His emotions warred like a raging storm in his dark eyes and across his handsome face. He looked torn as to what to do, for his emotions were at the extreme. He either loved or hated, and right now Reena was in his arms.

He captured her mouth with a kiss that left no room for her to respond, and his hands held her firm.

She understood his pain and his need, but he left no room for her to comfort him; he took and took like a man who ached to lose himself in someone he trusted and knew loved him and could take him to a place where pain and hurt did not exist.

He rushed her up against the stone wall, her feet unable to touch the floor, and he kissed her with a frightening need. His kiss turned more demanding than she thought possible, and after a few moments she found herself unable to breathe.

She tried to tell him, but he would not free her

lips. It was as if he needed her breath to survive, the very essence of her soul to help ease his anguish.

She grasped his arm and dug her fingers into his flesh as hard as she could, his taut muscles making it difficult to penetrate the skin, and she wrenched and pulled her mouth from his until finally she was free.

"I can . . . not . . . breathe," she said, pushing at his chest.

He tore away from her and she fell to the ground, her breath labored and her heart beating madly. She placed a hand to her chest, feeling as though her heart was ready to burst.

He reached down in haste, and she instinctively drew back away from him, needing a chance to breathe.

He bent down beside her, his clenched hands remaining at his sides. "I will not hurt you."

Tears pooled in her eyes. She hesitated, and then she reached out to him.

He scooped her up into his arms and held her tight as he walked with strong strides out of the confining room.

She was relieved and grateful that they left the tower room, and she was not surprised or upset when he took her to his bedchamber. He shut the door behind them with a shove of his boot and sat on the end of the bed with her in his lap, cradling her in his strong arms.

He touched her face so gently that it almost seemed he thought she would break. "You are pale; are you all right?" Before she could answer, he rested his forehead to hers. "Good God, Ree, I am so sorry; can you ever forgive me?"

Her heart continued to pound madly in her chest,

but she looked into his dark eyes. His anger was gone, replaced by despair, and she suddenly realized he needed her concern, her gentleness and, most of all, her love.

She placed a tender hand to his face. "There is nothing to forgive. You suffered a hurt so shocking—"

He placed a finger to her lips. "I had no right, no matter what I suffered I had no right to abuse you."

She took hold of his hand and kissed his palm. "Your anger took hold."

"A fatal mistake to any man or warrior. Sound reason is a better weapon."

"Pain, hurt and revenge blind many, and in the end it is the innocent ones who suffer the most."

He closed his eyes a moment and Reena thought that he battled tears, but when he opened them not a tear shone in his eyes. He had won the battle—or had he?

"My mother was an innocent. I thought she had endured misery beyond reason, but this . . ." He shook his head. "I do not know how she retained her sanity."

"She had you to protect, the son of the man she loved with all her heart and always would."

He remained silent, heavy in thought, and Reena rested a gentle hand on his shoulder, letting him know she was there and would remain by his side always.

"My mother taught me about love. She spoke about how love would find me when I least expected it, for she insisted love was unpredictable and could strike at the strangest times. She told me not to have any expectations but to accept the love that was sent to me and cherish it and never ever do it harm."

Thoughts of the anguish and pain his mother had endured choked the breath from her, and she sighed, hoping to ease her troubled emotions. To think that his mother had been forced to be intimate with the man who had killed her loving husband was incomprehensible. Her courage to endure such torture was remarkable, and to survive it all and encourage her son to love was even more remarkable.

"Your mother is a special woman, strong and courageous, and she taught you well of love, for I know you would never harm me."

Anguish surfaced in his dark eyes, and she knew he regretted his actions and that no apology would ease his regret. But she would not have him suffer, for he had suffered enough, now it was time for him to love.

"I—"

Reena pressed a firm finger to his lips. "Love you with my whole heart and soul. And did I ever tell you how handsome I think you are?" She rubbed her nose to his. "And how I love when you kiss me. Nibbles, I especially love nibbles, and touches, the slow lazy kind." She pretended to shiver. "Mmm, you make me tingle."

She faintly traced his lips as they slowly spread in a smile. "I am so very glad I found you to love."

"It is I who am grateful to have found you," he said and nibbled the tip of her finger.

"I think it is love that found us."

"And I intend to cherish that love and you forever and all eternity."

She rushed a kiss across his lips, leaving him aching for more, then nibbled at his ear and whispered, "I ache for the feel of you." She let her hand slowly travel down his chest to settle intimately over him. She squeezed ever so lightly, then slightly harder, lighter again, then harder until he enlarged in her hand. She laughed softly in his ear. "You ache for me too."

"You play with fire, Ree."

"That is good," she said with a nibble at his ear. "I like when you are *heated*."

His reaction was so swift that she did not realize what he intended until she was flat on her back on the bed, he looming over her.

"Now to heat you to a fiery blaze."

He had her naked in seconds, his own garments following with the same speed. And then he touched her slow and easy, running his fingers over every inch of her naked flesh and setting her soul on fire.

It was a torturous pleasure she never wanted to end.

His lips followed the same path in the same lazy manner, driving her completely insane with the want of him.

"Now," she insisted. "I must have you now." Her hands clung to his shoulders, her fingers digging into his hard flesh.

"Not yet." He moved down over her to taste her sweetness.

She grabbed at the covers on the bed, bunching them in her hands as her cries of pleasure radiated throughout the room. Finally she pleaded with him to satisfy her ache. "Please, Magnus, I want to feel you inside me."

He obliged her, his own desire to the point of eruption. He moved over her, slipped his arms beneath her back, and held her close as he entered her slow and easy.

Their passion took over and they held on to each other while the fiery inferno grew hotter and hotter and hotter and erupted in a blaze of blinding fury.

Their cries of pleasure swirled in the air and settled down around them in a breathless silence. They lay quietly clinging to each other, their bodies wet with the aftermath of lovemaking while the last ripples of pleasure faded away.

And as was their way, they both at the exact same moment whispered, "I love you."

They were dressed and looking over sketches of maps Reena had made of Dunhurnal land when a sharp knock sounded at the door.

"Enter," Magnus called out.

Thomas walked in. "A messenger from Peter Kilkern waits for you in the great hall."

"He is alone?" Magnus asked.

"No one was seen traveling with him, nor has anyone been seen since his arrival. It seems he carries nothing but a message."

"Where is Brigid?" Reena asked.

"With the weavers discussing a bridal veil." His words could not help but bring a smile to his face regardless of present circumstances.

Magnus grinned and walked over to him to slap him on the back. "Are you ready to be a husband?"

Thomas nodded vigorously. "Aye, and a good husband I will be to Brigid."

"Then let us go settle this thorn in our sides before the wedding so the celebration may be one of pure joy."

Reena smiled at the thought, for she and Magnus would wed the same day as Brigid and Thomas if all went well. She hurried to trail after them.

Magnus stopped outside the bedchamber. "Why do you not join Brigid and discuss your own bridal veil?"

Reena planted her hands on her hips. "You cannot get rid of me that easily, and besides, Brigid does not yet know of our plans to wed."

"Then this is a perfect time to tell her," Magnus urged.

She remained firm in her intentions to join them. "I want to know what goes on."

"I will tell you."

"I prefer to hear for myself."

Magnus stepped in front of Reena. "I am sorry, but I must insist. It would appear strange for my mapmaker to stand beside me while a message is delivered."

Thomas added his opinion. "He is right and we waste time."

Reena nodded, knowing there was no use in arguing. She turned to walk the opposite way.

"I will tell you all later," Magnus said. Reena simply waved as she kept walking.

The two men hurried off, their footsteps heavy on the wooden stairs. Reena turned in a flash and rushed after them, though she kept a safe distance behind so they would not see or hear her approach.

She crept slowly down the stairs, and once at the bottom she slipped around the stone wall that led to the great hall. Once there, she blended with the shadows along the wall and concealed herself in the dark corner of the hall where she could hear yet not be seen.

She thought of the Dark One and how he used the shadows and darkness to his advantage. She felt the comfort of the dark ease around her to conceal and protect her, and she felt safe.

The messenger bowed his head in respect when Magnus appeared before him, after he shivered. She could not say exactly how Magnus intimidated, but he did. He was tall and broad, but there were men taller and broader than he. Perhaps it was his confident strides or the set of his squared shoulders drawn back in pride, or it could have been his clothes, black as the blackest night, or his dark eyes that appeared to know all. Whatever it was about him, he was feared and regarded with respect, a respect he had earned at a costly price.

"You have a message from Kilkern?"

"I have a message from the earl of Culberry," the man corrected with a tremble.

"I will hear it," Magnus said and folded his arms over his chest to lean back against the edge of the table on the dais, his relaxed stance one of pure insolence, as if the message afforded him little interest.

The messenger appeared average in height but thick in muscle and looked as if he could best many in a fight, yet the Legend gave him cause to mind his tongue and manner.

Still, he held his head high when he spoke. "The earl of Culberry wishes to meet with you."

Reena furrowed her brow. Whatever good would a meeting between the two men accomplish?

Magnus gave no hasty reply; he waited as if giving thought to the suggestion. "Did Kilkern suggest a place for this meeting?"

The man stood straight. "He invites you to his home."

Reena thought to laugh. That would be like having the prey walk into the hunter's trap.

"When does he suggest this meeting take place?"

"Tomorrow."

Kilkern did not think Magnus foolish enough to walk into his keep as if in surrender. Why then the invitation? What did he have planned? Magnus would not be fool enough to accept, or would he force Kilkern's hand by placing himself in danger?

Reena grew concerned and placed a hand to her nervous stomach. A sudden thought that she could be with child filled her heart with joy and fear. Joy that they would be a family; she, Magnus and their child. Fear that Kilkern would kill him and she would be alone with their child—or completely alone, as Brigid had been when her husband had died. Reena felt an enormous loss for her friend, realizing now more than ever the hurt she had suffered.

She could not lose Magnus; she would not. She would do everything she could to keep him safe and protect him as he did her, even though he would protest. She would do what was necessary.

Magnus unfolded his arms and walked toward the man. The man retreated several steps before Magnus neared.

"What if I do not agree to his offer?"

The man's voice trembled. "Then I am to deliver another message."

"Which is?" Magnus demanded.

The man hesitated, swallowed as if gathering courage, then spoke. "I am to tell you that the earl of Culberry knows you for the coward you are; you being much like your own father."

At that moment Reena wished to race at the man and pound him with her fists, which she kept tight at her sides, but he was only a messenger, a messenger who presently was sweating profusely.

Magnus remained calm, his voice deep and his speech articulate. "Tell Kilkern I accept his invitation."

The man looked relieved.

"And—"

The man's eyes widened and a drop of sweat hung from his brow over his eye.

Magnus took several steps toward the trembling man. "Tell him that a man who knows no honor dies in shame—like his father."

The man's eyes widened in fear, and any fool could see that he realized the message he delivered to his lord would earn his wrath. He gave a quick nod, turned, and fled the great hall.

Magnus exchanged words with Thomas, their voices low and not reaching Reena's ears. They parted, and Magnus walked toward the staircase. She intended to stay where she was until he passed by. Once he was far enough up the stairs, she would take hasty steps to her room, explaining that she'd decided to map instead of discussing bridal veils.

She kept her breathing low and braced herself

against the stone wall, the darkness completely swallowing her. No one would know that she was there. She was safe in the recesses of the dark.

Magnus passed by, and she could not help but smile. She waited, giving him time to climb the stairs, and when she was sure that all was safe, she walked out of the shadows and around the stone wall to race up the stairs.

Her foot never hit the step; Magnus stepped out of the shadows in the corner by the staircase and grabbed her around the waist.

She cried out in shock, then punched his arm—not that he felt her meager attempt at revenge. "You frightened me."

"You should not have hidden in the shadows."

"I wanted to hear for myself."

"You do not trust me to tell you all?" he asked, lowering her to the ground but keeping firm hands on her small waist.

"Nay," she said softly. "I trust you, but . . ." She turned her head from him.

"Reena," he said gently and forced her to look at him. "Tell me."

The traitorous tears she feared would spill started, and she could not fight them.

He wiped them away one by one. "Tell me, Reena."

She answered with reluctance. "I had to listen for myself and hear so that I could protect you. I could not bear to lose you."

Magnus leaned down and kissed her with a tenderness that made her spill more tears. "You will not lose me."

"Aye, I will not," she said adamantly. "I will be by your side when you visit with Kilkern."

Her tears were as stubborn as she was, and he wiped them away, only to have more follow. "You will not be with me." He held up his hand before she could argue. "You will not go with me, and you will not hide and travel along in secret or follow in secret."

"I will not remain behind," she said, as if threatening.

He raised a brow. "How foolish would it be to take you with me when you are the very person who could help him achieve his goal?"

"How foolish of you to go to him when you know it is a trap?"

"Do you think me a fool?"

"Nay—" She stopped and stared at him. "You have a plan."

He nodded.

Excitement stirred in her. "You will tell me of this plan?"

"For your own safety, it is better you do not know."

Her excitement quickly deflated, replaced by annoyance. "Should I not have a choice in this matter, since it is me he seeks?"

"Nay, this is between Kilkern and me, and I will have no interference," he warned in a sharp tone.

Reena would not concede. "You do as you must and I will do what I must."

"Reena," he warned again, his dark eyes swirling with a mist of anger that would soon erupt if she was not careful.

"This argument needs to wait for another time," said the familiar harsh voice of the Dark One from the shadows. "There is someone who needs your immediate help."

Chapter 30

The three retired to the solar, the Dark One finding his own passage there while Reena and Magnus climbed the stairs. Once inside, the door was latched, more candles lit, and questions asked.

Magnus looked to the darkest recesses of the room.

"I am here," the deep voice confirmed.

"Then tell me what this is about. Who needs my immediate attention?"

"Mary."

"What of Mary?" Magnus asked, his body tense, his eyes focused on the dark, shadowed corner.

Reena walked to stand closer to Magnus, at a distance where she could at least reach her hand out to him if need be.

"I will tell you all that I know." His deep voice lost some of its harshness as he spoke. "I met with a man who told me that he was a friend of Mary's family and that she is in immediate danger. She has been safely hidden for over ten years due to the generosity of her benefactor, but those who wish her harm are close to discovering her whereabouts.

"He does not know her location, only that there are three possible places the woman could be hiding, and it is imperative that she be found before it is too late."

"When I sought a safe shelter for Mary, I purposely misdirected my path so that none would be able to find her," Magnus said.

"I found Mary's true location."

Reena's hand went out to Magnus, and he took firm hold of it as soon as he felt the brush of her skin against his.

"And what did you do with this information?"

"I kept it to myself until I could discover if this man spoke truthfully to me or if he himself meant the woman harm."

"He confided the truth to you without any persuasion?"

"He needed no persuasion. He was visibly upset when I reported my findings to him and he confessed that two men were after Mary, one protected and the other was out to do her harm. Knowing both men's reputations, he did not feel that either could be trusted, so he sought my help. He asked that I take Mary to a safe place until he could determine her true benefactor and seek his help."

"And you returned here because I am one of the men whose name was mentioned."

"Aye, you were one of the two."

"And the other?" Magnus asked.

"Decimus."

Reena felt Magnus tense, and she tightened her grip on his hand.

"I fear he will find her soon, which is the reason I returned here. You have much that concerns you now and it would not be wise for you to leave here. I can see to this matter for you and take Mary somewhere where she will be safe and where no one will find her."

"Decimus will make her suffer if he finds her."

"Then I will make certain he does not find her."

"You should waste not a moment," Reena said. "If you fear for her safety, then go now. See that she is kept well."

"Tell her that her father sent you to her," Magnus said. "When I first hid her away I explained that she must stay where she was until I came for her. And if I could not come myself then I would send someone and he would say, 'Your father sent me to you.' Say those words or she will go nowhere with you."

"I will do as you say and you, my friend, take care. Kilkern will stop at nothing to take your land."

His warning brought a smile to Magnus's face. "He is a fool who will meet a foolish end."

"Take care, mapmaker, and I will send word when Mary is safe."

"Godspeed," Magnus said and heard the door close, though he never heard the latch being lifted.

Magnus turned to Reena and took her into his arms, holding her to him while his hands stroked her back. She was safe here with him and he would make certain she remained safe. He would see to Kilkern on his own terms and settle a long-owed debt when he took Kilkern's life. Then it would be done, and then he and Reena would wed and he would worry no more on the Kilkerns.

For now he would trust the Dark One to protect Mary and know that she was in safe hands. But he would not wait long to hear from the Dark One. Mary was his responsibility: he had given his word to his teacher to protect her, and his honor would allow him to do nothing less than to protect her with his life.

Reena rested her head on his chest. "Who is Decimus?"

"You do not want to know."

"Is it safer that I do not know?"

Magnus took her by the shoulders and held her away from him. "It annoys you that I wish to protect you?"

"It annoys me that you do not let me help protect you."

Magnus almost grinned, but a warning look from her blue eyes, which looked ready to storm, brought his grin to a sudden halt.

"You think to have your vengeance at any cost, you have planned for it, counted on it, and now the time is here and you can almost taste the victory. But you failed to realize one thing."

Magnus waited in silence, curious as to what she thought he failed to consider.

"You failed to realize that falling in love changes everything. Now there is a reason for concern, for there is a person who loves you with all her heart and worries over your safety, praying every day that you remain well and alive, praying that she will share a long life with you. And when that is considered, then vengeance can be more costly than you thought possible and victory bitter in its futility."

She pushed his hands off her and took a step closer. "I love you and will do whatever is necessary not to lose you, so do not tell me that keeping me ignorant to your plans is better for my safety, for there is no safety in ignorance."

With a brief shake of his head and a slow smile surfacing, Magnus stared at the strong-willed woman he loved with an intensity that sometimes frightened him. "You are a rare woman."

"Nay, I but speak my mind more often than most women."

"And why do you think that is?" he asked, wanting to understand what made her different and thus all the more appealing to him.

She rested a hand over his heart and he covered her hand with his, sending a warmth of emotions racing through them.

After a brief moment of considering his question, Reena answered. "I think it is because I thought little of wedding and pleasing a man. I thought more about myself and what I wished to do, wished to accomplish, so therefore I could speak my mind without thought of offending a possible husband. I lived more for myself."

"How can you say that when you placed yourself in danger, traveling to my land for the sake of all the tenants?"

"That was for the good of the whole, not one person. I had the foresight to see that there was a way that could possibly rectify a horrible situation. It would have been wrong of me not to at least attempt to try." She shrugged. "Besides, I wished a bit of my own adventure. My mapping trips had been solely with my father, and my trip to your land was solely on my own, the beginning of my own mapping quests."

"And that is the life you envisioned for yourself? A dangerous one?"

"Not if I mapped for the Legend." She was fast to correct with a smile.

"So you came to find me *not only* for me to help your village but also to help free you to follow your dream?"

Her smile turned soft and she nodded. "And I found what I never expected or sought."

"Love," he said and leaned down to brush his lips across her moist ones. "That will never confine."

"Not so," she whispered before she tasted his lips. "You confine me when you do not share your plans."

"Try to understand, Reena," he said as though he pleaded with her. "I watched helpless as Robert Kilkern abused my mother and could do nothing. I will not have the same happen to you. If by chance I should suffer at Kilkern's hands, then it is me who suffers—"

"Nay," she said adamantly, tears rushing to fill her eyes as she pulled away from him. "I suffer along with you."

She silenced any opposition with a gentle finger to his lips. "Aye, for that is love. I feel what you feel. I fear what you fear. I ache when you ache. I suffer when you suffer. Love will have it no other way, for we are part of each other, you and I. So do not tell me I will not feel your pain if you are made to suffer, for I know you will feel mine, therefore it remains for us both to protect, for in protecting one, we protect the other."

He eased her finger away from his lips and held

her hand in his. "I understand what you try to say to me, but my way is to protect what is mine—"

"You are mine, can I not protect you?" She sounded impatient and a bit fearful.

Magnus kept his patience. "Reena, listen to what you say. How can you ever protect me?"

She stepped away from him and pounded her fisted hand lightly to her chest. "By making me aware of everything that goes on, by trusting me, by loving me."

"I do trust you and love you, but I believe that there are things you should not know for your own safety, and that is the way it must be. You must understand that and accept it."

She stared at him and refused to shed the tears that gathered like a raging storm in her eyes. She could not speak, the lump in her throat constricting her voice, her stomach growing upset. She shook her head, choked back her tears, and fled the room as if being chased.

Magnus did not try to stop her; when she calmed down she would come to understand his decision and accept it. He thought on the wisdom of her words and realized how deeply she loved him, and he hoped that when she thought on *his* words she would realize how deeply *he* loved her.

Her tears blurring her vision, Reena could barely see the steps down which she fled. She was grateful when she entered her room and latched the door behind her. She flung herself on the bed and let herself cry long and hard, hoping the tears would ease her aching heart.

She did not hear the first tap on the door. The second was more a knock, and she sniffled, coughed and wiped away the last remnant of tears before answering it. Her hand was on the latch before she realized it could be Magnus, and at the moment she did not wish to speak with him, especially after crying. She did not care if her eyes were swollen from her torrent of tears—she cared that he would know that their disagreement upset her terribly.

"Who is there?" she asked, keeping her voice as clear and calm as possible.

"Brigid. Let me in."

Reena had never heard Brigid demand, and she immediately opened the door to her friend and stepped back, turning away toward the fireplace so that Brigid could not see her red-rimmed eyes.

"What is wrong?" The demand remained in Brigid's tone. "Magnus entered the great hall only moments ago more temperamental than I have ever seen him, snapping and yelling at his men. He even became annoyed with Thomas, and I have never known him to do that."

Reena turned with a flourish, a faint smile on her tear-stained face. "He was upset?"

Brigid rushed to her friend's side. "You have been crying. What is wrong?"

More tears gathered in Reena's eyes and she wiped at them with annoyance. "I am in love and about to wed."

"And this causes tears?" Brigid shook her head. "You must explain, for I am confused, though happy." She scratched her head. "Should I be happy for you?"

"Aye, you may be happy, but you can tell no one

of the wedding. I am certain that all in the keep and village will know soon enough, but the wedding must remain a secret."

Brigid reached out and hugged her friend. "I am happy for you and I will tell no one of the plans for you and Magnus to wed, but can you tell me why?"

Reena sat in one of the two chairs near the hearth, and Brigid took the other, ready to listen.

Reena detailed the events that had led to the decision to keep their wedding a secret, and by the time she finished, Brigid was nodding her approval.

"A wise decision for sure. Kilkern would see that he used such information to his advantage."

"True enough, that was why I thought to postpone the wedding, but Magnus insists that we wed along with you and Thomas."

Brigid pressed a hand to her chest. "Reena, it would be wonderful to share a wedding day with you and Magnus. Think of the celebration. And Thomas and I can wait until things settle down and this matter is seen to."

"Magnus is certain this matter will be resolved shortly and that there is no reason to delay wedding plans."

"You think otherwise?"

Reena jumped out of the chair and began pacing in front of the hearth. "He places himself in danger by going to Kilkern." She bit at her bottom lip, knowing she could not reveal all she knew to Brigid: she had given her word. "He will be sure to imprison Magnus or, worse, kill him."

"Magnus is the Legend. Kilkern would be a fool to think that he could capture the Legend," Brigid said.

Reena stopped pacing and stared down at the

flames. No one understood that Kilkern did not see Magnus as the Legend but as his half brother who was depriving him of land he felt rightfully belonged to him. This was about brother against brother and revenge, the worst kind of battle, for neither would settle in agreement. Blood would certainly be spilled.

"I love him," Reena said softly.

Brigid stood and went to her friend's side, placing a gentle hand on her shoulder. "I understand."

Reena turned and her tears started once again, but this time they fell for Brigid. "I suffered along with you when John died, but until now ... until I have loved myself, I never truly understood how deep your pain and suffering was, and I am so terribly sorry for you."

The two women hugged tightly before parting and wiping their tears away.

"I am lucky to have found love again and with such a kind and caring man. Thomas means the world to me and I love him dearly, but if I had the chance to go back to the day Kilkern attacked John I would have responded differently. I instinctively knew something was amiss and that John should have remained silent. I would have been more brave and stepped forward to silence my husband so that he did not have to lose his life so senselessly." Brigid paused and fought back her tears.

Reena had to wipe at her own tears.

"I tell you this, Reena, for I understand your plight, and while I love you as a sister and do not wish to see any harm come to you, I would warn you to do whatever is necessary to protect the man you love. Death comes to us all, but unnecessary death, senseless death, is difficult to accept and understand. There was no reason for John to die. He died simply because a powerful and greedy man grew angry. And that man will kill again if he thinks it serves his purpose.

"After John died I blamed myself for not defending him and not dying along with him—"

"Nonsense," Reena said, fast to correct her friend. "There was nothing you could do, and dying along with John would—"

"Would be a senseless death." Brigid nodded. "It took me a while to understand that my living gave more meaning to John's death. Falling in love with Thomas made me realize how important it was to live my life, to love again, to wed and have children. John's love, my loving John, allowed me to love again. And I finally feel alive once more. But if you asked me if I had the chance to go back and change that fateful day, then I would tell you aye, most loudly. I would defend my husband at all costs."

Brigid reached out and took hold of Reena's arm. "So I tell you, Reena, defend the man you love at all costs and let no one stop you."

Chapter 31

Reena needed to clear her mind after Brigid left her bedchamber. She needed to think on what to do. What choices did she have in this matter? Was there anything she could do to keep Magnus safe? Or how could she make him see reason and inform her of his plans, at least easing her mind and heart?

He probably felt that if she did know of his plans it would only cause her more worry. If that was so, then his plans were definitely dangerous and perhaps foolhardy. Either way, she wanted to know.

She decided to map in order to clear her mind completely. Her jumbled thoughts did her no good, and until she could settle them and think more rationally, she would get nowhere. So with candles lit across her drawing table and quill in hand, she proceeded to finish the map of the dungeons. There was not much left to complete: she had worked sporadically on it, the map intriguing her, as each time she returned to it her memory would recall another detail for her to add.

She was meticulous in her details and in attempting measurement. She wanted to draw the dimensions of the rooms and his land on a smaller scale yet provide adequate knowledge for him to understand the depth and width—not an easy task, but one she continued to work on.

After an hour she stopped and rubbed the back of her neck, the painful ache she suffered from bending over the table annoying her.

"You should stop and rest more often."

Reena was not startled by Magnus's presence. She'd lost all track of time, and she would hear nothing, not even the latch on the door being lifted, when she was deep in her mapping. And she had been expecting him—or at least she had hoped he would come to her.

"I needed to map."

Magnus had come to realize that Reena's work actually soothed her and she would often seek it out if feeling troubled or concerned. When he had entered quietly after receiving no response to his knock he had seen that she was concentrating deeply on her work and he had not wanted to disturb her. But as she needed to map to ease her upset, he needed to see her, if it was only to watch her work to ease his own concerns.

"I needed to see you," he admitted to his own surprise.

Reena walked around the desk toward him, and Magnus met her as she rounded the edge of the bed.

"I do not wish to argue," he said, his hands remaining at his sides though he ached to hug her tightly and to taste her sweet, warm lips. He would know she wished the same before he kissed or touched her. He wanted no anger between them when they loved, and he wished to love her, he ached to love her.

"Nor I," she agreed, her hands itching to touch him, taste him and snuggle in his warmth.

"I do not like when we disagree. We often think much alike you and I," he said, taking a step closer.

"Aye, we do." She took a step that caused them to almost touch.

"I want to love you, Ree."

She collapsed in his waiting arms, which he wrapped tightly around her. "And I want to love you, Magnus."

"Then there is no longer any need for words," he said and claimed her mouth with his in a kiss that went on and on and on as their hands frantically tugged and pulled at each other's garments.

Their mouths only left each other's long enough to rid themselves of their clothing. Once naked, they fell on the bed together, eager to touch and taste. And touch and taste they did, each one not seeming to get enough of the other.

It continued until Magnus finally slipped over Reena, threading his fingers with hers and drawing her arms up above her head.

"I am going to love you hard and long and until you beg me to stop."

Her soft laughter drifted up and around him. "You will be the first to surrender." She ground her hips against his and moaned with the hard feel of him against her.

He nipped at her lips. "We shall see who wins this."

She laughed and wiggled against him. "There can be no loss in this."

He nuzzled her neck. "Then on to victory."

He settled himself inside her and kept his promise, loving her hard and long. In the end she begged, and he surrendered at the exact same moment, their united cries of pleasure filling the room and drifting down around them to wrap them in a gentle glow of contentment.

They snuggled in each other's arms, neither making mention of their earlier debate, both wanting to linger in the satisfying aftermath of their lovemaking.

"You will map more before the evening meal?"

Her head rested on his shoulder, her hand on his chest and her leg across his leg, and it felt good being there and knowing they loved. "Aye, I wish to finish the dungeon before I eat. It is almost detailed, I have but one cell left and it is done. And you?"

"I have things to discuss with Thomas."

She instinctively knew what things he would discuss, but she said nothing. He had made a choice and now she would make hers.

They dressed and hugged tightly.

"I love you, Ree, and I always will, no matter what happens."

She squeezed him to her as best she could. Her strength was meager compared to his, but strength came in different ways. "And I love you and always will, always my heart will belong to you."

He smiled and kissed her. "Thank you, I needed badly to hear you pledge your heart to me." He reluctantly stepped away from her, holding her hand until finally he was too far away to keep hold of it. "I look forward to the evening meal together, so go finish your work."

"I will see you in the great hall later."

He closed the door on her smile, looking forward to the evening ahead.

Reena returned to the map, working on the last cell in the dungeon. She was adding the two metal rings in the stone wall when she stopped and stared at what she had just drawn.

What were two metal rings doing in the wall, and at such odd angles? She had not given it thought when she had first seen them in the cell, though she had thought it odd that one cell contained two metal rings when the others did not. Of course the rings could have fallen out of the walls in the other cells.

She shook her head, doubting the possibility. The rings were held by metal stakes driven into the stone wall. They were there permanently; therefore, the other cells never contained them.

They also were set at odd angles to chain someone to the wall. She tilted her head to the left, then to the right, then back and forth she went, raising her hands as if grasping the metal rings until . . .

Her eyes widened and she jumped off the chair and ran out of the room.

Neither Magnus nor Thomas was in the great hall. She thought to see if Brigid would join her, then she realized her friend feared the dark too much to investigate the dungeon. She would, however, let Brigid know of her whereabouts so Magnus would not worry if she should be late for supper.

She found Brigid in the cook room, Horace sitting

right beside her as she busily stirred a batter in a wooden bowl.

"You what?" Brigid said so loudly that all in the room turned to stare.

Reena kept her voice low. "I am going down to the dungeons to take a look at one of the cells. I think I may have discovered something, and I wish to see if I am right."

"You are crazy."

"Nay, I tell you of where I go to be safe and ease Magnus's concern."

Brigid put the bowl down on the table, Horace's eyes following its descent. "Magnus will be angry."

"It is safe in the keep, what could happen to me?"

"I do not know, but the dungeons do not sound like a place you should go to alone. Why not wait for Magnus to return? He went with Thomas to Daniel the bowman's cottage. They should return shortly."

"I do not want to wait, I must see this for myself now, to see if what I believe is true." Reena headed to the door. "Tell Magnus where I am as soon as he returns."

"At once I shall tell him, and don't be surprised if he follows you."

"That will be good—then I can show him my discovery." She gave a wave and was off in a hurry.

"I do not like this, Horace," Brigid said to the dog, whose eyes remained fixed on the bowl. "I do not like it at all."

Reena grabbed a torch from the metal sconce on the wall before descending the stairs down into the dungeon. Her steps slowed as the damp darkness reached up to grab at her, and she had to drive back her fear to proceed. While the flame of the torch chased away the darkness in front of her, it but circled and crept up to follow behind her.

It seemed that there had been more light when Magnus had brought her here, but he was much taller than she, and he had carried the torch high, casting more light around them. She remembered several torches being lit along the wall where the cells were located, but none were lit now. Then she recalled how Magnus had told her that he had had them lighted for their visit to the dungeon so that she would have sufficient light for her work.

She had not taken the thick darkness into consideration when she had begun her decent down into the dungeon, but she was here now and would not turn back. Besides, she was much too excited to abandon her investigation.

She made her way along the familiar path, having trailed it many times in her mind while mapping it. She stopped suddenly, thinking she heard a noise, and she shivered at the thought that rats could be her only companions in this dismal, dark place.

The thought set her into action, moving more hastily to the cell in question so that she could ascertain whether her idea held any merit or she was crazy, as Brigid had suggested. Either way, she would have her answer.

She entered the cell and held the torch high, the light chasing the darkness to impatiently hover in wait in the corners. She spotted the metal rings and hurried over to the wall. With no place to put the torch inside the cell, Reena had to hold on to it, making her examination of the rings more difficult. She needed two hands.

She tugged at the one ring but nothing happened; she knew it would take two hands to accomplish anything. The lack of mortar around the stones led her to believe she was correct in her thought about the rings, but she needed to prove it to herself.

Another noise had her turning her head, but all she saw was darkness, and she wished Magnus were here with her, not only to help but also to comfort. She felt safe with him near, but then she was in his keep and safe from harm, so there was nothing to fear.

She returned her attention to the metal rings in order to determine her best course of action. She realized she would get nowhere on her own: she needed Magnus's help, she needed his strength. It was best she return to the hall and wait for him.

That was when she heard footsteps and sighed with relief—Magnus was here and would help her.

"Look what I have found," she said, her smile wide as she turned, holding the torch high. Her smile vanished in an instant when her eyes set upon Peter Kilkern.

"You are intelligent for a woman."

She ignored his insult and focused on her situation. Kilkern had her trapped; there was no chance of escape. He blocked the entrance to the cell, and he most certainly had not come here alone. Her heart began to beat faster, and she forced her fear to remain hidden. She would not let Kilkern think her frightened. Her only chance was to survive until Magnus arrived to rescue her. He would rescue her, she had no doubt.

"Your father built the escape route from this cell, did he not?"

Kilkern was a fair-sized man and impeccable in his dress, but now he stood before her dirt-smeared and disheveled from crawling through the secret escape passage in order to enter the keep.

"How did you learn of it?" Kilkern asked, sounding impressed. "No one but my father or I knew of its existence. He had it built in case he required a hasty escape or if he should ever have found himself imprisoned in his own cell. He never thought that one day it would be used to gain entrance to the keep."

She shrugged as if it had taken nothing on her part to discover the secret passageway. She attempted to hold her tongue and not remind him that his father had met his end in the torture chamber only a few feet away from the passage he had built to help him escape.

"The metal rings are fashioned in a way to grasp hold and pull, opening the escape route, and I would imagine your father had metal rings placed on the opposite side to help in replacing the outside wall so no one would be the wiser."

Kilkern clapped his dirty hands slowly. "I applaud your brilliance. I would never have thought that a woman could have the depth of intelligence that you do."

She wanted to keep him talking; she needed time, time for Magnus to rescue her.

"How often have you been in the keep without anyone's knowledge?"

"I saw no reason to come here until I was ready, and besides, Magnus's men keep watchful eyes on the land. If it were not for the trench, purposely overgrown with shrub, my father had built to aid his escape, I would never have been able to gain entrance here without notice. I spent the winter months making plans and, more importantly, gaining the king's support. Now when Magnus cannot produce the map of Dunhurnal land and I can, the matter will be completely and permanently resolved. Then I shall enjoy myself with that beautiful peasant woman until I tire of her and—" His eyes narrowed and his expression turned to one of complete rage. "I shall make every tenant pay dearly for having deserted my land. That is, of course, after I kill Magnus and you?" He placed a finger to his cheek as if in thought. "After you create a map designating my land as encompassing Dunhurnal land, I shall torture you for a while, then dispose of you. Your punishment for seeking the Legend's help."

Reena refused to show him any fear, though her legs trembled violently. Nor would she plead for mercy. He was without care or sanity, a madman, and there was no reasoning with a madman. She stood tall and straight and with confidence the Legend would come for her: he would rescue her. She held firm to her recurring thought, giving her the courage to face her plight.

"What of your plan when you entered the keep?" she asked, knowing she gained time by keeping him in a discussion. "What did you hope to gain?"

"Beware the belly of the beast," he said with a laughing grin.

She realized then his intentions. "You planned on kidnapping Brigid and me as soon as Magnus left to meet with you. You had no intentions of meeting with him. You not being there to welcome him would be an insult and a revelation that something was amiss and he would return—"

He interrupted to correct her. "You have it partially correct, Magnus would return to find you on his own torture rack and he would gladly surrender the map and marriage agreement to save you, thus surrendering himself. The original map would be immediately disposed of, and you would draw me one that would satisfy the king, thus making Dunhurnal land rightfully mine."

"You altered your plan when you discovered we loved each other."

"It was obvious to many, but it was confirmed by the men who tracked you while you mapped, they reporting back to me that you and Magnus spent a night alone in a cave. The Legend was now vulnerable and I revised my plan, as I must do again due to your curiosity. I had not expected you to deliver yourself so easily into my hands. You have made my plan much simpler and alleviated my need to spend a night in this dreadful place."

He stepped aside, a nasty grin distorting his features and making him appear a frightening demon.

Reena kept firm control of her fear, reminding herself over and over that Magnus would come for her. Even when two of Kilkern's men entered the cell, grabbed her, and dragged her to the torture chamber she didn't doubt he would rescue her. She knew he would and she held firm to her belief in the man she loved.

"Chain her to the rack," Kilkern ordered and stood to the side while the men did as instructed.

She did not fight: her efforts would have proven

useless, and she would have wasted valuable energy and courage she would need to survive.

"You go willing to the rack thinking Magnus will rescue you." Kilkern laughed. "He could not rescue his own mother, how then can he rescue you?"

She thought to remind him that Magnus's mother was his mother as well, but it was better not to enrage an already enraged beast. Discussion with him was her only weapon—or perhaps it was her shield.

"How can you hope to leave here after you are done and not have Magnus's men slaughter you?"

"Who will lead them once Magnus is dead? Without a leader warriors have nothing. They will pledge their allegiance to me or they will die."

The metal wrist clamps did not fit her small wrists as they should. When Kilkern's men stretched her arms up above her head, her wrists rubbed against the metal and continued to scrape as they fastened her to the table.

She could feel her skin being rubbed raw, and she knew it would not be long before her wrists and ankles bled. That would serve Kilkern well, for her bloody and painful condition would infuriate Magnus when he saw her.

"His men will stop you," Reena said confidently.

He laughed. "Their leader will be dead and they will have no choice but to surrender to me."

"Thomas will never surrender."

"That large idiot of a warrior that Magnus calls a friend will be done away with fast enough, and his death will only hasten the cooperation of the other warriors. I will make an example of one or two of the villagers, and fear will then have them obeying me without question."

Kilkern's vengefulness knew no bounds. She only hoped he remained the arrogant fool he was, for his plan was doomed to fail. Brigid would make certain Magnus and Thomas knew of her whereabouts and Magnus would come for her. He would rescue her, and she clung to that thought every time Kilkern ordered his men to tighten her chains.

The torture rack was situated so that it caught the eye of anyone entering, which was Kilkern's purpose. He expected Magnus to lose all sense and reason when he saw her lying there in pain and bleeding.

And the pain came fast and furiously, rushing through her arms and legs and flooding her with a tremendous pressure that felt as if her limbs were about to be ripped from her body.

She attempted to remain silent, not wanting to give him the pleasure of seeing her suffer. Then a thought came to her.

She let out a bloodcurdling scream.

Chapter 32

M agnus entered the keep, his thoughts on Reena. He looked forward to talking with her this evening, sharing the evening meal and sleeping with her wrapped in his arms.

He suddenly could not wait to see her. He hurried to the stairs and climbed the steps in quick strides, promising himself he would only take a minute of her time. A hug and kiss was all he wanted and then he would leave her to map.

He knocked on her door, and when he got no response, he smiled. She was lost in her mapping as usual. He entered quietly and was surprised to see she was not at her desk or anywhere in her room.

She had mentioned mapping the dungeon, and he walked over to her table and was surprised to see that one of the candleholders that lined the edge sat on the drawing. Reena never sat a candleholder on her maps for fear of wax or flame destroying it. Whatever had made her leave it here?

He studied the map hoping it would give him a clue to her hasty departure when he noticed the metal rings in the one cell. It did not take him long to rush out of the room.

She would hear of her foolishness from him. Whatever had possessed her to go to the dungeon alone? He rushed into the great hall at the same time Thomas entered from the front doors with Brigid close behind, followed by Horace, who was barking and growling uncontrollably.

Magnus had never seen the dog so upset and so ready to attack.

"He started a few minutes ago and I cannot calm him down," Brigid said. "It is so unlike him."

Horace jumped up and down in front of Magnus, turned to run, and then jumped up in front of him again.

"He tries to tell you something," Thomas said.

"Brigid, do you know where Reena is?" Magnus asked, though only to confirm his own thought.

"Aye, she foolishly went to the dungeons insisting she had discovered something of great importance. I told her I would inform you and Thomas as to her whereabouts as soon as you both returned."

"Trouble," Thomas said.

Magnus nodded. "Kilkern is in the keep."

"What?" both Thomas and Brigid asked in unison.

Magnus detailed his opinion on the situation and Brigid grew upset.

"He will hurt her," she said, close to tears.

"He will not have the chance." Magnus turned to Thomas and nodded for the man to step away from Brigid so that they could talk in private. He instructed Thomas as to what was to be done, then he turned back to Brigid. "I need you to do something. Do you feel strong enough to help Reena?"

Brigid swallowed back her fear. "I often wished I had had a second chance to have helped my husband when Kilkern attacked him. I do not wish to regret not helping Reena. I will do whatever you wish of me."

"This is what I need of you. It involves Horace," Magnus explained, then, making certain all was understood, he hurried to the dungeon, Brigid keeping a firm hand on Horace.

Thomas took Brigid's free hand. "I am sorry that you regret not helping your husband, but I am not sorry that you did not, for if you had helped him Kilkern would surely have killed you, and then I would have never known you. I love you, Brigid."

"Oh, Thomas, I love you too," she said and squeezed his hand.

He hugged her tight, then stepped away. "Now we must help Reena. Do as Magnus instructed—no more or less, understood?"

"I understand, and do not worry, Thomas. I know Magnus and you will save Reena. I will do nothing foolish. I will wait and release Horace at the signal."

"Good, then I go save your friend and mine."

Magnus heard the muted scream as soon as he reached the partially open door to the dungeon. It speared his stomach like a red-hot iron ready for branding; he took a quick flight down the steps, torch in hand and ready for battle. He knew it was necessary for him to remain as calm and in control of his anger as possible. Reena would only be in more danger if he allowed his anger to interfere, a difficult task knowing she suffered because of him.

His only weapon was the knife in the sheath at his

side, but it mattered not, for he would kill Kilkern with his bare hands if necessary.

He rushed down past the empty prison cells and into the torture chamber, where he stopped abruptly, his eyes going immediately to Reena. Her wrists and ankles bled raw from the scraping of the metal against skin, and her slim body was drenched with the pain of being pulled in opposite directions.

"The Legend is here," Reena said, smiling through her pain.

Kilkern did not care for her caustic warning, and with a simple pointing of his finger her chains tightened. She bit at her lip so she would not scream.

"Let her be, Peter, it is me you want," Magnus demanded.

"Is this not what you did to my father?" Kilkern asked in anger.

"And what of your father's actions against my mother?"

Kilkern shrugged. "She was a woman who did her duty and bore him a child. She served her purpose."

"The purpose being Dunhurnal land," Magnus said, remaining where he stood and glancing occasionally to Reena. When this was done he would see to tending her. He would wash away the blood, bandage her wounds, and ease her pain. He would do it himself; no one else would touch her. He alone would see to her care and make certain she healed and suffered no more, *not ever again.*

"I will not debate this issue with you, *brother*," Kilkern said on a laugh. "Dunhurnal land will be mine, and you will pay for killing my father. You will pay with your life, and if you wish to save the life of the woman you love—"

Reena ignored her pain to warn Magnus. "He plans on killing me after I map the land for him."

Kilkern grew furious and walked over to her, grabbing hold of her mouth and squeezing it until it pained her. "You are a brave one, though foolish."

"Get your hands off her."

Kilkern turned to face Magnus. "It is not wise to demand of me when I can cause Reena substantial pain." He stepped away from her. "Shall we see how much pain she can bear?"

Magnus wanted to charge at Kilkern and break his neck, but the guards would reach him before he reached Kilkern, and then Reena would suffer for his stupidity.

"Tell me what you want so this will be done," Magnus said, hoping to divert his attention away from Reena.

"You are quick to choose death." Kilkern shrugged. "But then it will not be a quick death." He took another step forward. "Bring me the marriage agreement and the map of Dunhurnal land."

"Let Reena go first."

Kilkern laughed, his men joining in. "You must think me a fool."

"I know you a fool. Hurt Reena once more and I will kill you." He stepped forward, his shoulders squared, his hands fisted at his sides.

He was a formidable sight, arrogantly confident of his skills and ability to take on three men and win. And his dark clothes made him appear like an avenging dark lord of the underworld ready to defend his mate and lair.

Magnus took another step forward; Kilkern took a step back.

"Get the map and wedding agreement now, for the longer you take the longer Reena suffers," Kilkern warned. "And bring any of your men with you and Reena dies."

"You think I would leave the woman I love to suffer while I submit to your demands? You truly are a fool. And you were even more a fool when you invaded my keep, for now it places you on Dunhurnal property, and I have every right to defend against those who invade my land."

"You will die a coward like your father," Kilkern all but screamed.

"It is a coward who shoots another man in the back with his bow and arrow, and a coward dies a coward's death—like your father."

"We shall see who is the coward." Kilkern raised his finger. "And if you take another step forward I will have my man cut off one of her fingers."

Reena answered. "How then will I draw your map for you?"

Kilkern looked ready to kill. Magnus knew his time was limited, but by now all should be in place—he need only give the signal.

"I will enjoy watching your tongue cut out of your mouth, then you will know your place as a woman," Kilkern said through gritted teeth.

That was enough for Magnus to hear; he looked to Reena and gave her a barely noticeable nod. Then, in a strong, resounding voice, he said, "I love you."

She understood and waited for all hell to break loose.

It did, though far differently than she would have imagined.

Horace led the attack, racing into the room growling, his teeth bared. The large dog leaped over Reena and straight for the man who had been causing her pain, going for his throat and knocking him to the ground. Reena heard the man's screams and Horace's snarls. He sounded as though he was tearing the man in two.

Thomas was quick to launch himself at the other man, wrestling him to the ground.

Reena quickly looked to see if Magnus was safe, and her eyes widened in fright. Magnus and Kilkern circled each other, knives in hand, preparing to battle.

"I am going to enjoy killing you as much as my father enjoyed killing your father," Kilkern said with a confident grin.

"It appropriately ends here, Peter. You die where your father died and by my hands."

Kilkern laughed like a madman and beckoned Magnus with his knife. "Come, let us see who dies this day."

Both men were skillful fighters, and Reena watched in fear as they launched themselves repeatedly at each other, both striking blows that tore garments but did not puncture the skin.

Thomas was quick to release her from her chains after knocking his opponent unconscious, and Horace kept a snarling guard over his prisoner.

Reena was in no condition to move, though Thomas assisted her in her struggle to sit up to watch the man she loved fight for his and her lives.

Kilkern did not fight fairly, though Magnus instinctively knew his every move and blocked several blows. Kilkern grew frustrated with his useless attempts and lashed out at Magnus, missing his target.

After several moments it was obvious that Magnus toyed with Kilkern, and the man's anger grew to a rage. The more Magnus inflamed that rage, the more careless Kilkern became until it was evident that Magnus need only reach out and end the battle.

But he did not. He toyed with Kilkern like a cat with a mouse, letting him think he had a chance, then showing him he had none. He was trapped and would die when Magnus so chose.

"For my mother," Magnus said after slicing his cheek.

Kilkern grew more enraged. "Worthless whore."

Magnus remained in control and lashed out again, slicing his other cheek. "For my grandfather."

Kilkern grabbed for his face, the blood smearing on his hand. He gritted his teeth and raised his weapon. "You will pay."

With a slice of his knife so fast that Reena did not see it, Magnus cut across Kilkern's chest.

"For Reena," Magnus said.

Stunned, Kilkern looked down at his chest and the blood that seeped into his white shirt. For a brief moment fear raced across his face. Then his face turned bright red as though his rage boiled over, and he launched himself at Magnus, knocking Magnus's knife from his hand.

Reena's heart stopped beating and her breath caught, and in that brief moment Magnus grabbed Kilkern by the wrist, shook the knife loose, twisted him around, and slipped his arm around Kilkern's neck.

"This is for my father." He snapped Kilkern's neck with ease and let him drop to the ground.

Magnus did not waste a second glance on the dead man; he walked directly to Reena, though he spoke to Thomas. "Get rid of the stench."

"With pleasure," Thomas said and turned his attention to the two prisoners.

Magnus said nothing. He gently picked up Reena and cradled her as tenderly as he could, though he knew from her pained expression it was not tender enough. He cursed beneath his breath and took her out of the dungeon and up to his bedchamber, where Brigid waited with Old Margaret.

Tears came fast to Brigid's eyes, but Old Margaret was ready to heal when she saw Reena's bleeding wrists and ankles.

Magnus placed Reena carefully on the bed. Before the two women could reach her side, he announced, "I will not be needing your services. I will tend to Reena myself."

Brigid attempted to protest, but Old Margaret placed a gentle hand on her arm.

"He needs to do this, let him be."

The two women left, promising to check on Reena later.

After locking the door and ridding himself of his shirt, Magnus returned to the bed. With a gentle touch he began to cleanse Reena's wounds. He was grateful he had all he needed at hand, the two women having prepared well for Reena's needs. A pitcher of fresh water, a bowl, a crock of salve and clean cloths to wrap her wounds were at his finger-tips.

He would make certain she healed, seeing to her every need, helping to ease her pain and making sure she suffered no more. He was, however, not prepared for her tears. They cut at his heart.

He dropped the cloth into the bowl of water and carefully took her small hand in his. "I am so sorry, Ree, for not reaching you sooner, for you having to suffer for me. When I saw you there on the rack I thought my heart would split in two and I thought I would go mad."

Her tears rushed from her like a dam that had burst, her sobs heavy and mournful and cathartic. "I am sorry," she wept. "I cannot stop crying. I am so relieved that you are all right. I knew you would rescue me."

"You had no doubt even when he chained you to the table?"

She shook her head. "I only knew I needed to survive until you came for me."

"Listen to me, Ree," he said calmly. "I have waited long for the day I could face Peter Kilkern and make him pay for all the hurt and suffering he has caused my family. But when I saw you on that rack nothing mattered more to me than you. I would have done anything, and that included letting Kilkern go free if it meant saving your life."

Her tears quieted as he spoke.

He smiled and patted her wet cheek with the end of the blanket. "And my heart filled with love and relief when you threatened Kilkern upon my arrival. Your courage astounds me, and I feel so very lucky that you have chosen me to love."

She sighed, and a smile crept across her face. "You never had a chance once I did fall in love with you. I am determined, you know."

He laughed. "The Legend finally met his match."

She gripped his hand. "The Legend finally found love."

Chapter 33

❦❦**I**t is your wedding day, your wounds have yet to fully heal in the last three weeks, and you want to walk in the woods when there is much yet to be done here?" Brigid asked, then threw her hands up in the air. "Why should that surprise me?"

Reena wrapped a blue shawl around her shoulders, having dressed in an old skirt and tunic for her foray into the woods. Spring was pleasantly upon them, and a cool breeze joined a sunny sky. She looked forward to being outdoors, having been confined to her bedchamber and the keep while she healed.

Magnus had tended her well, being there to serve her every need, but now she wanted to be off on her own if only for an hour or so. Soon she would exchange vows with the man she loved and she would be on her own no more. She would be wife to the Legend, and the thought filled her with joy.

"It does not surprise you," Reena said. "You understand me, Brigid, and you know I much prefer to walk the woods than plan a wedding. You, however, enjoy planning celebrations, and you have done an excellent job. I am grateful, but I need this time alone."

"Go," Brigid ordered with a gentle shove. "All is in good hands here, and when you return you need only dress for the ceremony and celebration."

Reena sighed in relief. "You are truly a good friend."

Brigid returned to seeing that the great hall was ready for the special occasion, and Reena marveled at her friend's talent to handle a multitude of tasks all at once. Brigid had planned the wedding feast, seen to the stitching of the wedding veils and dresses, and she now saw to the great hall and filling it with flowers and garland greenery and a multitude of white candles.

Reena slipped unnoticed out the door, leaving the chaotic scene behind. She was not alone, though; Horace followed on her heels. He had grown from a tiny, plump, and cowardly pup into a large protective beast of a dog. And ever since that day in the dungeons, he had remained by her side wherever she went, Magnus pleased and proud of the courageous animal.

Reena took a deep breath of fresh air and grew excited about her walk. Perhaps she would find quills for drawing or find an area of land she wished to draw. The next hour or so belonged to her, and she intended to enjoy it.

She had not walked far when she heard laughter in the near distance. It sounded like a couple that had sneaked off for a moment of private fun, and she thought to turn around and walk in another direction, not wanting to disturb them.

"Who goes there?" the voice demanded harshly.

Reena jumped, startled that the laughter had stopped so suddenly and that the man should hear her. She approached, intending to make herself known to someone she probably already knew then be on her way.

She was surprised when she entered the small clearing a few feet away and did not recognize the couple standing there, the man in a protective stance, with sword in hand, in front of the woman.

She did not think to fear the man though he was large and powerfully built. His long, dark hair was heavy with gray, and his face was handsome.

She greeted them warmly, feeling them no threat. "I am Reena, and you are on the Legend's land and most welcome."

The woman quickly stepped out from behind the large man and rushed toward her. She was tall and slim and more beautiful than Reena thought possible. Pure white long hair, smooth, almost wrinkle-free skin, and dark eyes that looked ready to burst into tears.

"Reena," she cried and opened her arms wide to throw around Reena for a hug. "I have been so looking forward to meeting you."

The man walked up behind her. "Then let her go before you smother her, she's just a wee bit of a thing."

The woman stepped back but took solid hold of Reena's one hand, as if making certain Reena remained by her side.

"Magnus has told us much about you, and you are as beautiful as he claimed," the woman said.

Reena was momentarily stunned silent, then she realized the woman beside her had to be Magnus's mother, her son having inherited her dark eyes. She meant to introduce herself properly, but instead she asked, "Magnus told you I was beautiful?"

"Aye, he did," the man said and stepped forward. "I am James and pleased I am to meet you."

The woman released her hand, and Reena's small hand disappeared into his large grasp.

"And the woman who almost hugged you to death is—"

"Catherine, Magnus's mother." And she hugged Reena again with the same abundant enthusiasm.

Reena was pleased to meet them both and overjoyed that they had come here for the wedding. "I was not told of your impending arrival."

"A surprise for you," Magnus said.

Reena turned around to find him standing directly behind her. She had not heard his approach, but then she'd been too busy speaking with the couple to pay heed to anything else.

She immediately went into his outstretched arms.

"Are you certain you feel well enough to walk the woods? Brigid told me your intentions, and I worried that your ankles may still pain you."

She stepped out of his embrace but took hold of his hand, his warmth and strength comforting and his concern touching her heart. "I am fine, there is no need for worry."

Magnus nodded, though concern remained evident on his handsome face. They both knew that her one ankle would be left with a scar, forever reminding her of her ordeal. It had upset him when Old Margaret had told him of this, but it did not bother Reena. She had simply pronounced the scar her badge of courage, which she would wear proudly.

"I am very pleased with my surprise," Reena said. "I have been impatient to meet your mother."

"And I you," Catherine said, walking over to her son and kissing his cheek. "When we arrived this morning he did nothing but talk of you—"

"Sing her praises is more like it," James said with a grin.

"Aye," his mother said, her grin as wide as James's. "He told us of your strength and courage and your many talents."

"Claims you are the best mapmaker in all the world."

"And that you can speak several languages," his mother added.

"I speak the truth proudly of the woman I love," Magnus said, squaring his shoulders as if ready to defend, though a smile showed he joined in the good-natured teasing.

Catherine slipped her arm around Reena's. "I wish a moment with my new daughter."

Magnus and James walked off, leaving the two women alone.

"I wanted to thank you," Catherine said.

"For what?"

Tears pooled in Catherine's eyes. "For loving my son."

Reena smiled. "He is easy to love."

"Not many would agree, and I had feared that because of all that had happened to him his heart would turn cold."

"How could you think that?" Reena asked with surprise. "It is because of you he can love so strongly. You protected him, took him away from harm and kept him safe until he was old enough to protect himself. He never once doubted your love, and that love taught him to love with courage."

"You are all that Magnus claims you are, and I am so proud that you will be my son's wife." Catherine hugged Reena tightly.

The two women returned to the men. James and Catherine joined hands and walked in front of Magnus and Reena.

Magnus and Reena locked hands. Magnus made certain they walked more slowly, when Reena suddenly stopped.

"You are all right?" he asked anxiously.

"Aye, but I have something to say."

Magnus grew anxious; Reena's tone was serious.

Reena took both his hands in hers. "The heavens shine brightly above us on this beautiful day, and I want to pledge my love to you here and now and let the heavens know that I will love you forever; and no matter what happens in our life my love for you will only grow stronger with each passing day. When my time is done here I will take my love to the heavens and wait for you, and never ever stop loving you."

Magnus stood speechless, and tears threatened his eyes. He reached down and cupped her face in his hands. "You and I will go to the heavens together

Reena, for I could not live one day without you, my love for you is that strong. I pledge that love here and now and forever."

They kissed, sealing their love, and the heavens shone down upon them.

Be prepared to be swept away by these April romances from Avon Books.

IT TAKES A HERO by Elizabeth Boyle
An Avon Romantic Treasure
"Sure to leave you smiling."—Stephanie Laurens

The publication of the notorious *Miss Darby* novels suddenly has every eligible debutante in London refusing to marry . . . ever! It is up to Rafe Danvers to unmask the unknown author and end scandalous scribblings, and the trail leads to the enticing Rebecca Tate.

HOT STUFF by Elaine Fox
An Avon Contemporary Romance
"Fox writes romance in a fresh and vibrant voice."—Nora Roberts

Love is for losers . . . and Laurel has no problem telling anyone her new philosophy, including the gorgeous coffee guy, Joe. But Joe has strong opinions of his own on the subject, and he's determined to prove to her that head-spinning, knees-weakening love *is* possible.

THE PRINCESS MASQUERADE by Lois Greiman
An Avon Romance
"Lois Greiman delivers."—Christina Dodd

Megan wishes she'd never laid eyes on a certain gentleman . . . or his shiny pocket watch that found its way into her hands. When the dashing Nicol Argyle tracks her down, he makes her an unbelievable offer she'd be a fool to refuse . . .

IN MY HEART by Melody Thomas
An Avon Romance
"I couldn't put it down!"—Karen Hawkins

After his brief and scandalous marriage to the daughter of an aristocrat, Christopher Donally is determined to put the past behind him . . . if only he wasn't undone by one single, soul-stirring kiss.

Avon Romances—
the best in exceptional authors and unforgettable novels!

Have you ever dreamed of writing a romance?

*And have you ever wanted
to get a romance published?*

Perhaps you have always wondered how to
become an Avon romance writer?
We are now seeking the best and brightest undiscovered
voices. We invite you to send us your query letter to
avonromance@harpercollins.com

What do you need to do?

Please send no more than two pages telling us
about your book. We'd like to know its setting—is it
contemporary or historical—and a bit about the hero,
heroine, and what happens to them.

Then, if it is right for Avon we'll ask to see part of the
manuscript. Remember, it's important that you have
material to send, in case we want to see your story quickly.

Of course, there are no guarantees of publication,
but you never know unless you try!

*We know there is new talent just waiting
to be found! Don't hesitate . . . send us
your query letter today.*

*The Editors
Avon Romance*

Avon Romantic Treasures

*Unforgettable, enthralling love stories,
sparkling with passion and adventure
from Romance's bestselling authors*

Discover Contemporary Romances
at Their Sizzling Hot Best
from Avon Books